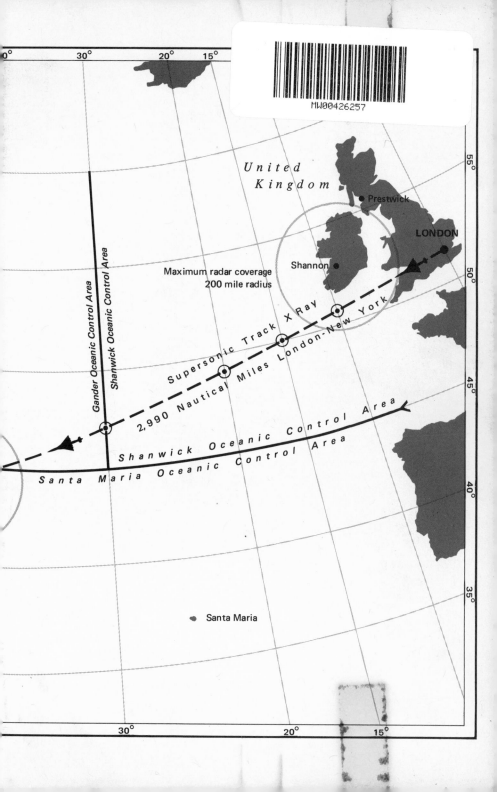

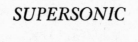

SUPERSONIC

By Basil Jackson

EPICENTER
RAGE UNDER THE ARCTIC
SUPERSONIC

BASIL JACKSON

SUPERSONIC

W · W · NORTON & COMPANY · INC ·

NEW  YORK

C 4

FIC
Jackson

ALL RIGHTS RESERVED
Published simultaneously in Canada
by George J. McLeod Limited, Toronto

Library of Congress Cataloging in Publication Data
Jackson, Basil, 1920–
  Supersonic.
  I. Title
PZ4.J127Su3.[PR9199.3.J37]   813'.5'4   74–28005
ISBN 0–393–08701–8

Map by Fred Haynes.
This book was designed by Robert Freese.
The typefaces are Century Nova and Janson.
The book was manufactured by Vail-Ballou Press.

PRINTED IN THE UNITED STATES OF AMERICA

2 3 4 5 6 7 8 9 0

To the unknown air traffic controller who brought me
and my fellow passengers safely to earth one fogbound
night at Gander . . .

ACKNOWLEDGMENTS

The experience and knowledge of many people have gone into this book.

Thanks are due to the Boeing Company, Seattle, Washington for data on the Supersonic 2707 project. Also to the British Aircraft Corporation, Bristol, England, for supplying technical background, including the captain's checklist for takeoff, cruise, and final approach for the Anglo-French Concorde supersonic transport, and for the courtesy of company officials during my visit to inspect this aircraft.

To Peter N. Waitt, public relations manager for Canada, Japan Air Lines, I owe a special note of thanks for arranging a trip on the flight deck of a DC-8 bound from Vancouver to Tokyo, and to Captains Veyran and Williams, who explained the workings of transoceanic navigation during the flight. I am grateful to Japan Air lines for other arrangements that the airline has made for me in the past, and specifically to Mel Scott, JAL's sales manager, Western Canada.

Officials of the Ministry of Transport, Ottawa, kindly gave permission for me to visit the Air Traffic Control centers at Gander International Airport, Newfoundland, and Toronto International Airport. In particular, I thank Jack James, Gander's airport manager, who hospitably bedded me down in the airport's VIP suite when I could not get hotel accommodation.

I also owe Jack James an explanation. One fogbound night, when all aircraft were grounded, in the quiet of the VIP suite,

ACKNOWLEDGMENTS

he told me about his adventures when piloting a Tiger Moth biplane in the early days of flying. I have retold his story of bravery and coolheadedness, putting his words into the mouth of a fictitious character, and I have added a blind landing to his tale. I have also attributed another of Jack's airborne exploits to my fictitious copilot. I hope Jack, who has been an airport official at Gander since before World War II, will forgive this method of retelling his story.

Paul Richard, Ministry of Transport operations officer, Gander, whose work for the Trans-Oceanic Plane Stop (TOPS) program is known to hundreds of air crews regularly flying the Atlantic, was untiring in supplying information.

To C. R. Rowsell, chief, Area Control Center, Gander, I am grateful for explaining the complex workings of computerized navigation checks, the operation of radarscopes and the radio communications system for trans-Atlantic flying, for which Gander is the western headquarters.

Fred Brock, Precision Approach Radar controller at Toronto International Airport, was most cooperative in demonstrating how he talks down an airliner under blind landing conditions. (A word of thanks to the Air Canada DC-9 captain who, in good visibility, suddenly found himself talked down to the runway threshold for no logical reason. Like the well-trained pilot he was, he asked no questions, obeyed instructions and played it cool.) W. J. (Bill) Ellwood, operational supervisor, Toronto Area Control Center, made my visit to the inner sanctum possible.

A special word of gratitude to Hugh Whittington, pilot and editor, *Canadian Aviation,* for supplying aeronautical charts and explaining radio operations from an airman's viewpoint.

Basil Jackson

SUPERSONIC

ONE

"Captain Thomas A. Bartlett, American Arrow Airlines. Please pick up the nearest telephone." The voice on the PA was urgent. Since the nearest phone was in the Flight Operations Room, he pushed open the door and went inside. Kowsky and Nardini were already there, chatting with the dispatcher at the counter. He crossed to an unoccupied desk and picked up the phone.

"Captain Bartlett speaking."

"Long-distance call from New York, Captain," said a female voice. "Person-to-person. I'll connect you."

He took off his cap and put it on the desk. In the background he heard the operator say, "London's ready with Captain Bartlett, New York," followed by a click and the voice of the American operator. He sat on the desk, tapping his foot against it, staring out of the window. A British Airways Super VC-10 taxied past, obscuring the terminal building in the distance. As it cleared the window, the London Airport sign on the terminal building glinted in the sunlight.

"Go ahead, New York."

"Tom?"

"Yes, Cathy, it's me. What's happened?"

"They operated at two o'clock this morning." His wife's voice sounded strained. "Dr. Lieberman phoned a few minutes ago to say he's in the recovery room and . . ."

"What about the biopsy?" Bartlett interrupted. As soon as it was out, he regretted being so impatient. After the last few months of shared anxiety, it had been Cathy who had borne the final worry alone.

"They expect the report very soon." She paused and sighed. "Will you be home on schedule this afternoon, Tom? Dr. Lieberman said we can visit as soon as he's out of recovery."

"Sure, honey, the usual time. We're just preparing for takeoff." He waited a moment before asking, "Did he say the fall in the gym made it worse?"

"I asked Dr. Lieberman about that but he wouldn't commit himself—you know how he is." Another pause, followed by a quick intake of breath. "I'll be waiting for you, Tom, we can drive over together. I'm glad I caught you in time."

"It's sort of a relief now that they've done it at last," Bartlett replied. "Try not to worry, hon. Everything's going to be okay now." He slid down from the desk. "Oh, Cathy."

"Yes, Tom?"

"Thank you for phoning. See you soon, hon. Good-bye."

He put the phone down and looked across at the others. Kowsky, his first officer, said, "Couldn't help overhearing, Tom. How's Gary?"

"They operated last night. He's in recovery and doing okay. They're still waiting for the biopsy report," Bartlett replied. He put on his cap and carefully adjusted it.

"You could have begged off last night's flight on compassionate grounds, Captain," Nardini, his flight systems management engineer said.

SUPERSONIC

"We had no idea last night just when they were going to operate, Nick. It was no use hanging around the hospital after he'd gone in." He grinned, showing even teeth. "Besides, you wouldn't have liked it. Remember who was down as alternate."

Nardini and Kowsky laughed. A senior check pilot with a reputation for being a flight deck martinet had been on the crew list as Bartlett's alternate for last night's flight.

Bartlett nodded at the dispatcher, glad to divert attention from himself. "What have you got for us this morning, Mr. Simmonds?"

Simmonds, a thin, sad-faced man, indicated a chart lying on the counter. "Met reports the warm front you overflew last night has pushed up north of latitude forty. It's generating thunderstorm activity in a large area west of longitude thirty. Scattered clouds to thirty-five thousand feet. It won't affect you, of course, but we're rerouting the subsonics farther north."

He looked up, the corners of his lips drawn down, giving the impression that he personally was to blame for the imperfect weather at the altitudes at which the subsonic aircraft flew. He slid a film cassette and a sheaf of papers across the counter. Bartlett picked up the cassette and handed it to Kowsky, who put it with care into his briefcase. He then examined the top sheet of paper headed "AAA Flight Plan, FL. 01, LDN-JFK/NYK" and followed by rows of figures and coded symbols of computer print-out. Bartlett read the figures from top to bottom.

"Has the nav cassette been checked with these figures?" he asked Simmonds.

"Yes, Captain. A-okay right through."

Bartlett rechecked a line at the top of the page. "Ramp fuel's close to maximum, isn't it?"

"Temperature's up," Simmonds replied. He waved a bony hand at the window. "Our English weather," he said apologetically.

"For a change," Kowsky grinned.

Bartlett put the Flight Plan to one side and looked at the met report. "Uneven temperature gradient south of the thunderstorm activity," he read aloud, thinking of the fuel reserves shown on the Flight Plan. Supersonic aircraft were uniquely sensitive to temperature variation: If the temperature rose only a few degrees over the course of a long flight, the rate of fuel consumption substantially increased above the normal, which, for Bartlett's aircraft, was five thousand gallons an hour. He studied the load sheet, peered again at the fuel load figures, and went over the computerized calculations for the fuel reserves to their nearest alternate, Gander.

Simmonds put a finger on the meteorological report. "You might want to make a note of this, Captain. If the warm front coming up from the Gulf accelerates, it will hit the cold air in through here." He indicated a region on the map off the Newfoundland coast.

"Fog?"

Simmonds nodded. "You'll be well south of it. But that's the whole picture." He folded a small facsimile of the weather chart and slid it across the counter. "And here's a Notam," he said, taking a sheet from the Notices to Airmen file tray on the counter. "It's a Class One. Came over the teletype an hour ago."

Bartlett looked at the Notam and turned to Kowsky. "A reminder about the joint war exercises off the Grand Banks by the U.S. Air Force and Canadian Armed Forces. Now extends down to Nova Scotia. Antisubmarine warfare aircraft with helicopters on standby search and rescue." He glanced at Nardini. "Restricted area for civil aircraft below ten thousand feet for twenty-four hour period beginning ten-zero-zero hours."

"That altitude excludes us, Captain. And we'll be far south of Newfie and Nova Scotia," Nardini added.

Bartlett nodded, gave the Notam to Nardini, and turned to the Load Sheet.

"Sixty percent payload," he remarked, lifting the page and looking at the passenger manifest. "Only five passengers in first class."

Kowsky tilted the cap on his head, revealing blond hair combed straight back. "That'll make it easy for the cabin crew."

"We've got a couple of VIPs this trip," Bartlett interrupted. "Vincent A. Maxwell."

"The Secretary of State? Something serious must have happened in Moscow to take him back to Washington in such a hurry," Nardini said. He turned to Kowsky. "When did you say they're going to trade in Air Force One for a supersonic?"

"I heard it's already been delivered to Andrews, but ran into teething problems."

"Who's the other VIP, Captain?" Nardini asked.

"Sir Leonard Wheeler-Carthert." The name seemed familiar to Bartlett, but he couldn't place it.

"Never heard of the guy," Nardini said. "I wonder who *he* is."

"Lydia'll know," said Kowsky. "She knows everybody."

Lydia Olsen looked up from the ticket desk. The door to the VIP lounge was only steps away and she wondered how her distinguished passenger had slipped away unnoticed. She tapped carefully manicured nails on the counter before once again putting the microphone to her lips.

SUPERSONIC

"Will Sir Leonard Wheeler-Carthert, passenger on Flight Zero-One, Arrowhead supersonic service to New York, please report immediately to American Arrow Airlines counter?" Her voice sounded imperative as it came from the overhead speakers in the Oceanic Terminal Building. She peered over the heads of the people hurrying through the vast concourse, hoping to catch a glimpse of the tall, lean figure of the famous surgeon.

She switched off the microphone, covered the mouthpiece of the telephone she held to her ear, and said to the ticket clerk at her side, "I made him a cup of tea less than five minutes ago. He hasn't touched it."

"Did you check the lav, ducks," the clerk replied. "Sometimes those professor types fall in." He grinned mischievously.

Lydia's lips thinned. Limeys had a queer sense of humor, cracking jokes when things went wrong. And things had started to go wrong the moment she had awakened, half-frozen, that morning. The hotel's central heating system had failed during the night—the result of a strike of gas workers. Then she'd torn her pantyhose as she lost her balance standing on one foot in the chilly room. Luckily she'd packed a spare pair. Her breakfast had been stone cold, and the coffee . . . When would the British learn to make a decent cup of coffee? Now she'd lost a passenger, one of the two VIPs she had been detailed to receive and escort aboard Arrowhead. The voice in the telephone spoke again, more insistently this time.

"Will you kindly endeavor to bring Sir Leonard to the telephone, miss? It's of the utmost urgency. I repeat. This is Ten Downing Street."

"We're doing everything possible to locate him, sir. Please hold the line while I page him again." As she wondered how Downing Street kept track of the prime minister's personal medical advisor, the lanky form of Sir Leonard appeared at the far side of the concourse, striding from the newsstand. She waved the phone to attract his attention. When he came up to the counter she said in a low voice, "It's Ten Downing Street, sir."

Sir Leonard dropped a copy of *Yachting World* on the counter. "Thanks so much," he said, taking the phone. Lydia handed the microphone back to the clerk who rolled his eyes toward the ceiling and surreptitiously tapped his ear with a forefinger, mistakenly believing Sir Leonard to be hard of hearing. She ignored him and turned her attention to her copy of the passenger manifest. Thank goodness there were only five first class passengers; it would be an easy flight, although, as senior stewardess, she'd still have to check on the stewardesses in the economy section.

She glanced at her watch. In about three hours she'd be in a New York taxi on her way to the apartment. She'd be able to cook something nice by the time Steve got back from the university. The thought of sitting curled up in the warm apartment waiting for his footsteps to sound down the corridor caused a glow to settle inside her.

Sir Leonard Wheeler-Carthert's voice drifted across the counter. "Then put him on." There was a pause. "Hello, Jenkins? He *must* rest if he's to last out the session. And make sure he takes the medication I prescribed." Another pause. "Good Lord, no! Under *no* circumstances will I countenance his going down to Cowes. He's got to stay off that yacht. Is that clearly understood?"

She smiled and ran her eye down the passenger list. The passenger agent had printed the letters VIP against another name: Vincent A. Maxwell. Her eyebrows arched. It would be the second time the Secretary of State had been on one of her flights. A year ago Maxwell had been on a Boeing 747 on which she'd served, going on a brief vacation before attending a meeting of NATO powers in Brussels. She wondered if he would recognize her.

Sir Leonard put down the phone. "Thank you." He sighed, and with a quick movement touched his gray bristle of moustache.

"If you'd like to return to the VIP lounge I'll bring you a fresh cup of tea, Sir Leonard," Lydia said.

"That sounds like an offer I can't refuse." He smiled and picked up the magazine. Lydia ushered him into the lounge and rechecked her watch. "We'll be ready to board in fifteen minutes, sir."

She retired to the little kitchen discreetly hidden by a planter partition and poured boiling water into the teapot. She arranged some things on a silver tray and took it to him. "Milk first, sir?" she inquired.

"Of course! We're still on British soil." He grinned and she felt his eyes on her as she put in the milk and poured the amber thread of tea.

"You pour very well—for an American," he said.

"Thank you, sir." She looked up and saw the amused sparkle in his blue eyes. "That's the nicest thing anyone's said to me this morning." It slipped out unintentionally. "I froze last night. The hotel heating system broke down. The . . ."

"This damned country discovered the smallpox vaccination, invented penicillin, the steam engine, radar, jet engines—and still hasn't recognized the fact that the human body in normal health is comfortable when maintained at 98.6 degrees Fahrenheit. That's one thing I admire you Americans for. You recognized the fact long ago. By the time this country gets around to . . . I say, this *is* a jolly good cup of tea."

"I was going to say the heat went off because of the strike."

"Labor'll be the death of England," Sir Leonard said

gravely, putting down the cup. She noticed the smooth white skin of his fingers and the short-clipped nails with translucent crescents, and wondered what miracles of surgery they had performed on operating tables around the world.

The door swung open and she recognized Vincent Maxwell, hatless, hands jammed into the pockets of his topcoat. Behind him was a willowy, blonde young woman dressed in a light tan suit and carrying an attaché case with the seal of the United States stenciled in gold near the handle. Lydia saw the flash of the safety chain on her wrist, securing the case to her body to foil snatch thieves. Sir Leonard politely half-raised himself from the chair when he saw her, then turned to his magazine.

"Good morning, Mr. Maxwell," Lydia said, and in an aside to the ticket clerk who held the door, "I'll look after everything."

"You're Miss Olsen," Maxwell said in a matter-of-fact tone, taking off his topcoat with a quick movement. He nodded toward his companion. "This is Miss Lindenberg, one of our embassy officials. Miss Lindenberg will be traveling on an official courier's pass."

"I understand, sir." Lydia looked at the young woman. She was beautiful, probably in her late twenties. She gave Lydia a friendly smile.

"May I get you coffee, or perhaps tea?" she asked.

"Thank you, neither," Miss Lindenberg replied. Lydia turned to Maxwell. He raised a pudgy hand and strode to the window, taking a silver cigarette case from his pocket.

"Mr. Maxwell, may I introduce another passenger on Flight Zero-One." She indicated Sir Leonard. "This is Sir Leonard Wheeler-Carthert." She was about to add, "the famous surgeon" but checked herself. "Sir Leonard, this is Mr. Vincent Maxwell."

Sir Leonard got to his feet and the two men shook hands. "I see you're a sailor," said Maxwell.

"Yes, indeed. Do *you* sail?"

Maxwell lit a cigarette and tossed the match into an ashtray. "No time for it."

"That boss of yours rides you too hard," the surgeon remarked. Miss Lindenberg looked from one to the other in embarrassment. She appeared to be surprised at the familiar attitude of the Englishman.

"That's what I tell him," Maxwell said, puffing a cloud of smoke toward the window. It was one of those London spring days when the air was crystal clear and blue sky spread from horizon to horizon. He sighed and turned to Sir Leonard.

"How's the PM's health? I haven't seen him for a month."

Lydia slipped away to tidy the cups and saucers in the kitchen and to add Miss Lindenberg's name to the manifest. Her mind went over the seating arrangements. She'd put Maxwell and Miss Lindenberg up forward facing the bulkhead so that they could talk state secrets privately, and steer Sir Leonard to the window seat on the other side of the aisle. That way they would be close enough to cross over if they wished to chat, but they could easily stay within their own territory if they wanted to keep to themselves. She glanced down at the clipboard that held the manifest wondering what the three other passengers would be like.

Bartlett gathered up the papers, slipped them into the folder Simmonds had produced, and put it in his briefcase.

"Thanks, Mr. Simmonds," he said. He turned to look at the counter at the far end of the room. "Where's Gerrard?"

"He stepped out for a minute," Simmonds replied, looking around. "Ah, there he is now."

Bartlett led his crew to the counter on which a sign read, "Radiation Weather Service." Gerrard, a solidly built man with a smooth, pink face, hurried up, tore off the paper slip that rolled from a clacking teletype machine built into the counter, and read it before acknowledging Bartlett's presence.

"Morning, Captain," he said briskly. He looked at Kowsky and Nardini and murmured, "Gentlemen." Then his eyes moved to the instruments recessed into the countertop, where a chart of the Atlantic Ocean was pinned, with the British Isles on Bartlett's right, the Azores at the bottom where Bartlett's elbow rested, Iceland and Greenland at the top, and at the far left the United States and Canadian eastern seaboards. None of the subsonic captains and their crews stopped at the Radiation Weather Service counter; the data it presented and the service Gerrard provided were of no interest to them. But for Bartlett and his crew, the data center was a mandatory briefing stop before takeoff.

Gerrard and his instruments provided data on the strength of cosmic radiation—the type of radiation opponents of commercial supersonic transports had predicted would jeopardize operations, before the aircraft had gone into service six months ago. Originating from stars in the depth of space, eons before man had appeared on earth, galactic radiation continually bombarded the earth with an invisible rain of high-energy protons, alpha particles, and heavy nuclei. Human beings and animals exposed to them suffered the same effects as to an overdose of X ray or nuclear radiation: disintegration of tissue and premature death. Some experts had predicted that the fetuses of pregnant women traveling in supersonics would be stillborn or born deformed. All life on earth was protected from this bombardment from outer space by the blanketing effects of the atmosphere, but at the extreme altitudes at which the supersonics traveled, thirteen miles above the earth's surface, the aircraft were above the protective air layer.

As Bartlett waited for the physicist to speak, he found himself fingering the exposure rate badge worn by all supersonic crew members. The photographic strip changed color according to the amount of radiation absorbed. Once a week the badges had to be turned in to the airline's Radiation Check for evaluation and the results sent to the Atomic Energy Commission in Washington.

Gerrard consulted a dial. "London's recording eight milli-rems dose rate at ground level; New York seven. Ground stations at Shannon and Gander both show six."

Bartlett jotted down the figures, which Gerrard received by teletype daily from the United States Space Disturbance Center at Boulder, Colorado. The Center gathered data on galactic radiation from monitoring devices in different parts of the world, correlated them, and flashed the information to airports from which the new breed of aircraft, the supersonic transports, operated, and to various research centers. The readings were taken from radiosonde balloons released into the upper atmosphere, and from earth stations to measure the amount of radiation penetrating to ground level.

But galactic radiation readings were practically nonexistent for the area of the Atlantic, mainly because of the lack of recording stations. Bartlett had heard Gerrard himself worry about this huge unmonitored area, and Bartlett had often been on the point of asking why detectors couldn't be placed on board ships, which could relay regular readings to land stations. Probably too simple a solution for the scientists, he'd concluded. He was not too worried about the lack of pre-flight radiation information from the Atlantic, since a radiation detector was mounted on Arrowhead's flight deck, continually monitoring the strength of the radiation on the two hour and fifty minute flight to New York. But he would feel more at ease if they could produce *forecast* radiation weather maps like the conventional charts Simmonds provided, which predicted wind velocities, temperatures, and atmospheric pressure over the whole ocean.

Gerrard glanced at another instrument. "Boulder says to expect more solar flares within the next forty-eight hours, Captain." He looked up at the trio around his counter, doubt creasing his face. "But you know nobody can forecast these things. It's been a heck of a year for flares. A KLM supersonic crew came through this morning complaining about a partial radio blackout. Did you have any problems yesterday?"

"Clear all the way across," Bartlett said. "What flight level were they flying?"

"Seven-six-zero," said Gerrard, using airmen's abbreviation for seventy-six thousand feet.

"We were cleared for seven-one-zero at destination. Could that account for it?"

Gerrard looked doubtful. "Probably a localized flare. Anyway chaps, keep close tabs on your radio." He looked at another instrument.

In addition to his airport duties, Gerrard, a physicist by training, had done some theoretical work on cascade effect, an obscure and little-understood phenomenon that puzzled scientists specializing in galactic radiation. At Britain's National Physical Laboratory, he had focused radiation rays on targets of empty tomato juice cans, with meters inside, to measure the intensification of radiation that was suspected to take place inside a shielded capsule. Later, he'd had the metal-working shop make him specially shaped containers to emulate the sleek metal fuselage of a supersonic airliner, which he knew was the ultimate perfectly shielded enclosure.

Bartlett was aware that Gerrard secretly yearned to spend a month traveling back and forth daily on an Arrowhead to gather definitive data for a paper he was writing on his research. Since the aircraft traveled almost outside the earth's atmosphere, where passengers and crew were exposed to nearly three hours of natural radiation on each trans-Atlantic flight, it would be a perfect laboratory. Bartlett, listening to the physicist's theories, had shuddered and changed the subject.

Gerrard looked up. "That's it, Captain. I'll send a radio message via Shanwick Control if Boulder teletypes an imminent solar warning."

"Thanks," Bartlett said. He turned to Nardini. "Any questions?"

"No, Captain," replied Nardini, patting his briefcase.

"Then let's get aboard."

"Have a good flight, Captain," Gerrard called before looking down at his instruments.

"What time did you take Evelyn in, Bill?"

Charlie Wilson jumped from the ground test monitor truck as Bill Timlett braked it near Arrowhead's drooped nose.

"Three o'clock this morning," replied Timlett, yawning. "Cool as a cucumber she was. You'd never think she was expecting twins again." He uncoiled a spooled electric power line from the back of the flat-decked vehicle and handed it to Wilson. Timlett remained in the vehicle, rubbing his eyes and blinking at the electronic testing panel above the dashboard. " 'There's time for a nice cup of tea,' she said," he called over to Wilson, "and blow me if she didn't make me brew a cuppa before the taxi came."

"You'll have to put in for a rise to support two sets of twins, two other kids, and a wife," Wilson said, searching for the correct socket in Arrowhead's underbelly. He walked along the center line of the aircraft behind the nosewheel until he found the spring-loaded panel. "Systems Test. 28 Volts Only" was stenciled in black letters and figures. He gripped the panel, pulled it down, and checked that the multipinned plug was pointing the right way—there was a thick neutral pin on one side to prevent accidental insertion of the plug the wrong way around—and pushed it home.

"Okay, Bill," he called. "Select twenty-eight volts and turn the switch to check fuel transfer solenoid valves and visor test circuits for transition to supersonic." He walked around to the back of the vehicle and slid aside a panel under the weather hood, revealing electronic test instruments. He heard a click as Timlett moved the switches. Needles on the instruments flickered and steadied as a row of green lights lit up.

"Reading all greens," he called. "Now the same circuits for transition to subsonic."

"Okay, Charlie. Subsonic it is," Timlett said, stifling a yawn.

A red warning light flashed. "Jesus Christ, Bill! That can't be twenty-eight volts. It's at the top of the scale," Wilson cried.

"Sorry, Charlie. I shoved the voltage selector to fifty-six."

Wilson popped his head above the weather hood and saw Timlett's arm shoot out toward the voltage selector. There was a snap as Timlett moved the switch to the correct position.

"For Christ's sake, be more careful!" Wilson admonished. "You'll blow a bloody fuse."

"I said I was sorry, Charlie. How's she reading now?"

"Okay. Power off while I move the plug."

"Power off."

Wilson moved under the aircraft, pulled out the plug, checked that the hinged flap snapped back, tested the automatic catch for security, and inserted the plug in the next socket.

"Fifty-six volts, Bill. And don't bugger it up this time. Fifty-six. And switch to the flight director computer."

"Fifty-six it is, Charlie."

Wilson walked back to the test control panel at the rear of the truck. Shouldn't be too hard on him, he reproached himself. The poor fellow's had no sleep and he must be worried to distraction with another set of twins on the way. He inspected the readout for the on-board flight director. Thirty-three electronic functions automatically checked as he held down a button on the panel. Thirty-three typed symbols, all reading AAA, appeared. He moved his eye along the row. If any symbol showed AAB it would mean the flight director computer on the aircraft had developed a minor fault; a set of dials would indicate precisely where the fault lay. In that event, the computer package would be swiftly unbolted from its storage bay behind the flight management systems officer's position on the flight deck and replaced with a computer package taken from the airline's maintenance section. The operation, including check-out, would take fifteen minutes.

Wilson took a ball-point pen from his pocket and entered a check mark in the appropriate space in the electronics test logbook. He then switched to another mode and tested the engine intake-nozzle control computer system. Everything checked AAA. It took him another few minutes to run through other tests. He slid back the panel cover and called, "Power off, Bill."

He removed the plug from the underbelly, checked that the hinged lid locked, thumped his fist against it, and recoiled the cable. He looked up as a ground service vehicle drove up.

"All through?" yelled the driver of the other vehicle, applying the hand brake as he parked near the tip of Arrowhead's nose.

"She's all yours," Wilson shouted. He turned to Timlett. "Find yourself a quiet corner and curl up for a couple of hours before the 2:30 Arrowhead's due out, Bill. You look as though you could do with some shut-eye." He gave a friendly wave to the driver of the other vehicle as they drove past, but the other driver didn't notice. He was plugging a ground interphone cable into Arrowhead's underbelly, ready to speak to her captain for last-minute checks before takeoff.

"Here's the flight systems engineer now," Wilson said, seeing Nardini emerge from a door of the terminal building.

Timlett drove toward him. "Morning, sir," Wilson said politely. "Grand day." He stepped down and gave Nardini the test report logbook. Nardini passed his eye down the column of AAAs, checked that the readings recorded from Wilson's other tests were within the safety margins; he noted that Wilson had added his signature and the date to the bottom of the test sheet. He scribbled his own initials and handed back the book.

"Cheerio, sir. See you tomorrow," Wilson said.

"You won't see us until Friday. We're off-duty for three days after this flight," Nardini said. He waved and walked toward a door leading up to Arrowhead's loading bridge. Looking up, he could see the figure of Bartlett settling into the left-hand seat on the flight deck.

"How about here, sir?" Lydia asked.

"It'll do very nicely." Sir Leonard Wheeler-Carthert lowered his thin form into the seat and fastened his belt with accustomed ease. Lydia smiled at Maxwell and his companion on the other side of the aisle and returned to the forward vestibule. A frail, elderly woman, wearing a tweed suit and a gray hat trimmed with flowers, entered. She had white cheeks, with the skin pulled taut over a pert nose, and faded blue eyes that peered through steel-rimmed glasses under a lined brow. Lydia took the boarding pass she thrust into her hand, glanced at the passenger list, and spotted the initials GG embroidered on the flight bag the woman carried.

"Good morning, Mrs. Glinker. Welcome aboard Arrow-head." The woman's eyes widened in surprise.

"Oh, thank you very much, Miss. Good morning to you, too."

Lydia led the way into the cabin. The old lady looked the talkative type. Better keep her clear of the VIPs.

"You'll be comfortable here," Lydia said, stopping about three-quarters of the way down the cabin and pointing to a window seat.

"That's nice. I do like to look out and see what's going on." The old lady beamed.

"Shall I put your bag on the seat beside you, Mrs. Glinker? You can spread yourself out then."

"Thank you, Miss."

The woman fumbled with her seat belt, and Lydia bent to fasten it.

"There. That's it."

She straightened up as a well-built man appeared at the entrance. He wore an expensively cut spring coat and his bald head shone under the ceiling lights. A new leather briefcase was under his arm.

"Good morning, Mr. Ives. Welcome to Arrowhead service," Lydia said, intoning the line from the stewardess training school. She took his boarding pass, tore off the bottom part, handed him the top portion, and preceded him along the aisle, stopping about half way down. She wasn't sure about Ives—he didn't look the garrulous type but you could never be sure. It might be better to keep him clear of the others.

"There, how's this?" she said.

"Fine, just fine," Ives said, sliding into a seat on the oppo-site side of the aisle from Mrs. Glinker without removing his topcoat. He fastened his seat belt with a loud snap. He seemed to be in a hurry; perhaps he had an important business meeting in New York. Lydia was about to ask him if he'd like to remove his topcoat when her attention was diverted by the appearance of a young woman about twenty-two, in patched blue jeans and a grimy zippered jacket. Her jeans had been adapted to accommodate the swelling home of a fetus that seemed to threaten at any moment to transit from the dark world of the womb into the bright, plush surround-ings of the first-class cabin. Lydia thought about the interna-tional air regulations that prohibited airlines selling a ticket to a woman more than eight months pregnant, unless she had a medical certificate saying she was not likely to give birth in transit, or was accompanied by a physician. But then, she reflected, it took a strong staff at the ticket counter to tell a woman in such condition, who fulfilled neither of the re-quirements, that they were sorry but they couldn't allow her on the flight. As a result, many women more than eight months pregnant were allowed to board flights. But Lydia had never seen one *this* pregnant.

The woman shook her ponytail over the back of her jacket and thrust a boarding pass at Lydia.

"Good morning, Mrs., uh . . ." Lydia tried to recall the name on the manifest. ". . . Browne," she said. She was sure the manifest had her listed as Miss.

"Perhaps you'd like a window seat," Lydia suggested, lead-ing the way, but Browne sat down in the aisle seat in the same row as Ives.

"Are you sure you wouldn't prefer to sit near a window, or a seat farther back?"

"Thanks, but this is great," Browne said, shifting gum from

one side of her mouth to the other and throwing a haversack on the floor. She glanced at Ives, but he turned away and stared out of the window.

"Would you like me to put your coat in the rack?" Lydia asked, indicating the stained jacket.

"No, it's okay," Browne replied, running the zipper down the front and over her protruding form.

"If there's anything you want, just press." Lydia indicated the overhead call button.

"Thanks," the girl said, and Lydia caught a gleam of excitement in her eyes. She turned and went forward, re-checked the manifest before pressing the button that controlled the closing of the forward door, and then surveyed her make-up in the mirror on the front of the medicine cabinet in the vestibule.

TWO

Bartlett adjusted his shoulder harness and tested it for security. Kowsky put his briefcase on the floor, extracted the film cassette, and slid it into a slot in the center instrument console. Bartlett heard Nardini shut the door and settle into his seat at the flight systems management position.

"Nav film home and locked," Kowsky reported.

"Switch on and stabilize for London Airport," Bartlett said, switching on a cathode ray tube—like a small television monitor—and beginning to read off the pretakeoff check items that appeared on it.

"Landing gear lever."

"Down and locked," replied Kowsky.

"Nose and visor standby switches."

"Off."

"Brakes."

"Parked," said Kowsky.

"VHF—NAV—DME." Bartlett turned to the radio panel on the center console.

"Checked and set," Kowsky replied, switching on the special distance measuring equipment. The digital readout spun to JFK, 2,990 nautical miles; GDR, Alternate, 2,036. When they were airborne the numbers would automatically change to show their decreasing distance to New York and Gander.

"Transponder."

"At standby," Kowsky said, leaning forward to snap on a switch that insured Arrowhead's radar equipment would respond to interception by air traffic controllers en route.

"Cabin 'No Smoking,' 'Seat Belt' signs."

"On."

"Auto throttle."

"Off."

"Fuel transfer switch."

"To rear tank."

Bartlett's eyes moved to the panel before him. He heard Nardini clicking switches as he went through his own checklist for the three inertial guidance navigation systems, the autopilot, and engine control systems.

"Stall captions."

"Out."

"Throttles."

"Checked—shut."

"Reheat."

"Off."

"Landing gear horn."

Kowsky momentarily pressed a button and the raucous sound of a warning horn, simulating a condition with wheels up and throttles closed, shattered the quiet of the flight deck.

Bartlett glanced at the ground intercom light indicating that the man on the ground had plugged in his phone jack and was standing by. He pressed his face against the small side window but couldn't see the man. He moved a switch and spoke into the microphone.

"Signalman, move forward to port."

SUPERSONIC

"Yes, sir."

A man in white coveralls, with protectors over his ears, appeared below. Bartlett gave him the thumbs-up sign.

"Fuel on board."

Kowsky examined the fuel gauges and consulted the Flight Plan. "As stated."

"Doors and hatches."

"Secured. Lights out."

"Flight documents."

Kowsky touched his briefcase. "On board."

"Flight data recorder."

Again Kowsky moved a switch. "Running. Battery on."

Bartlett felt the familiar glow of a shared achievement. He and Kowsky had been together on the same flight decks for three years now, since they'd met on a Boeing 747 conversion course. Last October they'd both applied, and been approved, for training on supersonic transports at which time they'd met Nardini. The three men had spent several hundred hours in the flight simulator before being sent up to Boeing's Renton plant for training on the real thing, a shining new production Arrowhead that had been wheeled out of the test hangar the morning they'd arrived.

Kowsky had made a big sacrifice in applying for training on the faster-than-sound birds. If Pete had stayed with the 747s he'd have moved into the left-hand seat in a couple of months. Now he'd have to wait another year before assuming his own command. Nardini, on the other hand, was considerably younger and more impatient. Although also a first-class pilot, he had evolved into a systems specialist, one of the new breed of flight engineers that had developed with the era of the supersonics, a man trained to apply complex theories of aerodynamics, physics, thermodynamics, and electronics to the computerized integrated systems that drove Arrowhead above the rim of the world at three times the speed of sound. Nardini had passed the course at the top of the class and his performance as flight management systems engineer had been faultless.

Nardini, the theorist, stubbornly defended systems; while Kowsky, a practical man like himself, took action first and analyzed problems later. Bartlett pressed the transmit button and spoke into his microphone.

"American Arrow Flight Zero-One to tower. Request start-up clearance." He took a ball-point pen from his shirt pocket.

"Tower to American Arrow Zero-One. Cleared to start up," replied a Cockney voice.

The man on the ground stepped back and pointed to number three engine. Bartlett turned to Kowsky. "Engine feed pumps."

"On," replied Kowsky. "Warning lights out."

"Start three."

Kowsky pressed a button on the center console below the throttle levers. Despite the earphones, Bartlett heard a howl followed by a subdued whine. The engine rev indicator for number three engine on the center panel came alive.

"Start two."

Kowsky pressed the next button. Bartlett glanced at the man outside, thumbs raised, peering under Arrowhead's slender fuselage.

"Start four." The sound on the flight deck increased.

"Start one." A tremor passed under his feet as the fourth engine caught. He checked the needles on the jet pipe temperature gauges, and switched the checklist on the monitor to After Start.

"Weather radar."

"On and standby," Kowsky intoned through the earphones.

"Powered flight controls."

"On and checked."

"Droop nose to fully down." Kowsky moved a lever and Arrowhead's nose dropped out of sight below the dashboard coaming, giving clear visibility to compensate for Arrowhead's thirty degree angle of climb during takeoff.

Bartlett spoke to the man on the ground. "All ground vehicles cleared?"

"Cleared and away, sir."

"Ground locks."

"Removed, sir." Red flags fluttered as the man waved the undercarriage external locks above his head.

"Disconnect jack."

"Disconnect jack. Good flight, Captain."

Bartlett switched off the ground interphone and waited for the man to reappear from under the nose. He came into view, held the interphone jack and its cable high, and moved clear. Bartlett called over his shoulder, "Engineering checks, Nick."

"Completed. All A-okay, Captain."

"American Arrow Zero-One to tower. Request taxi clearance," Bartlett said. He took a message pad from the top of the dashboard.

"Tower to American Arrow Zero-One. Cleared for taxi to Runway Twenty-eight Right. Ceiling and visibility unlimited. Contact tower on one-one-niner-decimal-five in holding bay Runway Twenty-eight Right. Twenty minutes delay."

Bartlett, obeying the international regulations for air traffic control, repeated the message from the notes he'd scribbled. He peered through the side window. The man held out his left arm horizontally and waved with his right.

"Release brakes."

"Brakes released."

Bartlett pushed the two outer throttle levers forward and

turned the nosewheel handle to the right. The terminal building swung away. He glanced at the center console where a map display had lit up with a pink glow. In the center of the picture was a bright spot of light that represented Arrowhead, superimposed on a map of southern England. To the left of the screen, Land's End and the ragged Welsh coast opened like the jaws of a prehistoric monster through which Arrowhead would shoot after takeoff. The longitude line for Greenwich, marked with a large zero, passed through the bright center dot, and other lines of latitude and longitude gridded the moving map display that had become alive as the film cassette projected. Linked to the inertial guidance navigational systems, the cassette was a living map simulator of the earth's surface directly under the aircraft's track. Guiding the two-hundred ton aircraft by the nosewheel steering handle, Bartlett continued to run his eye down the checklist, which he had switched to Taxi.

"Flight instruments and nav aids."

Kowsky, eyeing a Japan Air Lines 747 taxiing into a holding position ahead, glanced down. His eyes took in a row of green lights. "Checked. All operational."

Bartlett moved the yoke from side to side and pulled it fore and aft. He pressed the rudder pedals until they hit the limit stops. "Flight controls functioning," he said.

There was a moment of silence on the flight deck. "Check reverse thrust," Bartlett said, moving the nosewheel handle to follow the JAL 747 onto another taxi strip.

"Checked."

"Center of gravity indicator."

"Balance in limits."

"Select weather radar range for three hundred miles." Even with unlimited visibility Bartlett did not want to take chances with the weather. At three times the speed of sound Arrowhead could run into deteriorating weather in a few seconds.

SUPERSONIC

"Weather radar three hundred miles."

The JAL 747 braked in the holding bay at the end of Runway 28R. An Air India 707 and a Swissair Caravelle were waiting for takeoff clearance ahead of it. Bartlett pressed the brake toe pedals and Arrowhead stopped behind the high tail of the 747, bouncing as the nose dipped. He glanced at the Flight Plan, rechecking the fuel reserve, and found himself tapping his fingertips on the yoke and thinking of Gary in the recovery ward. His thoughts returned to the morning six months ago when Cathy had drawn his attention to the barely discernible slur in his son's speech. The disadvantage of flying as a career, for a family man, was the irregular hours—the days away from home that prevented constant contact with the people closest to you. Yet one would think that after being away for several days he would have been the first to notice the creeping impediment in his son's speech. Gary's garrulous and exaggerated talk, to him at least, sounded just like any other eighteen year old babbling with his buddies. But when Gary complained about his dragging left foot, he acted. Dr. Lieberman had been direct.

"Brain tumor."

"Can you operate? I mean . . ."

"It's lying in a very sensitive portion of the brain . . . can't operate until we do more tests."

Fate was a funny thing. He'd probably fallen in the gym because of his foot. So they'd *had* to operate sooner.

"American Arrow Zero-One. After takeoff fly Supersonic Track X ray Kennedy. Transit to supersonic at longitude ten west, fifty nautical miles south of Irish coast."

"Roger." Bartlett repeated the instruction into his microphone, and settled down to wait his turn for takeoff.

Three miles away in London Airport's Air Traffic Control, in the village of West Drayton, a controller assistant named

SUPERSONIC

John Gregory picked up sheets of paper that flip-flopped into folded bundles from a chute in the computer room. Gregory gathered up the sheets and, with practiced ease, tore along the perforations until he had a small stack of white paper strips each measuring eight inches long and one inch wide. The progress of an aircraft's flight across the Atlantic was recorded on these strips, called flight progress strips. Each strip bore the airline code letters and the flight number, and was divided into numbered sections. The numbers progressively became higher from right to left—beginning with 10, for meridian of longitude 10, followed by 15, 20, 30, 40, 50, and 60. These were the meridians at which each captain radioed his aircraft's position as he crossed them.

The en-route controllers, receiving this information, scribbled in the time in the appropriate longitude section, noted if the aircraft was early or late according to the captain's earlier estimated forecast of when he expected to cross the meridians, and jotted in other relevant data.

Gregory sorted the strips. He looked at Flight Zero-One's strip, noted it was the forty-seventh westbound flight of the day, and went into the adjoining Air Traffic Control Room, whistling as he walked between the aisles of green lit radarscopes, his face glowing from the diffused light from the backlighted airways maps above the controllers' positions. He placed bundles of flight progress strips on trays at different controllers' elbows, putting Flight Zero-One's strip in the tray belonging to a terminal controller named Allan Mondshead. Mondshead didn't notice: He was handling a strip for another flight, inserting it into a plastic holder before positioning it in a rack on the console before him. There were already fifteen strip holders in his rack, which was divided into various flight levels so that he knew at a glance how many aircraft were at flight level 390, how many at the 370 flight level, and how many at 350. He had a half-dozen aircraft ascending through the medium levels, having taken off from London Airport minutes ago, and now climbing to their cruising altitudes for the westbound flight.

Mondshead finished what he was doing, picked up the strip Gregory had put down, and placed it in a standby tray. He took a quick look at the console: There were five supersonics westbound at 71,000 feet and three eastbound at 74,000 feet, transiting to their cruise levels.

As Mondshead surveyed his console, other terminal controllers at the Shannon and Prestwick air control centers placed identical flight progress strips for Flight Zero-One into their console racks. Shannon and Prestwick worked together, and were combined under the name of Shanwick Air Traffic Control Center. At Gander and Kennedy International Airports, and at American Arrow Airlines Flight Operations Room in New York, identical flight progress strips for Flight Zero-One had popped out of computers and were put in standby trays.

Mondshead reached out to grab a plastic holder for Flight Zero-One's strip as a TWA captain requested letdown clearance. He adjusted his headset, lost his grip on the holder, and it fell to the floor, making a hollow sound. Checking the blips crowding the face of his scope, ignoring the sound of the other controllers' voices in the stuffy room, he spoke into his stick microphone.

"London to TWA Eight-Two-Two. Cleared for letdown to flight level two-five-zero," Mondshead said, as the drawl of a Pan Am captain sounded in his headset. The Pan Am flight was westbound over the Brecon radio beacon and letting down before he overflew the Woodley beacon a few miles from West Drayton. The aircraft, a DC-10, moved into the inner circle on his scope. As he replied to the Pan Am captain, he kicked the fallen plastic holder out of the way, picked up another, and slipped American Arrow Zero-One's flight progress strip into it ready for positioning in the rack on the console.

Bartlett's earphones came alive with the tower controller's voice giving instructions to the Air India captain. The 707 moved from the holding bay and taxied to the end of the runway. He turned down the volume as the exchange of instructions from the tower and the readback by the pilot began and checked the clock. There'd be less than a twenty minute delay before takeoff, after all. The 707 gathered speed, passed out of sight, and the Swissair Caravelle and JAL 747 nudged forward. While the Air India plane set course south across the equator, the JAL aircraft would head north over the Pole to Tokyo, he thought. Admiring the sleek lines of the Caravelle, probably bound for some European capital, he mused about this first jet to have its engine pods attached to the fuselage instead of the wings. The logic of the French, so obvious, to keep the wings free of drag-inducing nacelles. Yet Arrowhead's designers had put the four engines in snug twin pods built integrally with the wings, one pod on each side, and had faired them into the wings so skilfully they actually contributed to the overall lift of the delta-shaped wing.

The Caravelle thrust forward and disappeared down the runway and the 747 lumbered into position. Again he found himself tapping his fingers on the yoke as the JAL captain, with the characteristic exactitude of the Japanese, waited a full minute after his compressor revs came up before releasing the brakes. "Tower to American Arrow Zero-One. IFR clearance to Kennedy Airport from London on high-level Supersonic Track X ray. To maintain flight level six-niner-zero. Taxi into takeoff position Runway Twenty-eight Right."

SUPERSONIC

Bartlett released the brakes and grasped the steering control. Mondshead's voice came over the radio.

"ATC to American Arrow Zero-One."

"Roger. American Arrow Zero-One," Bartlett replied.

"ATC clearance American Arrow Zero-One to Kennedy," Mondshead confirmed, checking Arrowhead's flight plan that had been handed to him earlier. He proceeded to read off the aircraft's waypoints along Supersonic Track X ray while Bartlett ran his ball-point down the figures on the Flight Plan as Mondshead intoned them; at the same time, Mondshead picked up the flight progress strip holder and crosschecked the computerized position figures corresponding to the imprinted longitude figures. "Fifty-two north, ten west; fifty north, fifteen west; forty-niner north, twenty west; forty-seven north, thirty west. Gander Oceanic Control," he added, to remind Bartlett that at longitude thirty, geographically halfway between Shannon and Newfoundland, Arrowhead would pass to Gander ATC. He continued his litany, "Forty-four north, forty west; New York Oceanic Control, Delta weather ship; forty-three north, fifty west; forty-two north, sixty west; forty-one north, seventy west." Mondshead scribbled the numerals on the flight progress strip and waited for the readback.

Kowsky grabbed the nosewheel steering control while Bartlett read back the way points. When Bartlett looked up, Arrowhead was on the runway, positioned for takeoff.

"ATC to Zero-One. Your readback is correct. Contact tower one-one-niner-decimal-five when ready for takeoff. You are cleared for position."

Kowsky turned the radio frequency control to 119.5. The voice of the tower controller replaced Mondshead's in Bartlett's headset. "To maintain flight level six-niner-zero climbing to seven-five-zero as burn-off requires. Altimeter setting three-zero-zero-niner." Bartlett adjusted the knurled knob at the bottom of the barometric altimeter. "The wind calm. Zulu one-zero-one-four," the controller added, indicating Greenwich Mean Time.

Bartlett scribbled the instructions on his pad and read them back.

"Zero-One. Your readback is correct. Cleared for takeoff. Contact Shanwick Center one-two-seven decimal six-five at twenty thousand feet."

Bartlett repeated the new information and saw Kowsky make a note of the high-level radio frequency on which he would talk to the controller at Shannon as they passed through twenty thousand feet. He put down the Flight Plan and turned to the checklist monitor, switching to Takeoff.

"All engines, 71 percent power."

"Seventy-one percent. All engines," Kowsky said.

"Arm takeoff monitor."

"Takeoff monitor armed." Interconnected with the flight director, the takeoff monitor automatically fed electronic signals into the flight controls, making takeoff semiautomatic.

Bartlett could feel Arrowhead fighting the brakes now, like a whippet eager to be out of the starting gate. He looked down the twelve-thousand-foot concrete ribbon that was Runway 28R. "Brakes released," he said quietly, taking his toes off the pedals and placing his feet on the rudder pedals. The aircraft surged forward; the airspeed indicator needle moved upward. At sixty knots Kowsky called, "Engine power captions four greens."

The airport buildings vanished and the white dashes on the center line of the runway became a blur. "Angle of attack indicating," Kowsky said, scanning the sky. "Overhead clear."

They were halfway down the runway. He could feel the nose lifting in response to the signals from the takeoff monitor. The end of the runway was visible. There was always the temptation to pull back the yoke at this point and lift the aircraft clear. Kowsky, eyes glued to the airspeed indicator, said "Vee one." They were committed to flight now. Ten seconds later he called, "Rotate," and Bartlett eased the yoke back. It came toward him easily, effortlessly. The distant rumble of wheels on concrete ceased and Arrowhead pointed upward at thirty degrees.

He switched the checklist to After Takeoff. There were twelve items. He knew them by heart, but he always flew by the book. The airspeed indicator showed one hundred and seventy knots when he said, "Wheels up."

"Wheels up," repeated Kowsky, moving a lever. A distant clunk told him the gear had locked up. "Wheel lights out."

"Wheel *temp* lights."

"Out," said Kowsky. Now that the undercarriage was retracted, a stream of cold air from special intakes under the wings played on the tires. As far as Bartlett was concerned, it was the most important item on the After Takeoff list. Without the cool air, at supersonic speed the rubber tires would be burned off the wheels by the heat, generated by skin friction, transmitted through the aircraft's structure.

Bartlett called off the remaining items. At five thousand feet he turned on course, selected a button on the flight director, pressed it, and watched the airspeed indicator needle climb. The Woodley Beacon beeped through the earphones.

"Droop nose fully up."

Kowsky pressed a switch and waited expectantly. "Droop nose fully up and locked." The black, nonreflective upper surface of the nose ahead of the windshield appeared, its finely tapering point reminding Bartlett of a hummingbird's beak.

"Audio mute." There was no need to listen to the chatter from other traffic now.

"Audio mute," Kowsky said, adjusting a radio knob.

"Radio altimeter, check."

He waited for Kowsky to select a test switch.

"Radio altimeter checks."

" 'No Smoking' cabin sign off. 'Seat Belt' remains on."

" 'No Smoking' sign off. 'Belt' sign on."

Clarence Ives reached for a cigarette the moment the 'No Smoking' sign went out. His fingers trembled as the match flared. He inhaled deeply and puffed out a smoke cloud that drifted toward the young woman on the aisle seat. She wafted it away with her hand.

"I'm sorry," Ives said, and reached overhead to adjust the ventilator outlet. He glanced covertly at her and turned to the window. When she went to the john he'd move back a bit. He sighed and took another drag on the cigarette, thinking of the blue suitcase in the baggage hold. For the hundredth time since takeoff he wished he'd been more insistent with the checking-in clerk at London Airport.

"Sorry, sir. It's too big for carry-on baggage. It'll have to go in the baggage compartment."

All his fifty-five years had been a succession of "Sorry, sirs," but that would change as soon as he got through Customs at Kennedy. His mouth eased as he thought of the look on Callahan's face when he showed him the contents of the secret compartment. "Clarence, for once in your goddamned life you've done something real." And he'd add—of course he'd add, he always did—"With your know-how and my skill we'll go far."

Yes, we'll both be rich. But the price of wealth was more than know-how and skill. The hair on his neck bristled as he recalled the moment of terror in the Lombard Street bank director's office.

"If you'll kindly sign this receipt, Mr. Ives, I'll have our messenger deliver everything to your hotel in accordance with this authorization from our New York office. Where are you staying in London?"

"Uh, the Dorchester." He'd leaned over and signed with a shaking hand.

"Would three o'clock this afternoon be convenient, sir?"

"Yes. Very convenient."

He took another puff on the cigarette and wiped the sweat from his forehead with the back of his hand. Jesus, it was warm in here. Wish I'd taken my topcoat off before sitting down. Too late now, have to pass the damn kid to get it off and put it in the overhead rack.

The most agonizing moment had been before the director had stood up and handed him the pen to sign the receipt. If Callahan's little speech hadn't come back to him at that precise moment, his nerve would have cracked. "Take a look at yourself, Clarence. Thirty-five years with Smithers, Smithers, O'Donnell, and Rose—thirty-five years devoted to making *other* guys rich, investing their fortunes, making *them* richer. And what's been in it for you? Eighteen grand a year? Maybe twenty, huh? This plan's foolproof. But only *you* can do it. You're the front man. For once in your life you've got to stick your neck out or stay in the back room until you rot." Until you rot. He licked his lips; he wasn't going to rot. Not now. Travel and vacations in Bermuda, Hawaii, Europe lay before him like an attainable dream.

"Excuse me, sir. Would you like a magazine or news-paper?" He jerked his head up. It was the stewardess.

"Uh, no. I mean, have you got the *Wall Street Journal?*"

"I'm sorry, sir." He felt his body tighten from an old habit. "The *New York Times* and the London papers."

"No, thanks." He uncrossed his ankles and tried to relax, but the director's face swam into his inner vision and he saw him peering again at the letter of authorization. Had he suspected anything? The English were cool, never showed their feelings, even when they had a hunch something was wrong. He moved his head around the cabin. Everybody was deeply engrossed in their own affairs, but the tall man up front, in the window seat. He was staring at him, raising his hand. Supposing they'd put someone on his tail?

"Coming, sir," the stewardess called as she hurried past to hand a newspaper to the tall man. Take hold of yourself; your imagination's on the run. Callahan was the world's best forger; there was nothing to fear. The cigarette stub burned his fingers and he rammed it into the ashtray. With a sidelong glance, he studied the passenger in the aisle seat, noticing for the first time that she was pregnant. He let his eyes drop, saw the gym shoes on her feet, the haversack on the floor, and he had a sudden feeling that somebody was watching him. He raised his eyes and found himself looking into a small white face peering from behind a seat on the opposite side of the aisle. Although only part of the face was visible, the portion he could see struck him as being excessively alert to its surroundings. Too late, he blinked and turned away.

"Hello there. I'm Gladys Glinker. How are you enjoying the flight? Your first time in supersonics?"

"Hi. Fine, thanks." He hesitated and added, "No, I've, uh, been across several times by supersonic." He congratulated himself. It sounded as convincing as yesterday's encounter in the bank.

The face came completely around the side of the seat and a frail old woman's body appeared. She stood up, came toward him, and sat in the seat directly across the aisle.

"I always say, 'If you've got to travel, travel first class,'" she said, looking past the younger woman at him. Then her eyes examined the girl; sharp, beady eyes behind the glasses, taking in the slouching form. "Hello, I'm Gladys—Gladys Glinker," she said, extending her hand and smiling.

Alex Browne stretched back as far as the seat would allow. She took Mrs. Glinker's hand. "Hi. Alex Browne, Browne with an E."

"Pleased to meet you."

Ives turned to the window and pretended to stare at something below.

"You didn't mention your name, ah, Mr. . . . I always say 'If you're going to have a pleasant cruise or flight you must get to know your fellow passengers.'"

He swung around. "My name's Ives. Uh, Ives." Damn. Now they knew his name. Before she asked his first name —her mouth was already opening to inquire—he added, "Pleased to meet you." He took the small hand and jerked it once. The girl smiled. "Hi."

He nodded, peering around with a trapped look at the unoccupied seats. He could make an excuse and go to the john, but he hesitated as he looked at Browne stretched out in the seat. He felt in his pocket for another cigarette, found a squashed package, and lit up. Then he unzipped his briefcase and extracted a file folder. He ran his eyes down the copy of the letter of transmittal he had given to the bank director and shoved it behind the other papers. His heart started to pound. He swallowed and took a deep drag on the cigarette.

"Won't be long now, eh?" The old woman's thin voice broke into his consciousness.

"I guess I'll make it," the younger woman replied, grinning.

"Where are you going?"

"New York. I've a sister there." Alex looked at Mrs. Glinker curiously. "Been visiting London?"

"Just a short visit this time. Old friends, you know."

"You a New Yorker?"

47

"Yes."

Ives looked at the tip of the cigarette, pretending to be deep in thought. But his attention was distracted by the girl passing her hand over her abdomen.

"I want her to be born Stateside," she said.

"I understand the second part of your sentiment perfectly, my dear. But medical science has no way of guaranteeing the first," said Mrs. Glinker.

The girl said simply, "I want it to be a girl."

Gladys Glinker looked at the stained jeans and soiled shirt.

"You're probably wondering how come I can afford to fly first class," Alex said self-consciously. Mrs. Glinker's eyelashes fluttered.

"My sister sent me the money. I was broke after bumming around Europe for ten months." She scratched her nose with the tip of her finger. "I thought I might never get a chance to fly in a supersonic, so I decided to travel back to the States in style."

Mrs. Glinker nodded. She appeared lost in thought. Then she asked, "Did you get to Greece?"

"Yeah. Some country. I didn't go for that Acropolis stuff, but they've got some super bars and discos in Athens. And out on the islands it's for real. Have you been there? Athens, I mean."

"Yes. And to the islands. The Dodecanese."

"Dodeca—what?"

"Dodecanese. They're a group of islands in the southeast Aegean Sea," she replied. "Used to belong to Italy at one time."

The old biddy sounds like a schoolteacher, thought Ives, rolling the cigarette around in his fingers and studying the wording near the filter tip.

"Been to Italy?" asked the girl.

SUPERSONIC

"About twenty years ago." Gladys Glinker looked up at the ceiling reflectively. "Must have been in the early fifties. We were on our way from Madrid to Turkey, before we caught a ship through the Golden Horn for Alexandria. That was before the Arab-Israeli bother got really going, of course. Then we went to, uh . . ." she turned to Alex Browne. "When you get to my age you begin to forget the details of itineraries."

"You don't sound old," Alex said ingenuously.

"I'll be seventy-seven next July," Mrs. Glinker replied, the crinkles splaying up from the corners of her mouth.

"You don't look a day older than, uh, sorta middle-aged." Alex paused and added, "Did you travel on a tour?"

"Me on a tour? Never! Just me and my husband. Can't stand to see those tourists abroad. Herded like sheep from one museum to another, from this art gallery to the next. I always say, 'If you're going to travel, travel like a traveler. Either alone or with someone you like.' On a tour—never!" She paused and added, "What does your husband want? A boy or a girl?"

"I'm not married."

That'll knock the old lady for a loop. Ives ventured a careful sideways glance.

"In that case only you'll be disappointed if it turns out to be a boy," Mrs. Glinker said philosophically.

Alex Browne fell silent. Then she said, "Where else have you been, Gladys. You don't mind if I call you Gladys, do you?"

"Not at all. Where shall I start? From Alexandria we went down the Nile—the Blue Nile, that is—and the Valley of the Kings and spent a few days at Victoria Falls." She jerked her head toward the front of the cabin and stared at some distant spot. "When my husband was alive I shot lions

49

in Africa—but I wouldn't do that now, not with all these 'vanishing species.' " She turned back to Alex. "Once we went up the Amazon in a canoe, without an Indian guide, and found ourselves surrounded by crocodiles. I've starved at twenty below zero in a tent in the Himalayas and I broke a leg jumping from a moored blimp in France, before the war, when it caught fire."

"A blimp? What's that?"

"An airship. They used them for army reconnaissance. My husband was at one time a military advisor to the French government. I went up in a balloon, too, in Switzerland. We tried to fly over the Matterhorn." She paused and took a breath. "Do you know the Matterhorn is also known by the name of Mont Cervin and is more than fourteen thousand feet high?"

Alex shook her head. "Wasn't very good at geography at school. Say, you've really been around, Gladys."

Mrs. Glinker shrugged. "A bit," she replied modestly. She leaned over and looked out of the window. Straightening up, she checked her watch, drawing her lips together as if to whistle. "I hope this plane gets to New York on time. I don't want to miss my connection."

"I thought you lived in New York."

Gladys Glinker shook her head. "I said I was a New Yorker, dear. I'm bound for Yokohama."

Alex's eyes were saucers. "Yokohama! Isn't that some place in, uh . . . ?"

"Japan. I catch a freighter out of 'Frisco in the morning."

"A freighter?"

Gladys Glinker studied her fingernails. "It only takes twenty-one days," she said in a disappointed voice. "Once my husband and I went from Belem—that's in South America—

across the South Atlantic and through the Indian Ocean to Ceylon on an old converted banana boat. It took six weeks, we stopped everywhere after Capetown." She paused to take a breath. "Went ashore on all the exotic islands in the Indian Ocean."

The old girl wasn't such a nobody after all, Ives reflected. She'd been around. He glanced at Alex Browne, staring at Gladys Glinker with her mouth open, and leaned back in the seat. He replaced the papers in the folder and put it back in the briefcase. His muscles, drawn taut by the tension of the past twenty-four hours, began to relax, but his body ached. He stubbed the cigarette in the ashtray and closed his eyes, with a last image of the stewardess laughing with the dignified looking man up front. As he drifted off to sleep, he wondered what they were talking about with such animation.

Bartlett scanned the sky for traffic, then glanced down at the moving map display. London, with longitude zero cutting through its center, had moved to the right of the screen and the pinpoint of light at center screen was south of Pembroke, in West Wales. The coast of Cornwall fell away abruptly at the bottom. The airspeed indicator showed 540 knots; the altimeter digital readout indicated twenty thousand feet. He waited for the falling-behind feeling as the flight director automatically cut the raw fuel pouring into the afterburners behind the turbines, where it was ignited like a blowtorch for added power during the climbout. Arrowhead eased back.

"Reheat off," Kowsky said, observing four lights change from red to green.

The needle on the combined Machmeter and airspeed indicator steadied and then surged upward.

"Engage autopilot."

Kowsky pressed a button on the center console. "Autopilot engaged."

"Visor up," he said, taking a final look at the empty sky. The flight deck darkened as the steel visor slid upward, completely covering the windshield. All sound on the already quiet deck ceased. Bartlett saw his reflection in the windshield and turned the dimmer switch for the overhead lights to Bright.

"Shanwick frequency."

Kowsky twisted the radio frequency knob to 127.65, checking his scribbled figures. Bartlett pressed the transmit button.

"American Arrow Zero-One to Shanwick. Climbing through flight level two-zero-zero." Ninety seconds later he said, "Flight level three-five-zero."

"Shanwick to American Arrow Zero-One. Roger," replied an Irish voice.

In the subdued light of the Air Traffic Control center at Shannon Airport a controller named Sean O'Reilly peered at the blip that had appeared on his radarscope. He watched it move swiftly from the scope's edge toward the top center. With a radar range of only two hundred miles' radius, he knew he could hold the supersonics for only a few minutes. He reached for the plastic strip holder and placed it in a slot under the three-five-zero flight level control sector. There were nine strips in this sector of his console as he checked several subsonic aircraft to their cruising altitudes. He looked up at the screen. The FL 350 flag that accompanied Arrowhead's blip across his scope had already changed to FL 450. Holy Mother o'God, these supersonics climb faster than angels soaring to heaven! His eye lingered for a moment on the fast-moving blip; the speed label flashed from Mach .75 to Mach .85. His eyes swept the screen in a careful pattern as the voice of an El Al Israel captain came through his earphones, requesting clearance through Airway UG-1 into London Airport. O'Reilly checked the blip of the El Al plane and spoke into the microphone. At the same time he picked up Zero-One's flight progress strip holder and slid it into the flight level 450 control sector on his console, noting that it was the only aircraft there.

As he did so a controller at Prestwick ATC two hundred air miles northeast of Shannon picked up his copy of a flight progress strip headed AAA-01 and moved it into flight level 450 on his console. Since he was busy working five 707s, two DC-8s and a Lockheed L.1011 that were converging on Airway UA-1 he didn't have time to follow the progress of Flight Zero-One's blip across his scope, so he pressed a red button by the side of his seat and spoke to O'Reilly. "Prestwick to Shannon high-level controller. AA Flight Zero-One to you."

"Roger. AA Flight Zero-One to Shannon control," said O'Reilly.

To the south the curvature of the earth revealed a ragged line of cumulus clouds, indicating the point where the sea merged with the sky. By shading his eyes from the bright sunlight that poured through the side window Bartlett could see the outline of Cornwall, laid out like an atlas, and farther south the dark smear that was Finistère, the northernmost part of France that jutted into the Atlantic. He glanced back as Nardini punched keys on the navigational computer, feeding in the latitude and longitude waypoints of their track, rechecking the figures he'd fed in at takeoff. After he pressed a series of keys, Nardini checked the displays on the console that showed Arrowhead's ground speed, track, and true airspeed. Bartlett turned back to the center console and his eye fell on the radiation detector. The amber alert and red take-action lights were out, as he expected them to be at fifty-five thousand feet, but the counter built into the dial of the instrument showed eight millirems. Safe enough, but to reassure himself, he pressed the test button at the top of the instrument. A white light appeared in a tiny window, indicating that the system was working properly. The amber light came on when the dose rate exceeded ten millirems per hour and the red lamp when it rose to one thousand millirems an hour. He glanced at the Machmeter. It showed Mach .93.

"Announce climb, Pete," he said, tightening his grip on the control yoke.

Kowsky switched on the cabin PA system. "Good morning, ladies and gentlemen. In a few moments we will be starting our supersonic climb to cruising altitude. Those of you who are unfamiliar with flight procedures in supersonic transport aircraft will be aware of the more than usual tilt of the cabin floor as the aircraft climbs. This is perfectly normal. Please be sure that your seat belts are tightly fastened and all loose objects such as handbags and carry-on baggage secured. There will be no sensation when the aircraft transits from subsonic to supersonic speed. Thank you."

Bartlett caught Kowsky's nod as he switched off the PA. This was the part of the flight he liked, overriding the flight director, which stayed on to perform other functions, and flying the aircraft under manual control.

"Disengage autopilot."

"Autopilot disengaged," said Kowsky.

The radio altimeter showed sixty thousand feet. Bartlett pulled back the control column and pushed the four throttle levers forward, feeling the back of the seat press against his body. The artificial horizon indicated the vertical movement as he pointed Arrowhead's nose to the sky. The Machmeter nudged 0.98 . . . 0.99 . . . and flashed to unity. The pressure on his hands increased as the control yoke moved forward. An orange light winked on the overhead panel.

"Fuel transferring," Kowsky said, glancing up.

Pressure on the yoke increased as the nose-down movement caused by transiting through the speed of sound pressed Arrowhead's nose down. Computerized signals from the flight director triggered electric pumps in the fuel tanks, causing fuel in the eighteen tanks in the aircraft's wings and below the cabin floor to surge through a complex gallery of pipes from the forward tanks into amidship collector tanks. From these tanks hundreds of gallons of fuel a minute poured into a big tank in the extreme tail cone of the aircraft. The mass of the fuel acted as a weight that swiveled Arrowhead through her center of gravity to counteract the characteristic nose down tendency of supersonics when transiting from subsonic to supersonic speed.

Bartlett checked the overhead lights, which now showed green, indicating that the transfer of fuel was complete. The yoke pressure fell off. Nardini called, "Fuel transfer complete."

The artificial horizon leveled and he continued to move the throttles forward. The Machmeter turned to 1.7. It passed through Mach 2.0—twice the speed of sound. 2.2 . . . 2.4 . . . 2.6 . . . 2.8 . . . He eased the throttles, the counter turned to 3.0 and steadied. The altimeter read 69,100. He moved the yoke forward until the figures showed precisely sixty-nine thousand feet. There was nothing like being exact. The aircraft would steadily rise to 75,000 feet as the fuel burned off. By that time they'd be approaching Nantucket and preparing for a fast descent into the regular approach pattern with several score of subsonic jets, under New York Oceanic Control.

"Engage autopilot."

"Autopilot engaged."

"What's the burn-off, Nick?"

Nardini tapped the keys on his calculator, tore off a paper slip, and compared the amount of fuel burned off since take-off with the computerized figures on his copy of the flight plan.

"Dead on," he said, handing the slip to Bartlett, who checked it and dropped it into the plastic waste container at the side of his seat. He slackened the buckles of his harness and stretched his legs to either side of the rudder pedals. Now that they were on course at eighteen hundred knots thirteen miles above the Atlantic the tension that had imperceptibly built up during the takeoff and climb-out slipped away. Arrowhead sat rock steady, without a tremor passing through her structure, only the faint hum of her engines reaching the flight deck. He looked out the side window at the violet vault of sky, in the center of which the flight deck appeared to be suspended, an illusion created by the fact that his eyes had no point of reference to earth. The horizon had vanished, swallowed by a deep blue smudge where space and the ocean's edge melded. He checked the moving map as London slipped off the right-hand edge and a wide, empty mass moved in to the left—the Atlantic Ocean. He decided to give an Air Report Position, although one wasn't due until he was at longitude fifteen degrees west. He slid down the transmit button.

"American Arrow Zero-One to Shanwick. ARP latitude fifty-one north, longitude twelve. Flight level six-niner-zero. Speed Mach three."

"Shanwick to Zero-One. Roger," O'Reilly's voice was

crystal clear. "Contact Shanwick at longitude thirty west on frequency one-three-three decimal eight."

"Contact Shanwick high-level frequency one-three-three decimal eight, at longitude thirty west," Bartlett repeated and switched off, while O'Reilly, still marveling at the rate of climb of Zero-One, watched Arrowhead's blip move to the extreme edge of his scope. He pressed a red button. "Shanwick high level controller. AA Flight Zero-One. Flight level six-niner-zero. Speed Mach three. Supersonic Track X ray to Kennedy. Passed to you," he said.

"Roger," replied the crisp voice of a high-level controller in another section of the ATC Center. From now on, until Arrowhead came within the radar range of the Delta weather ship plowing a ten-mile square course on longitude 40, the high-level en-route controllers would keep track of Arrowhead by radio only.

O'Reilly leaned forward, picked up the plastic holder from his console, removed Zero-One's flight progress strip, and slipped it into a small stack of other flight progress strips held together with an elastic band. On one of his frequent journeys between the rows of radarscopes, a controller assistant would pick up the stack, take it to the computer record room, and place it, with the other stacks of flight progress strips, on a shelf where it would be kept for thirty days before being destroyed. If some sort of what was euphemistically called "an occurrence" happened to Arrowhead, the paper slip, with the others from London Airport, Prestwick, Gander, and New York, would be handed to government air accident investigators. Together with the ground tapes and the cockpit voice recorder storing away everything spoken between Bartlett, Kowsky, Nardini, the tower, terminal, and en-route controllers, the flight progress strips would help them to reconstruct every second of Arrowhead's flight from the moment her wheels started to roll on London's Runway 28R, to the second any accident occurred. The other flight progress strips in the stack would enable them to represent on a dummy scope the exact position, altitude, and speed of every aircraft in all sectors through which they had passed that day, at any precise second of flight.

Before he re-examined the flurry of blips that crawled in an untidy formation across his scope, O'Reilly gave one last glance at Zero-One's blip before it vanished from the edge of the glass.

THREE

Sir Leonard studied the sky. He thought he saw the pale gleam of a star in the north, but dismissed the idea and turned back to Lydia. "How long have you been in the supersonics?"

"Six months, sir. Since American Arrow started flying them." He saw the flash of pride in her eyes. "Much better than the old 747s," she added.

"Fewer people to look after?" He laughed, wiped his lips with a serviette, and put it down on the luncheon tray.

"Oh no, sir. It's not that. We had plenty of help on the jumbos." She paused and added, "We get more time off between flights on the supers."

He raised his eyebrows. "Now *that's* interesting," he waited for her to go on, but she remained silent. "Why would that be?" he asked.

"On account of galactic radiation, sir," she said reluctantly.

His hunch had been right. Last year he had attended an international conference on aviation medicine at Copenhagen and had listened to a paper by an American physician on the irregularities of menstrual flow reported by stewardesses flying in long-distance subsonic jets. The disturbances had been suspected to be the results of diurnal rhythm—the effect on the human body when it traveled rapidly through several degrees of longitude, as when flying across the Atlantic or Pacific and the long haul across Siberia from Moscow to Vladivostok. Sir Leonard had developed his own theory about the disorders; he suspected they were due to the long time spent at elevated altitudes rather than diurnal rhythm, which never affected people flying from north to south or vice versa. Aeroflot and Lufthansa had done tests with control groups of stewardesses. The results, the Copenhagen expert had pointed out, had not been definitive, which made Sir Leonard more convinced that the cause was due more to galactic radiation at thirty-five thousand feet altitude than crossing lines of longitude. He'd promised himself that when he retired from medical practice, he would explore the subject in depth.

He smiled as he looked into Lydia's face, and wondered what effect galactic radiation had on businessmen and women who flew the supersonics between Europe and the United States two or three times a week. Some American executives, he knew, left New York by the morning plane; flew to Paris, London, or Rome; conducted their business; and were back in New York in time to catch the evening television news. Wouldn't their bodies accumulate more than the maximum millirems of radiation considered safe?

Another topic that had been discussed at Copenhagen had been the ozone hazard. His mind mulled over one lecturer's remark that ecologists had said the engine exhaust gases from supersonics would destroy the thin ozone layer that helped screen the earth from harmful ultraviolet radiation. There'd been a report from the American National Academy of Sciences that a five percent decrease in the average ozone concentration over the United States would cause a twenty-six percent increase in ultraviolet radiation and eight thousand more skin cancer cases a year, plus three hundred extra cancer deaths.

"How many trips a week do you do?" he asked Lydia.

"Twelve, sir." A lovely young woman, he thought, admiring her oval face and smooth skin. She'd be about twenty-six, the same age as his youngest daughter.

"It used to be eighteen. We cross three times a day now. That's why I stayed in London last night."

"Three single crossings a day?"

"Yes, sir. It used to be four. That made a four and a half day work week. Now it's down to four days." Her eyes suddenly became alight. "But after this flight I'm off for a month."

"A month? Some sort of accumulated leave?"

She nodded and smiled happily. "I'm going to be married day after tomorrow."

Sir Leonard leaned forward and touched the hand resting on top of the seat in front of his own. "Congratulations! He's a very lucky fellow, if I may say so."

"Thank you, sir."

He saw her fingering the brooch on her blouse, and his eyes narrowed. Wasn't that an exposure film badge cleverly worked into the brooch's design where the three A's representing American Arrow Airlines intertwined?

"Is that an exposure film badge?" he said, pointing to the brooch.

"Uh, yes." Lydia Olsen jerked her fingers away from the badge and pretended to tuck in the blouse around her waist. "It's just a safety check," she remarked casually, preparing to move away.

"I suppose the pilots wear them too?" he suggested.

SUPERSONIC

Lydia nodded. "But theirs are not as pretty as this." She laughed. "Are you sure you wouldn't like a drink, Sir Leonard?" she added, obviously changing the subject.

He gave her a smile. "It's still a bit too early in the morning. But I wouldn't mind another cup of tea."

"Certainly, sir."

He looked out of the window, blinking at the bright sunshine that poured from a purple sky, and marveled at the thought that he was streaking through the boundary of space at bullet velocity while sitting in a comfortable chair that appeared to be stationary. A few minutes later Lydia reappeared at his elbow. He took the tray with the little teapot and hot water jug. "Milk first?"

"Thank you." He smelled the aromatic steam that rose as she poured. At that moment, a musical chime sounded from the vestibule in front of the cabin.

"If you'll excuse me, Sir Leonard," Lydia said, filling the cup and putting down the teapot. "I'm wanted on the flight deck."

"Certainly. You attend to your duties and I'll enjoy my cuppa." As she hurried away he thought about the case that awaited him in New York. The long-distance call had been brief and to the point. "We need you for immediate consultation and possibly to operate," Gillespie had said. It was fortunate he'd been rearranging his case load and was about to go on holiday in Switzerland, otherwise he'd never have been able to fit in the trans-Atlantic trip. He sipped his tea and glanced out of the window again, fancying he saw a faint flickering far to the north and wondering if it was the aurora borealis. Imagination; he was tired. He pushed away the tea tray, pulled down the blind, and sank into the luxurious seat, enjoying the peaceful detachment from earth, its hurriedly called medical consultations, and its operating rooms.

SUPERSONIC

The purpose of his rushed journey across the Atlantic lost its urgency and the voices of the pregnant girl and the old lady behind retreated from his consciousness as he drifted into sleep.

Bartlett turned as Lydia's head appeared around the door.

"Bring Mr. Maxwell to the flight deck. There's a personal call for him on the airline frequency."

"Yes, Captain."

The dispatcher's voice at American Arrow Airlines' Kennedy office went on. "The message is being routed on a private line from Washington, Captain. The White House."

"Roger. Mr. Maxwell is coming to the flight deck."

"What're we supposed to do? Plug our ears?" Kowsky asked.

"Look busy and forget anything you hear," Bartlett said.

"Here's something to look busy with," Nardini said, passing a folded map to Kowsky, as the door opened and Lydia appeared with Maxwell. Bartlett swiveled around as far as the harness would allow. So this was Vincent Maxwell. He looked exactly like the pictures on television—the world-famous image, a stocky figure with a commanding face, and a thick neck. His outthrust hands made a characteristic grabbing gesture as he took the headpiece from Bartlett. Before he put it on he acknowledged Bartlett's presence with one word, "Captain."

"Pleased to meet you, sir," Bartlett said. Pointing to his own headset, he added, "We're on another frequency. Yours is private, sir."

In the reflection from the visored windshield Bartlett saw a thick muscle work under Maxwell's jaw. Despite the thick, foam-rubber pads that clamped his own headset over his ears he heard Maxwell say, "It's the time of day when the sun looks rosy," and guessed that it was a password phrase that identified him to the White House speaker, whom Bartlett could only assume was the president. No doubt they changed the code at prearranged periods throughout the day. Then followed a long period of silence. Bartlett inspected the moving map display, checked the fuel gauges, looked at the flight director panel, and wondered what was being said through the ether as Arrowhead sped toward Kennedy, overtaking at more than three times their speed the hundreds of Boeing 747s, DC-10s, L-1011s, and the older 707s and DC-8s that crowded the airlanes forty thousand feet below. The only traffic near their altitude would be the midday, eastbound Arrowhead service from Kennedy to Le Bourget, which they were due to pass as they neared a point three hundred miles south of Newfoundland. They never saw the other airplane. At a closing speed of thirty-six hundred knots it was impossible to spot it, despite warning of its approach by the chatter on the ATC frequency and the brief interchange of radio messages between the two captains.

Maxwell said, "Understood, sir. At the appointed hour." Then followed another period of silence, broken by the crinkling of the map as Kowsky refolded it. Maxwell said, "Good-bye, sir," removed the headset, and handed it to Bartlett.

"Thanks, Captain." He saw his reflection in the windshield, adjusted his tie, and pointed. "Doesn't it bother you flying blind like this, Captain?"

"We're only blind in the forward direction, sir. We have limited side vision." He indicated the small side windows, made of heat-resistant, toughened transparent plastic and quartz.

"How hot is it on the other side, Captain?"

"On the outside of the visor, sir? About one hundred and thirty degrees centigrade. It's hotter at the extreme nose. Approximately two hundred degrees."

Maxwell looked surprised. "I didn't know it got *that* hot. What about the rest of the airplane?"

"The wingtips are as hot as the visor, but the temperature drops as you come inboard amidships. The outside of the fuselage is about one hundred and forty degrees." Bartlett turned around. "What's the skin temperature forward of the leading edge, Nick?"

Nardini consulted one of his scores of dials. "One hundred and forty-two, Captain."

"That's outside the first-class cabin where I'm sitting?" Maxwell asked.

"Yes, sir."

The stubby man spread his legs apart in a commanding posture and thrust both hands into his jacket pockets. He emanated a sense of power and for a moment Bartlett imagined himself on the opposite side of an international meeting facing Maxwell. A feeling of unease passed through him that he shook off with difficulty.

"Captain," Maxwell said, his lips turned up puckishly, "have you ever landed one of these things and scorched yourself stepping out?"

"Someone worried about that before we started flying these fast birds, sir." He bent forward and adjusted a knob. "The structure cools off as we cut back to subsonic speed and descend to a lower altitude."

"Doesn't the alternate heating and cooling strain the structure?"

"Stainless steel, titanium, and special aluminum alloys take care of that problem, sir."

"Excuse me, sir," Nardini said, stretching across Maxwell and handing a paper slip to Bartlett. "Fuel flow into trim tanks A-okay, Captain."

Bartlett looked at the figures showing the number of gallons of fuel that the computer had directed the electric pumps to pass through the fuel-tank system, trimming the aircraft to compensate for the fuel burn-off. Maxwell waited until Bartlett had put the slip of paper into the waste container before asking, "What does that trim tank business mean?"

"There's a seat here, sir," Bartlett said, moving the folded jump seat into position between himself and Kowsky. He turned to Kowsky. "Take over position reporting, Pete."

Kowsky nodded, and Maxwell eased himself into the seat, his face attentive. "Well, sir," Bartlett commenced, easing the headphones away from his ears. "We use the fuel to trim the aircraft on a continuing basis throughout the flight. The most critical mode of flight, as far as the aircraft's weight and attitude to the ground are concerned, is when we transit to supersonic speed." He glanced sideways at Maxwell and was rewarded with an understanding nod. "At that point the center of aerodynamic lift swings toward the tail and this tilts the nose down. Now I can adjust that by pulling the control column back, but that moves up the elevons—they're the flaps on the wing trailing edge. Or I could adjust the elevon trim tabs. If we continued across the ocean with the elevons or tabs up we'd get a drag penalty—and use more fuel—because the air would be disturbed as it flowed over the uplifted surfaces, creating eddies. What we want is a smooth, nonturbulent flow."

"So you move the fuel around from one end of the airplane to the other. And keep the elevons flat?"

"Yes, sir. There's a large trim tank in the extreme tail of the aircraft, under the fin. The tank is almost empty at takeoff. When we go supersonic we pump fuel into it from the forward tanks."

"And I guess you do the reverse at the end of the flight when you reduce speed from supersonic to subsonic."

"That's correct, sir. The nose swings up as we slow from supersonic to subsonic speed, so we move the fuel in the rear tank forward to retrim the aircraft. There're eighteen tanks —in the wings and under the passenger cabins, plus the big tank in the rear. We transfer fuel constantly to trim the aircraft as fuel is burned off. Actually, we're gaining height as fuel is burned off. For instance," Bartlett turned to Nardini and held out his hand, "the Flight Plan, Nick."

Nardini handed him a pad with several sheets of paper gripped in a spring clip. Bartlett took off the top sheet. It was covered with the columns of figures and coded letter symbols.

"Here's the Flight Plan," he said, passing the sheet to Maxwell. "We went into supersonic cruise at sixty-nine thousand feet." He moved his finger to the bottom of the page. We'll be at seventy-five thousand feet two hundred and forty miles east of Kennedy."

"The airplane naturally gets lighter as you burn off fuel. I follow."

"And the higher we fly the thinner the air and the more efficiently the engines operate. They require less fuel per mile the higher we go, sir."

Maxwell looked surprised. "I didn't know that." He paused, stroked his chin thoughtfully, and studied the figures on the Flight Plan. At the top the computer had typed: "AAA Flight Plan, FL 01. LDN—JFK/NYK." Across the top of the page were headings: ZTM, TTG, POS, FL, TOW, and others that Bartlett could see meant nothing to Maxwell.

"What do these symbols mean, Captain? Across the top here."

SUPERSONIC

"ZTM means zone time—Greenwich Mean Time as we fly over the lines of longitude. Air Navigation has a language all its own. Time is called zulu, for example, always zulu, and it's always Greenwich Mean Time wherever we fly in the world. The next three letters, TTG mean time-to-go. We started to move from the ramp at London Airport at one-zero-one-four. Pete's jotted it down here as a crosscheck. If you follow the column of figures down you'll see TTG is zero-zero-zero-zero at the bottom of the page. At that point we'll be on the Kennedy ramp."

Maxwell, obviously impressed, said, "I guess this means your position," putting a finger on the symbol POS.

"Yes, sir."

"And this must mean flight?" Maxwell said, moving his finger to the letters FL.

"Flight level, sir. The figures below show the levels. We use only the first three numerals. Here's six-nine-zero, that stands for sixty-nine thousand feet where we started our supersonic cruise . . ."

"And this seven-five-zero near the bottom is the end of the supersonic portion of the flight, eh?"

"That's correct. Incidentally, we don't use the term *flight level* below seventeen thousand feet. At altitudes below seventeen thousand we say so-and-so many feet *altitude*."

"Now you've lost me," Maxwell said, his face easing into a smile.

"It's *flight levels* above seventeen thousand feet and *altitudes* below it. It's an international agreement. And incidentally, when descending through seventeen thousand feet every pilot resets his barometric altimeter—this instrument here—to twenty-nine decimal nine-two. That's the international *standard* atmospheric pressure. It's done so the poor guy who doesn't have a radio altimeter as well as a barometric altimeter as we do but has to rely on his barometric altimeter—which varies with barometric pressure—is reading his altitude correctly like everyone else. In other words, everybody descending through seventeen thousand feet resets his altimeter so that all altimeters read the same—thus reducing the risk of a mid-air collision."

"Huh," Maxwell snorted. "Wish other kinds of international agreements . . ." He broke off and consulted the Flight Plan. "What's TOW?"

"Takeoff weight. About half is for fuel. This column of decreasing figures shows how the weight drops off as we burn off fuel. The symbol FRMG means fuel remaining at each of the waypoints as the flight progresses."

Maxwell rubbed behind his ear with his forefinger. "About this fuel trim business, Captain. How do you know when to switch the pumps to move the fuel from one tank to another."

"It's automatic, by an on-board computer. The way this flight plan was drawn up . . ."

"These calculations were computerized before we took off?" Maxwell asked.

"Several weeks ago. The computer programmers know the airlines' schedules and input flights weeks ahead."

"I had no idea," Maxwell said.

"They feed in our flight data along with all the other daily five hundred. This gives everybody a flight path clear of everybody else."

"The daily five hundred, Captain?"

Bartlett laughed. "Sometimes called the wolf pack, sir." He glanced at Kowsky, who was speaking into his microphone. "Excuse me, sir," he said, and moved his earphones into place. Kowsky was giving a routine position report to Gander Air Traffic Control center. He looked at the moving map display. They were now entering Zone Seven, the strip of air space between longitude thirty west and thirty-five west. The tiny spark of light that was Arrowhead on the moving map was poised on longitude thirty.

"Now this is an interesting point in the flight, sir," he said, pushing the earphones to the back of his head. "We've just reached longitude thirty west and are passing from Shanwick Oceanic Control Area to Gander Oceanic Control Area. It's on the Flight Plan here." He pointed under the column headed POS on the Flight Plan. "Thirty west. That's the dividing line in the middle of the Atlantic as far as air traffic control is concerned, like a huge invisible cross in the middle of the ocean. My first officer is now reporting our position to both Gander and Shanwick. But from this point on, we report only to Gander. Later we'll report to New York air traffic control—that's below the horizontal line of the invisible cross, and farther west, of course."

"Shanwick Control. Is that a combination of Shannon and Prestwick?"

"Yes. It's a combined control center."

Maxwell pointed to the moving map display. "How does that map know at what speed to move?"

"It's plugged into the computer of the flight director, which is connected to the inertial guidance system. There's a film projected onto the screen from behind the dashboard."

"No reflection on you fellas, Captain, but it seems to me you've got an easy job. Sitting up here chewing candy," he nodded at a Dixie cup containing a few mints balanced on the dashboard coaming and winked at Kowsky, "and watching the figures on the clocks and reporting your position now and again."

Bartlett laughed. "That's just what the subsonic crews say. They're jealous, of course. A mint, sir?" He offered the Dixie cup. "But we can't report our position when we like, sir. Regulations call for a position report every ten degrees of longitude."

Maxwell declined the mint, looked around the instrument panels, and said, "You were starting to tell me about the wolf pack, Captain."

"There're about five hundred jets crossing daily from east to west and another five hundred from west to east. Mostly scheduled flights, but many charters and freighters, too. The airlines arrange their schedules to attract business: nobody wants to leave New York at six o'clock in the evening after a busy day at the office and arrive in London six hours later when it's around five o'clock in the morning London time."

Maxwell nodded. "You don't have to tell *me!*" he said grimly.

Bartlett smiled. "So the airlines try to fly out at about the same time to get their passengers to distant points at decent hours. And that goes for the westbound flights too." He paused, enjoying the explanation to his VIP passenger of the intricacies of his aircraft and flight scheduling. "As a result there's one hell of a problem giving everybody enough air space. In subsonics it's like being caught in rush hour traffic on the Long Island Expressway. You hear aircraft calling control all around you and you watch your altitude, position, and speed very closely. Especially altitude."

"Why's that?"

"There's only a thousand-foot vertical separation between you and the airplane above and the one below over land— that's why we reset the barometric altimeter at seventeen thousand feet—for safety. Naturally, the radio altimeter gives you your altitude more precisely. Nobody really likes being that close. By the way, over the Atlantic the vertical separation between aircraft on the same track is two thousand feet."

"What about the fellow coming up behind you? Isn't there a danger of him ramming into you?"

"Minimum fore-and-aft separation is one hundred and twenty miles over the Atlantic. Some pilots are uncomfortable about it—they say it is not enough to prevent ramming, in the event of flying at a wrong altitude. At six hundred miles an hour a subsonic swallows up those miles in twelve minutes."

"What about the sideways separation, Captain?"

"Sixty miles." Bartlett paused. "But up here, sir, we practically have the sky to ourselves. I don't expect it'll last now that so many of the airlines are buying supersonics. The old traffic jam will start all over again, up here at seven-zero-zero." He wondered how much of what he was saying would get back to the president. It wouldn't hurt to let important ears have some idea of pilots' beefs.

"Getting back to that fuel trim business, Captain. I had no idea supersonics were so difficult to, uh, balance."

Bartlett settled in his seat. "It's not a question of being difficult to balance. Just that matter of cleaning up the airplane aerodynamically to keep the drag low and the efficiency of the engines high and thus keep fuel consumption down." He nodded rearward. "You can get some idea of our consumption rate from the flowmeters on the panel there." He pointed to Nardini's flight systems management position. Nardini, pleased to show off his many dials and switches, put his finger on a row of whirling flowmeter gauges.

"We use the fuel for several other purposes."

"Other purposes?" Maxwell looked puzzled. "Surely its purpose is to drive the engines?"

"That's it's main job. But we also use it as a *heat sink*." Maxwell threw out his hands in a helpless gesture.

"The heat of the structure, due to traveling at supersonic

speeds, transmits itself to some of the systems. If we didn't cool them they wouldn't work. For instance, there's heat generated by cooling the cabin. So we pass the heat derived from the air-conditioning system through heat exchangers buried in the fuel tanks. This transfers the excess heat to the fuel . . ."

"Isn't that dangerous?"

Bartlett's eyebrows arched. "The fuel can absorb a lot of heat without danger. At the end of our run into Kennedy the fuel remaining in the tank will be about seventy-five degrees centigrade. We also use the fuel to cool off the hydraulic system fluid, the heat from the electrical generators, and engine lubricating oil—all by heat exchangers buried in the fuel tanks."

Maxwell, impressed, stroked his ear for several seconds. "I guess as the engines use up fuel, what's left in the tanks must heat up more rapidly," he said at length.

"Yes, sir."

"What you need is something to radiate the heat from those tanks," he went on, and Bartlett sensed his train of thought. He waited for it to reach its conclusion as Maxwell worked out the problem by his own logic. "Something like a radiator along the wing. But of course. I see. You can't do that because the wing surface is hot, about one hundred and forty degrees centigrade." He looked at Bartlett. "It's like flying inside a furnace."

"That's a good way of putting it. But, of course, when the hot fuel is pumped into the engines, it gives up its heat and is dumped overboard in the jet exhausts."

Nardini leaned over and gave Bartlett another paper slip. Bartlett examined it and turned to Maxwell. "Here's another report on the fuel transfer flow. My flight management systems engineer checks from time to time to make sure the computer's doing its job correctly. It must be in what we call Condition Triple A in all operating modes. It's checked on the ground before each flight."

"What about the fuel in the tail tank? Is that tank full until you need it to change from supersonic to subsonic flight?" Maxwell asked.

"Yes. It holds the biggest load of all the tanks. The computer'll switch the transfer solenoid valves and direct the pump to pump fuel through the amidship tanks and into the forward tanks at the end of our supersonic cruise. This trims the ship and makes it easier to handle on final approach and touchdown."

"This gets more interesting all the time," Maxwell said.

Bartlett smiled. "I don't want to bore you with a short course on the aerodynamic characteristics of delta-shaped wings . . ."

"It's fascinating. Please go on."

"The delta wing is practically unstallable in the ordinary sense. It's very stable on final approach and touchdown."

"Does that make landing easier?"

"That's about it, sir," Bartlett replied, a trifle evasively. He should back off on this technical stuff. It was better for Maxwell to remain ignorant of the fact that, while the delta-shaped—or triangular—wing was a most stable form at steep angles of approach, when landing the nose dropped slowly because the wing retained its lift to the very last moment of flight. If a pilot tried to get the nose down by moving the control column forward, the aircraft ballooned off because the elevons had an extremely powerful lift action, quite opposite to the action of the elevators in conventionally shaped subsonic aircraft. During her flight tests Arrowhead had repeatedly shown this characteristic. As a result, last-minute modifications had been made to reduce the elevon area.

SUPERSONIC

Another problem that occurred during the final moments of touchdown with most of the supersonics, including the Anglo-French Concorde and the Russian TU-144, was that the sheer length of the aircraft made it difficult for the pilot to feel for the runway as he came in over the threshold and cut throttles. Bartlett sat one hundred and ten feet ahead of the main wheels and forty feet above the ground at the moment of touchdown. Experiments had been made with closed-circuit television, using a camera mounted behind the nose undercarriage leg to face the main wheels with a monitor screen on the flight deck to allow pilots to see the main wheels touch the runway on landing. The experiments were abandoned after complaints from the test pilots. They said the operation had become too complex and the television pictures unreliable. But the real reason was pilots' pride, "We don't need an idiot box to tell us how to land."

"I've heard another word used to describe the delta shape," Maxwell said. "They used it on the Concorde, I think, in the early days. *Oh* something or other."

"Ogee plan form, sir."

"That's it, ogee. An odd name."

"It's what they used to call the shape of medieval cathedral windows," Bartlett said. "Those pointed Gothic arches." He glanced at Maxwell, not knowing that Maxwell, scholar and professor of history, had pretended ignorance to test Bartlett's knowledge, and added, "I'm no expert. But that's what I heard."

Maxwell sat silent, preoccupied in thought. "Captain, what about sonic booms? Have there been serious complaints since the supersonics went into service?"

Hell, he hadn't expected *that*. It didn't seem diplomatic for the president's personal advisor to refer to such a politically charged subject as sonic booms, especially to the captain of a supersonic. A cough behind him told him Nardini awaited his reply with interest. He wondered if Maxwell knew what had occurred when an Arrowhead aircraft had overflown a freighter in the Pacific on the airline's San Francisco to Hawaii leg en route to Tokyo. The ship's second mate, a man of forty-three, had been enjoying a quiet off-duty pipe leaning on the taffrail when the aircraft's shock wave burst on the ship. As an instantaneous reaction to the explosion he had thrown himself over the rail into the sea. By the time the captain and crew had recovered from their own shock, amid shattered glass and snapped guy wires, the second mate had drowned. Legal action brought by the ship's owners and the widow—Kowsky had told him they were suing for two million dollars—was pending. American Arrow, like all airlines, didn't like bad publicity. As with other cases of damage wreaked by sonic booms, the suit would probably be settled out of court to keep it out of the headlines and lessen its impact as material for the environmentalists to use in their continuing war against supersonics.

"Less than anticipated, sir," he said evasively, adjusting his headset. He hoped that a routine message from Gander ATC would come through to give him an excuse not to get involved in the subject of sonic booms.

"I mean other than the case where the seaman drowned," Maxwell went on. Of course Maxwell would know every detail on that; he'd have advisors and research assistants covering every aspect of anything even remotely touching on political issues. And sonic booms had become a hot political issue years before the Arrowheads had entered airline service, even before Concorde had pioneered the trans-Atlantic supersonic route in the mid-1970s. Conservation groups had picketed airfields when the supersonic transports were being tested, assailed senators and congressmen with petitions signed by thousands, and one group, the Boston-based Citizens' League Against the Sonic Boom, had been largely credited with the success in having the original Boeing 2707 supersonic project abandoned. Enlisting the aid of Senator William Proxmire of Wisconsin and other influential antisupersonic politicians, they had bombarded Washington at a time when the president, involved with extricating America from Vietnam, was looking around for government-aided projects to ax.

"Well . . . some people always complain," Bartlett said.

"Any specific cases, Captain?" Maxwell persisted. An inflection between a polite request and a command underlined the tone of his voice.

"Our public relations department has been called on several occasions, sir," Bartlett continued, thinking of the several writs that had landed on the desk of American Arrow Airlines' vice-president of flight operations since the Arrowheads entered service. His eyes made their accustomed traverse over the instruments, absorbing and evaluating their readings, and his mind went back to a lecture he'd attended sponsored by the American Institute of Aeronautics and Astronautics in New York, where a critical paper on sonic booms had been discussed. The original lecture had been given by an outstanding aeronautical expert, Bo K. O. Lundberg, an outspoken antagonist of supersonic transport aircraft. Lundberg was a respected member of the international aerospace technical community and, as director general of the Aeronautical Research Institute of Sweden, his opinions carried weight. The Lundberg paper had originally been delivered before the Royal Aeronautical Society in London and had caused a considerable stir and had been hotly discussed in learned aeronautical circles on both sides of the Atlantic.

"Lundberg now talks of superbangs," Edelman, the discussion leader from Berkeley had said. "These are strong overpressures from the original shock wave due to the focusing effects caused by sudden flight maneuvers, such as sharp turns on climb-out."

"But with straight-line takeoffs and fast climb-outs through transition to supersonic speed, that's unrealistic," Bartlett had challenged at question time.

"You're citing a perfect takeoff, Captain. I'm talking about a sudden maneuver during the fast climb through subsonic traffic to avoid a midair. Traffic control is, to say the least, not perfect."

A murmur of approval from flight crew officers had underscored Edelman's remarks. Despite new electronic aids for air traffic control, the number of midair collisions and near-misses had increased as airways and terminal approach areas had become more crowded in recent years.

"Superbangs can result from pitching, too. So watch those fuel trim maneuvers during transition periods. Especially when decelerating from supersonic to subsonic. That's a critical time for superbangs."

"What about weather, Dr. Edelman? Could that lead to superbangs?"

"I was coming to that, Captain. Lundberg says 'yes.' Unfortunately he's not specific. He simply says that adverse weather conditions could cause superbangs. The plain fact is that little is known about the effects *on the atmosphere* of maneuvering a two-hundred-ton aircraft at supersonic speed." Edelman had paused and continued, "Lundberg believes that air temperatures and wind velocity are the important factors in the creation of superbangs. But we should come back to the more conventional aspect of sonic booms. More specifically, the reactions of people on the ground."

The engineers in the crowded hall had leaned forward.

SUPERSONIC

Many worked for Boeing and the research establishments where models of strange arrow-shaped airplanes had been under tests in supersonic wind tunnels and components of titanium and stainless steel had undergone torture tests at the elevated temperatures and high-stress conditions of faster-than-sound flight.

"These are the results of tests done over United States cities to sound out public reaction to sonic booms," Edelman had gone on, turning to a large wall chart. "Flyovers were made at supersonic speeds at varying altitudes, as you can see from this table at the side of the chart. A total of forty-nine passes were made over Chicago. As a result, nearly five thousand claims for property damage were filed. Damage took the form of smashed windows, collapsed wooden buildings, loosened roof tiles and shingles, and sickness following erratic behavior of dogs, cats, and pet birds. The Air Force paid compensation in more than three thousand cases. As a matter of fact," Edelman bent to read the small print at the bottom of the chart, "in one three-month fiscal period the Office of the Judge Advocate General, claims division, paid out three decimal eight million dollars."

He straightened and adjusted his glasses. "Flights over St. Louis resulted in one homeowner being awarded ten thousand dollars to repair his damaged house."

A voice from the back of the hall had asked, "Has any specific research been done on the effect of booms on animals? And what about insects?"

"That's a very good question. Recently the Air Force, in conjunction with the federal Department of Agriculture, arranged for planes from Edwards to make passes over the Husbandry Research Division at Beltsville, Maryland. There's an experimental farm down there where they raise chickens, turkeys, and pheasants. Since nobody knew what the sonic boom would do to the birds, the pilots were warned to make flyovers in a narrow corridor three to five miles to one side of the actual farm."

Edelman adjusted his glasses again before continuing. "Pandemonium broke loose as the birds flew and scrambled in every which way, clawing at each other until scores were dead or mortally wounded. The turkeys suffered the most because of their weight and size."

Edelman had flipped the pages of a loose-leaf notebook on the lectern. "Nothing's been done on insects so far. But a pilot project's getting underway using artificially produced sonic booms. I made a note about it somewhere. Ah, here it is. Overpressures will be directed at irregular periods on fruit flies, ants, and spiders in an artificially created environment. It will be some time before we get a report on the results. The effect on breeding, longevity, and nervous reaction to overpressures will be studied."

And that had been it, Bartlett reflected. Mostly theory from the experts and loud noises from the supersonic antagonists, as well as from Arrowheads. Maxwell's insistent voice brought him back to reality.

"Were the complaints from people on land or from ships at sea, Captain?"

"Uh, mostly from sea, I believe, sir," Bartlett replied evasively. "As you know, supersonic flights over land are prohibited by most countries. But there's some talk now of okaying it for sparsely populated regions such as parts of Northern Canada and over the Pole. And, of course, the Russians are running their TU-144s across Siberia on the milk runs from Moscow to Tokyo."

"Wasn't there a complaint from Nantucket recently?".

"I didn't hear of one, sir."

Suddenly, Maxwell's posture relaxed, and the tension on

the flight deck eased as the VIP pointed to the display map. "How would you know if we flew over a ship right now, Captain?" he asked with an amused expression.

"We wouldn't," Bartlett replied. "We don't have downward pointing radar." He studied the bright spot of light at center screen, now five hundred miles northwest of Corvo and Flores, the most westerly islands of the Azores, which were moving off the right-hand side of the screen. The boom pattern the aircraft was laying down was at least five hundred miles clear of the tiny islands, Bartlett reflected. Maxwell stood up, and Kowsky leaned across to fold back the jump seat. He gave Bartlett a covert wink.

"That was interesting, Captain," Maxwell said, smiling broadly. "I had no idea supersonic flying was so complicated." He paused, his big head to one side, deep in thought. "One hundred and forty degrees, eh. Jesus, that's hot."

Bartlett smiled and readjusted the headset. As Maxwell moved toward the door he called after him, "Enjoy your flight, sir."

He waited to hear the door click before turning to Kowsky. "I thought he was going to give us a hard time about booms."

"Never did trust politicians," Kowsky said, helping himself to a mint. "There's only one left, Captain. Want it?"

Bartlett unwrapped the candy and popped it into his mouth as an indistinct voice crackled in his earphones. For a moment he thought his hearing had been affected by his teeth crunching the mint. He turned to Kowsky. "Did you get it?"

Kowsky shook his head. "Just TW. TWA flight, I guess —then it went."

"I'll get Gander to play it back," Bartlett said. "Nick, there'll be a message coming through your readout in a moment. Stand by."

SUPERSONIC

He turned the radio to another frequency. "Arrowhead Zero-One to Gander ATC. Please repeat in full TW transmission on your radio teletype. We didn't get it by audio."

The radio print-out on Nardini's desk clattered as the Gander high-level controller typed back a repeat of the message. Every radio message received at Gander, and at Shanwick Oceanic Control, was typed on a teletype machine as it came over the air. In three control points at Gander Air Terminal a roll of paper unwound from the teletype machines: in the Air Traffic Control Center, the Radio Center housed in a brown brick building outside the airport perimeter, and in the Weather Office on the third floor of the Terminal Building. Nardini tore off the slip and handed it to Bartlett. He scanned it rapidly.

HAG299 281506
FF EGGXZQ EIAAYE EINNTW CYQXYM CYQXZO
  KJFKTW
281505 EIAAZZ
TW891 RELAYING FOR TW811 RETURNING TO
  SNN AT F370

Ignoring the three top lines, symbols indicating the message number, the Prestwick, Shannon Oceanic, and Gander computer output codes, and the fact that a Trans World Airlines plane bound for Kennedy was involved, his eye took in the line beginning TW891. He spoke into the microphone. "American Arrow Zero-One. Thanks, Gander," and passed the slip to Kowsky.

"Solar flare?" Kowsky suggested.

Bartlett shrugged. "It hasn't affected us. And Gerrard said he'd radio if Boulder issued a warning."

Nardini leaned over to reread the message. "TWA Flight

Eight-One-One's with a radio blackout?" He scratched his head. "Bad enough to return to Shannon."

"If Flight Eight-Niner-One's relaying for him, it can't be a solar flare," Bartlett said. "Must be having trouble with his radio equipment. I'll double-check Gander."

"American Arrow Zero-One to Gander. Please report if solar flare responsible for TW Eight-One-One return to Shannon."

"Negative report on solar flare. TW Flight Eight-One-One has internal communications problem."

"Thanks, Gander."

Kowsky, listening on his own earphones, grinned. Bartlett snapped off the Transmit button and flicked on the Listening-Out switch. At that precise moment an amber gleam caught his eye.

FOUR

He jerked his head toward the radiation indicator. The numerals on the inset counter tumbled, raced to fifty millirems, jumped to one hundred, and became an unreadable whirl.

"Hell, that's high," he said, keeping his voice level. Kowsky leaned forward and touched the test button. The white light flashed above the amber. The whirling figures slowed until they were possible to read—720 . . . 790 . . . 810. The counter rotated uncertainly and came to rest on 830 millirems.

"Jesus! I've never seen it *that* high!" Kowsky exclaimed.

Bartlett, staring at the 830, was about to say, "Neither have I," but instead said nothing. He thought about reporting it to Gander. But the amber light was only an alert signal; there was no need to report an alert. As long as the millirems stayed below the one thousand level they were in no immediate danger. All the same, he wondered how long they should remain at their present flight level of seven-two-zero if the amber stayed on. He glanced at the time-to-go clock. The figures read 01:58:33—one hour, fifty-eight minutes, and thirty-three seconds to the Kennedy ramp. He rechecked the counter. It had started to spin rapidly. The rotating ribbon of white broadened from three digits to four, and a crimson light blazed from the radiation detector. At the same time the quiet of the flight deck was shattered by the take-action klaxon. Bartlett's hand swept into action. He snapped off the override switch to silence the shrieking klaxon, pressed the transmit button, and spoke into the microphone.

"American Arrow Zero-One to Gander. Request clearance for immediate descent to flight level four-five-zero. Galactic radiation detector shows action signal."

His hand moved to the Disengage button on the autopilot, putting the aircraft under manual control.

"Gander to American Arrow Zero-One. Cleared to descend to flight level four-five-zero." The voice in his earphones had a North American accent, and was even, and calm. Kowsky, listening on his own headset, flicked on the "Fasten Seat Belt" switch for the passenger cabins.

"Harness on, Nick," Bartlett called. He gripped the control yoke and pressed it forward.

"Fifty percent power."

He must avoid a full-power descent: Some passengers would still be fussing with their belts, others strolling back to their seats from the toilets. He looked at the Machmeter. It edged below Mach 3 and showed 2.8.

"Forty percent power."

"Forty percent power," Kowsky intoned, moving the throttles.

The radio altimeter passed through 69,000 feet. The red light on the radiation detector glowed steadily. He pushed the yoke further forward and glanced at the artificial horizon. The gap between the miniature replica of an airplane at its center and the fixed horizontal line across the instrument widened. With no spoilers on the wings to produce drag, and thus reduce lift, Arrowhead was an efficient lift-producing machine. No spoilers, no landing flaps, had been two of the aerodynamic essentials decided at the beginning of the design concept: Arrowhead's designers had been more concerned with straight and level flight at Mach 3 than the rare need to lose height quickly to escape radioactivity from outer space. Handbooks slithered across Nardini's desk and thumped on the floor. From the corner of his eye, Bartlett saw Kowsky tap the indicator glass.

"It's for real," he said between tight lips, glancing at the console. The Machmeter read 2.2; altimeter 68,500 feet. The red glow glared at him, an evil eye he had to put out. He pushed the yoke forward, the space on the artificial horizon widened, and he felt the harness restrain his body as he slid forward. The angle-of-descent dial swung through forty-five degrees. At fifty degrees he pulled back, feeling the pressure on the yoke increase. The Machmeter was glued to 2.2. A crazy notion passed through his brain: If he kept up this speed he'd burn off the wings as Arrowhead dived into the denser air at lower altitudes.

"Back," he called to Kowsky, now gripping his own yoke. The little airplane on the artificial horizon rose toward the fixed line, and the angle-of-descent dial fell to twenty-five degrees. The red light glowed steadily.

"Thirty-five percent power."

Kowsky's hand moved. "Thirty-five percent power."

The pressure on his body against the harness fell off as the speed slackened. Arrowhead passed through Mach 2, the altimeter showed 66,000 feet and dropping . . . 65,000 . . . 60,000. They were approaching subsonic speed and he felt the controls grow mushy. He didn't want to be caught in "Coffin Corner," where his cruise speed got close to his stalling speed. He pushed the yoke forward, feeling Kowsky release his grip. The nose dipped into a thirty degree dive, and the altimeter spun down . . . 58,000 . . . 55,000 . . . 52,000. At 49,000 feet the red light went out and the amber light glowed. At 47,000 the amber vanished and the numerals in the counter's tiny window flashed downward with lightning speed and stabilized on nine millirems.

"Christ!" Kowsky exclaimed, wiping his shirtsleeve across his forehead. Bartlett eyed the Machmeter, waiting for transition speed. The numerals tumbled . . . 1.3 . . . 1.2 . . . 1.1 . . . flipped to unity, and the control yoke pressed toward him as the aircraft eased through the sound barrier and the tail swung down. He waited for the pressure on his arms to fall off as the fuel pumps transferred fuel from the rear tank to the forward tanks to trim the aircraft. But the pressure increased as the aircraft's speed dropped to Mach .93. The pumps, fast-action boosters submerged in the tank, were taking a long time to start up under the computer's direction.

"Nick, check the flowmeter for the rear tank," he shouted.

"It's not moving."

Kowsky's hand shot to an emergency switch on the ceiling panel.

"Manual on," he announced.

"The bastard's not working," Bartlett exclaimed. He pressed the yoke further forward. "Check the circuit, Nick."

"The test dial shows zero," Nardini said in a strained voice.

"Circuit breakers! Check the circuit breakers."

He heard a panel snap open and a click as Nardini reset a circuit breaker. "Still zero."

Bartlett's body stiffened, his arms rigid against the control yoke. "Pete, switch off for five seconds, then on."

SUPERSONIC

Kowsky stretched up and moved the switch to the off position. He counted aloud "one thousand and one . . . one thousand and two . . . one thousand and three . . . one thousand and four . . . one thousand and five." Bartlett heard the switch snap on.

"Dead," Nardini called. "No voltage." He scratched his head. "I don't understand it, Captain. The circuits were ground-tested as usual at London Airport. I checked the test report myself after the ground crew was through. They were all Triple A okay."

"You're sure the circuit breaker's closed?"

A pause while Nardini checked. "Fully closed."

Bartlett swallowed. "Then the pumps have failed," he said flatly.

"A mechanical failure?" Nardini's voice was colored by a mixture of doubt and alarm. Bartlett was silent, knowing that the others knew what pump failure meant. With a major portion of the total fuel locked in the rear tank, Arrowhead would never make New York. He switched on the radio transmit switch.

"American Arrow Zero-One to Gander. Request clearance for diversion to Gander alternate. Fuel transfer trouble. Range curtailed. Flight level four-five-zero. Airspeed six-six-five knots."

The earphones hummed. He opened his mouth to repeat his call when the same reassuring voice came through.

"Gander to American Arrow Zero-One. Request to Gander alternate cleared. Give position."

Bartlett peered at the moving map display. "Latitude forty-five ten north, longitude thirty-five west. Zulu one-one-four-zero."

"Expected zulu to your next position reporting point?"

Bartlett took a breath. "Will call you when we pick up our new heading." He pressed a button on the center panel that switched the navigation film cassette for the moving map display to the alternate channel for Gander.

"Roger."

The owner of the even-toned voice at Gander Air Traffic Control center, George Mercer, was a fat man who, in the language of the ATC, was "working Arrowhead." He was one of ten high-level en-route controllers on duty and sat before a teletype keyboard on which he'd typed Bartlett's request for descent clearance a few minutes ago. Now, as he tapped out Bartlett's further request, to land at Gander, he checked what he'd typed with the cathode ray tube readout —like a small television set—on which flashed everything he typed. He tore the paper from his teletype machine and stuck it in an endless conveyor belt that ran between the two rows of controllers. A controller assistant at the end of the room picked up the paper when it reached him, glanced at it, raised his eyebrows, and put it with other teletype messages from the other controllers in a pile ready for filing, to be kept for the regulation time period of thirty days.

Mercer switched the cathode ray tube readout clear, his ears alert, waiting for Bartlett to announce Arrowhead's expected zulu to his next reporting point on the new course. He took a deep drag on the stub of his cigarette and mashed it in an ashtray by his half-filled coffee cup. It was noisy in the room, and the voices of the other controllers bore into his consciousness, despite the carpet that had been laid on the floor to muffle the sound. Since he was working several other aircraft as well, he hoped that the captain of the supersonic wouldn't take long to report. He took a swig of coffee and waited for the captain's voice to sound in his earphones, wondering what precisely had occurred to make a supersonic divert to Gander. It had never happened before.

Bartlett said, "Nick, work out the zulu to next position report as soon as we get on our new heading."

He moved the rudder pedals and the yoke, watching the compass and shifting his eyes to the turn-and-bank indicator. Arrowhead came around in a gentle turn onto her new heading, two hundred and ninety degrees, pointing well north of northwest. He heard Nardini punch the keys on his computer console as he himself touched a button on the DME console. He pressed the transmit button.

"Zero-One to Gander. On new heading two-niner-zero." He consulted the DME readout. "Distance to Gander niner-four-eight miles." Nardini handed him a slip of paper. "Zulu to next position report eleven minutes." The door burst open and Lydia Olsen appeared, her face tight. "What . . ."

Kowsky raised a warning finger to quiet her. Bartlett, ignoring the interruption, listened to George Mercer read back the estimated time to Arrowhead's next position, switched off, and turned to Lydia.

"Sorry, Captain, but there're casualties back there." She brushed the hair from her eyes. "We've attended to them as best we could."

Bartlett's lips tightened. "How many and how bad?" he demanded.

"Several banged heads and bruised sides. And there's an elderly lady in first class who appears to have a broken arm."

He nodded to Kowsky. "Take a look, Pete." He glanced over his shoulder at Lydia. "I know this sounds corny, but is there a doctor on board?"

"Yes, Captain. One of the VIPs is a famous surgeon—Sir Leonard Wheeler-Carthert."

"Ah yes. I remember who Wheeler-Carthert is now. Get moving, Pete."

"I've already had him take a look at the lady, Captain, but

there's a man knocked unconscious in economy," Lydia continued.

Kowsky slipped out of his harness and stood up. Bartlett wondered if he should use the PA system, apologize for the dive, and announce the diversion to Gander. He decided against it. Let Pete handle it personally, assess the injuries, and report back. As Kowsky slipped on his jacket and moved to the door he called him back. "Yes, Tom?"

"Don't mention we're diverting to Gander. I'll announce it later."

"Okay."

The door shut, he checked the instruments, and switched on the autopilot. When he looked up he saw his reflection in the windshield, mirrored by the protective visor. He selected a button, pressed, and waited for that queer sensation as the visor rode forward away from him on guide rails and retracted into its storage position, snug against the fuselage nose. His image stared back at him. Again he pressed the switch. Nothing happened. His fingernail chipped as he jammed his fingertip on the button. He whirled around, unaware of the harness cutting into his flesh.

"Check the visor circuit."

Nardini moved switches on a test panel and consulted his dials. "Christ, Captain. It's dead, like the rear tank pump circuit."

"Circuit breakers?"

He heard the familiar snap as Nardini yanked open the circuit breaker box. "Set solid."

"Check again."

He heard the circuit breaker click as Nardini reset it.

"Set. Positive," Nardini confirmed.

Bartlett pressed the button again. "Bash the windshield frame while I hold the button down."

Nardini stepped forward and thumped the heavy frame, but the visor wouldn't budge. "It's stuck solid, Captain."

Bartlett transferred his hand to the unyielding pressure of the yoke, thinking about the complex fuel-transfer system, trying to recall details of the fuel flow direction. "If we dumped fuel from the rear tank, it would straighten the trim and take the blasted pressure off the control column. If the fuel's locked in the rear tank we can't use it anyway. What say?"

Nardini shook his head. "The fuel dump valve's located in the amidship tanks. Fuel in the rear tank has to be pumped forward to reach the valve." He reached for a handbook, opened a foldout page of the fuel system diagram, and studied it. "No way," he concluded.

Bartlett's mind raced ahead. "What's the length of Gander's longest runway?" he demanded.

Nardini took a leather-covered book entitled *Canada Air Pilot* from the shelf where he had replaced the handbook. He flipped the pages over the metal ring fasteners to a plate showing the layout of Gander International Airport.

"Runway Zero-Four Dash Two-Two is longest. Ten thousand, five hundred feet. They lengthened it when they brought in their TOPS project."

"Goddamned good thing," Bartlett muttered.

"Excuse me, Captain."

"Nothing." He paused. "What the hell is the TOPS project?" he added irritably.

"Trans-Oceanic Plane Stop," replied Nardini, fingering an insert glued to the page.

"Must be something new. Haven't used Gander for years," Bartlett growled, futilely pressing the visor retraction button again.

"It's to attract the charter and freight traffic, Captain, the traffic from the West Coast bound for Europe. They lengthened the runway and reduced landing fees. And installed arrester cables in case of . . ." Nardini broke off abruptly.

"Bully for them," Bartlett said. Christ, he'd personally pay ten times the landing fee if he could get the visor unstuck.

"The way I heard it Bangor Airport in Maine was taking a lot of lucrative refuelling business away from Gander because they had more to offer in the way of longer runways and quick refuelers. Then Gander hit back with longer runways and . . ."

The door opened and Kowsky appeared. "The doctor confirms that the lady broke an arm and there's a man in economy who's got a concussion. The doc has fixed up the arm in a splint from the medicine chest and is standing by the unconscious guy. The lady's scared but she looks like a tough old bird." He took off his jacket, hung it up, squeezed into the right-hand seat, and buckled his harness. "Lydia and the others are working wonders back there." He looked at Bartlett. "Something wrong?"

"Select visor retract."

Kowsky hesitated, sensing something had happened during his absence.

"Okay. Visor to retract." He put a thick finger on the button. The expectant look on his face vanished. He turned to Bartlett. "Jesus! Not another circuit out?"

Bartlett nodded. "Nick's checked it. It's dead. Like the transfer pumps."

"How come the pumps and visor worked after takeoff? If both circuits were dead you'd have expected . . ." he broke off and passed a hand through his hair.

Bartlett shrugged. "I'm as mystified as you are. I'll call New York in a minute. See if they can sort it out . . ."

"A first-class case of Murphy's Law if I ever saw one,"

Kowsky said in disgust. "If something can possibly be installed incorrectly, someone will do it." He punched the visor retract button again, but the visor remained in position against the windshield.

"Maybe," Bartlett said doubtfully. On second thought, perhaps Kowsky *was* right. He remembered the hydraulic pump failure on a DC-6 he had been flying, where the filter elements, installed backward, trapped oil in the pump, causing it to overheat and disintegrate. If it hadn't been for his first officer's fast action in dousing the flames with the hand extinguisher they would never have made Honolulu. And he'd heard of a case of Murphy's Law in action when the rotor blade of a Navy helicopter had worked loose and cut off the tail section. The pin in the blade-locking mechanism had been turned to the right instead of to the left.

Was it humanly possible for aircraft designers to anticipate *everything* that could go wrong in such a complicated piece of machinery as a modern airplane? And for maintenance crews and even inspectors to avoid oversights? He remembered the time he climbed into the cockpit of a DC-3 and, while taxiing, discovered the control yoke wouldn't go completely over to starboard. Lucky thing he'd returned to the ramp and demanded the closing strip between the outer wing and the center section wing be opened up. They'd found a file handle jammed between the aileron control cables and the flange of a lightening hole in a wing rib. He wondered how many big jets were in the air right now with lost lunch pails rattling in the dark recesses of the outer wings or steel measuring rules that had fallen from an inspector's breast pocket flapping around inside an otherwise empty enclosure somewhere in an aircraft's structure. He looked across at Kowsky, a little envious. Kowsky wasn't in a hurry to get to New York; he didn't have a son in the hospital to worry about.

SUPERSONIC

Just Marie and himself in the ranch-style bungalow on Long Island, close enough to town, but conveniently near the mooring where Kowsky kept his thirty-two foot keelboat. On the other hand, Pete had been looking forward to the three days off-duty to start sanding the hull. Murphy's Law, he conceded, may have done it again.

"GCA at Gander," Kowsky said.

"How will we see the threshold with no forward visibility?"

"Through the side windows."

Bartlett shook his head. "You can't see more'n ten feet ahead."

Kowsky pressed his face against the transparent plastic pane. "I never realized that before. Not even in the simulator." He added, "That's a curve to throw us that they never dreamed up." He scratched his head. "And with a dragging tail at slow speed . . ."

"The economy section's a little more than half filled. We'll move some of them forward into first class before final approach. When will we know how serious the concussion case is?"

"Doctor didn't say. They've spread the poor guy out on three seats. One of the stewardesses is standing by with an oxygen cylinder." He saw Bartlett's straining arms. "Need a hand?" Bartlett nodded.

"She *is* heavy!" Kowsky exclaimed. He pushed and added, "Let's dump the rear tank. We don't need it now that we're diverting."

"We've thought of it. The dump valves are located in the amidship tanks. We've got to get the rear fuel into them first."

"Oh," Kowsky said. He fell silent, reflecting on how complicated the supersonics were. The technical jump between the Boeing 747s and the supersonics, a period of less than a decade, was equivalent, in terms of technology, to the know-how and experience accumulated between the Wright Brothers flight in 1903 and the first flight of the prototype 747. Complexity heaped on complexity until it took an army of skilled maintenance men, overhaul experts, eagle-eyed inspectors, and ground testers equipped with sophisticated electronic gear to keep the supersonics flying. Made one want to get back to fundamentals again, like the people who gave up cars for bicycles.

Kowsky blinked, and, looking back in time, he saw the back of Rod Ketchum's head, straining to see from the front cockpit of the little Stearman biplane. It had been a glorious, cloudless day just like this. In the distance, the sun glinted from the Oregon lakes like sapphires amid the green pines and dark firs. He picked up the speaking tube, a length of rubber hose pipe, and whistled into it. "Want to shoot up trains?" he yelled above the engine's roar. He shoved the mouthpiece over his ear.

"Sure!" Ketchum shouted back through the tube. Kowsky laughed and pulled the goggles over his eyes.

Since Ketchum had had his first flight last week the retired railwayman had delighted in Kowsky's simulated efforts to shoot up trains. He scanned the forest, searching for the tell-tale railway tracks, pulled the Stearman around in a tight bank, and spiraled down toward the verdant carpet below. Then he spotted the silver threads twisting out of the untidy brown patch that was the lumber camp. He straightened the wings and turned in a new direction as a freight train headed out of the camp, hauled by a black locomotive shrouded in a cloud of smoke. He shoved the rudder bar over, following the tracks of the Great Northern Railroad, looking for the spot where they swung west to a trestle bridge spanning the gorge of the Rogue River before it tumbled into the Columbia.

"Hold on!" he'd yelled, exhilarated by the sharp response of the little plane as the nose dropped. The slipstream shrieked through the bracing wires and the back of Ketchum's head fell against the cockpit coaming. He glanced over the side, judging the train's speed and the distance it had to travel before reaching the bridge. Dead ahead was the river, white where it splashed over a rocky bed, and there was the gorge and the bridge, seventy feet above the rushing tide. He shoved the control column to the right and the biplane leapt about the sky like a terrier. What joy to fly a machine that acted as if it were an extension of his body! The train picked up speed, its smoke billowing in the calm air.

He spun down to where the Rogue widened into a shallow bay a mile east of the bridge and put the aircraft into a tight turn until it was fifty feet above the torrent. If he gauged it accurately he'd arrive at the bridge at the same time as the train. Tall pines flashed past the wingtips. Jiggling the stick to follow the twist of the river, he saw the bridge coming up ahead, now level with his wheels. A flick of the stick would send the plane soaring above it. The locomotive thrust its ugly snout onto the bridge. His grip tightened. The bridge was a hundred yards away, seventy-five, fifty, the locomotive and its tender halfway across; the first of the flatcars appeared, loaded with huge tree trunks lashed down with chains. In a sudden impulse he rammed the stick forward and the train disappeared overhead in a jumbled blur of rotating iron wheels and open-mouthed faces staring from the footplate. A shadow flitted across the cockpit. The bridge had vanished and white water tumbling over jagged rocks streaked under the wings. The propeller disc shimmered and spray stung his face. He jerked the stick back to his belly, the water vanished, and he was staring at a broad expanse of blue sky. Ketchum's head had disappeared. The aircraft zoomed upward and he rammed the stick forward, feeling the seat belt bite his flesh. The top of Ketchum's head reappeared.

"You can look now," he yelled.

The old man gripped the coaming, knuckles white, and turned around, face distorted by the slipstream. The features shaped into a toothless grin.

"Jeez! Bet . . . 'em hell . . . of . . . scare!" The wind shrieked through the wires as Kowsky opened the throttle. "How much clearance . . . we have?" Ketchum shouted, still grinning.

"Enough!" Kowsky yelled.

He took a deep breath and smelled the odor of the flight deck, a mixture of freshly painted stringers and milled titanium, plastic coverings, and leather seats. Bartlett's voice telescoped twenty-eight years of flying and jolted him back to reality.

"It's time we told Gander we've got problems," he said, snapping on the transmit switch. "American Arrow Zero-One to Gander. Have two injured passengers requiring immediate medical attention on landing. Several others need first aid for bruises. Request approach and GCA on Runway Zero-Four if wind direction permits." He paused and, through his earphones, caught the faint tappety-tap of the keys on Mercer's machine. "We have a special problem. Fuel transfer pump for rear tank in the tail of the aircraft has failed. Unable to transfer fuel to forward tanks to trim aircraft on landing. Our attitude will be above normal nose up."

The full impact of what lay ahead struck him as he verbalized the problem, and he brushed the beads of sweat from his forehead with the back of his hand. What an understatement! With no landing flaps, not even the drogue parachutes they'd installed in the preproduction Arrowhead models to reduce the landing run, they'd come in fast as hell with the nose high. They might need those arrester cables after all. What if the drooped nose had gone blooey and wouldn't lower? When in the down position it created drag and helped cut their landing run. He fought to keep his feelings in check, remembering that the drooped nose was operated by an electric motor driving a screw jack. "And, uh, we've got a stuck visor. The visor won't retract away from the windshield."

Mercer's voice sounded in the headphones, calm and measured.

"Gander to American Arrow Flight Zero-One. Cleared for GCA on Runway Zero-Four. Wind gusting to ten miles per hour from two-seven-zero. Emergency services alerted. Will raise arrester cables if needed. Medical services at standby. Give present position and ETA Gander."

Bartlett studied the moving map display. "Position latitude forty-five fifteen north, longitude thirty-seven west. ETA zero-two-three-zero."

He listened to Mercer's talk-back. "Give position report at normal intervals." Mercer added, "There's a restricted airspace below ten thousand feet for combined United States–Canadian armed forces air exercises." Damn, he'd forgotten about that Notam. "Will advise you of any military aircraft movements in Gander control area when you arrive longitude forty west."

Kowsky, listening on his earphones, screwed up his mouth. "Balls! The Air Force has to play games right now."

"They've got helicopters out on search and rescue too," reminded Nardini, hunting for the Notam Bartlett had given him. He fished it from the drawer of his console. "Sub-hunting aircraft operating as far east as longitude forty-five west. That's nearly five hundred miles from the Newfie coast."

"We're okay as long as we stay above ten thousand feet," Bartlett said, slackening his harness in a deliberate effort to install some confidence on the flight deck. He rotated the radio selector to the airline frequency. He'd get the operations director in New York to contact the technical section to give him advice on finding the faults with the fuel pump and visor circuits. With luck it might be possible to track them down and correct them in flight before Arrowhead reached Gander. He was about to call New York when an orange call light winked over the Shanwick frequency sign on the radio panel. He switched from the airline frequency to Shanwick Oceanic 133.8. Who would call him from Shanwick now they were in Gander's traffic control area? In a flash the answer came. Gerrard—the radiation man in London.

FIVE

"Are you all right?" Vincent Maxwell asked, peering at Miss Lindenberg's head.

She felt her scalp and looked at her hand. "No blood at least," she replied, laughing nervously. "What about you, sir?"

"I only hit my arm on the side of the seat. But your head hit the bulkhead."

"I couldn't fasten my seat belt fast enough," Miss Lindenberg said, grasping the attaché case.

Maxwell turned and looked back along the aisle. The surgeon had left his seat and was bending over the elderly lady halfway down the cabin. He undid his seat belt and stood up.

"We'll have it in a cast as soon as we get to New York," he heard Sir Leonard say as he adjusted the sling supporting the woman's arm.

"Oh dear. I hope I don't miss my connection to San Francisco. I have to be on board the freighter by eight in the morning." That lady's got plenty of guts, Maxwell thought.

"You *must* have it set first," Sir Leonard insisted.

SUPERSONIC

Maxwell saw the stewardess come from the vestibule and hurry down the aisle.

"Oh, miss," Sir Leonard called. "What time is the connecting flight from New York to San Francisco? This lady has to get to San Francisco before eight o'clock tomorrow morning. But she must have her arm set in New York first."

"There's an Arrowhead service departs La Guardia at seven-fifty this evening, Mrs. Glinker. It arrives at San Francisco seven-fifty local time. We'll arrange ground transportation to La Guardia for you from wherever they set your arm."

A look of puzzlement passed over Sir Leonard's face, quickly changing to an expression of understanding. "The time difference is exactly the flying time. You arrive at the same local time as you left?" he asked.

"Yes, sir."

Maxwell turned and peered out of the window. A line of cloud now rimmed the northern horizon and he had the impression that the aircraft was heading in another direction. After the steep dive and the yelling had subsided he'd had a feeling that the aircraft had gone onto a different course. When the first officer had come back to reassure them that everything was all right—that they'd been forced to make the dive to avoid galactic radiation—he'd been evasive when asked if that would mean they'd be late arriving at New York.

"They can fix me up and I can get the plane to the West Coast on time?" Gladys Glinker said, her face brightening. Lydia and Sir Leonard nodded and the ends of Maxwell's lips dimpled, an upward movement of the mouth that did not reach the generous curve that characterized the broad smiles that showed up so well on television screens.

He'd never reacted with a spontaneous outburst of joy in

SUPERSONIC

his life and the thought produced a familiar heaviness in his spirit. Maximus Maxwell—the delayer—they'd dubbed him at Princeton, parodying Fabius Maximus, after those early debates on American foreign policy. The sobriquet had disappeared when he'd entered politics and become a senator. But his gut feeling for delaying action, based on a xenophobic feeling that American external policy must be based in distrust of the foreigner, had remained. This was the basic reason, a columnist for the *Washington Post* once remarked, with wry if corny humor, that he had been chosen as the president's *right*-hand man when the president needed a new security advisor after the near outbreak of war between the Chinese and Russians less than a year after he'd been elected. Since he'd become the president's chief envoy in the past few years, he'd clocked approximately one hundred thousand miles of air travel annually, conveying America's policy on external relations to top-level foreign officials, probing the mystic sanctums of Peking's rulers, the arcane rooms of Tokyo's Foreign Office, behind grim Kremlin walls, the Regency drawing rooms of Whitehall, and glittering palaces of former rajahs secreted in the mountains beyond New Delhi.

He had hidden his own feelings behind a smokescreen of statements and lectures cleverly contrived to tell people what *they* wanted to hear. To a senator from California, representing the big avionics and airplane armaments industries, he would say that maintaining an American military presence in Southeast Asia during the present Sino-Russian confrontation was essential to "protect the legitimate interests of the United States in that area." Speaking before an audience of distinguished academics with liberal leanings he would "doubt the advisibility of keeping an American presence in Southeast Asia at a time when China was flexing its muscles and indications showed a developing expansionist movement on the Asian mainland." To a coterie of cabinet members in the White House he "doubted the wisdom of maintaining the United States' demonstration of strength at a time of flux within heartland Asia." As a result, newspaper stories and magazine articles appearing in *Time* and *Newsweek* became a tangle of conflicting reports. Thus, partly due to Maxwell's double-talk from his place of power, rumor and counter-rumor shuttled backward and forward through Washington, canceling each other out, leaving only worthless hypotheses on which reporters based long articles that appeared in the national press and caused brows to furrow in puzzlement in the foreign offices of a dozen major countries.

All through his political career, and especially since he had been seated at the president's side, Maxwell had succeeded in giving the impression that he never disagreed with any of the president's policies. At first timid when approached by the press—he gave interviews in the early days of his climb to power in an anteroom in the White House—within a year he had reached a position of superstardom in the media. His characteristic smile had an enigmatic quality that exuded mystery, but emanated confidence, giving the impression that whatever was hidden behind the words was not at that particular moment good for the public interest, but would be revealed at the propitious time. In short, Maxwell, sitting next to the throne of power but not on it, gave the American people a feeling of righteousness that appealed to the Puritan streak that remained in the national psyche.

Now, in this aircraft that had suddenly lost height and, he suspected, altered course, the fragility of his physical condition flashed upon him. The things he'd seen and been told on the flight deck took on a new meaning—a moment of truth was at hand. The correct functioning of these new aircraft depended on so many interrelated systems that it was a marvel the things had set records for efficiency and punctuality. As he leaned against the side of a seat, he wondered about the hot fuel in the tanks beneath him. Now that they were at a lower flight level perhaps the fuel had cooled. The sun shone brightly through the windows, tipping the shadows of the vacant seats across the aisle as the aircraft rolled lazily from slight turbulence, the soft hum from the engines barely audible. A voice came over the PA system that he instantly recognized.

". . . is Captain Bartlett speaking. Due to the necessity to maintain a lower flight level and a technical problem with the fuel transfer system we are, in your own interests and safety, diverting to Gander International Airport. We apologize for the injuries sustained by some passengers and for the inconvenience caused by our diversion. Medical facilities will be on hand at the airport, which has been alerted, and connecting flights to New York will be available. Again, on behalf of American Arrow Airlines, I express apologies. Every assistance will be given by the cabin attendants. Thank you."

Maxwell clutched the top of the seat. The plane *had* altered course, and there must be something seriously wrong if they were arranging for other planes to take them from Gander to Kennedy. With an all too familiar insight, he recognized the weasel words from the flight deck, soft talk to lull them into a false sense of security. Weren't the supersonics supposed to have enough fuel to continue to their stated destinations even at subsonic speed if they were forced to fly at lower altitudes due to galactic radiation? There was something screwy going on. The president would have to be told; he was expected at the White House this afternoon and, after the call on the radio, it was imperative that he get there to attend the hastily arranged national security council meeting. He walked down the aisle with a purposeful stride.

"I must send a radio message to Washington. It's urgent," he told Lydia Olsen.

The girl's eyes widened. "It's rather busy on the flight deck right now, sir. I . . ."

"You understand who I am?"

"Yes, sir." She hesitated. Maxwell shot a glance at Sir Leonard Wheeler-Carthert, now bending over Alex Browne. "I'll, uh, see what can be done," Lydia said.

Smart girl, but not smart enough. *It's rather busy on the flight deck right now* was a dead giveaway. She must have known all along about the course change. He followed her to the flight deck door, which she cautiously pushed open and stood behind Bartlett and Kowsky. Nardini didn't look up from his array of dials and both the men in the front seats ignored him, although he could tell they sensed his presence. Bartlett, his hand dancing over the frequency band switches, pressed the earphones to his head with his free hand. Maxwell glanced at Lydia, who made an "I told you so" gesture. It was obvious the crew was having trouble with the radio.

Maxwell motioned toward the vestibule. As he followed Lydia from the flight deck he demanded, "What's going on? Level with me, Miss Olsen."

"I don't know any more than you do, Mr. Maxwell. Obviously they're having trouble with the radio."

"Didn't the first officer tell you what was wrong when he came back here?"

"Only that we were diverting to Gander and not to tell the passengers."

He searched her face. "I understood this plane could make

SUPERSONIC

New York even at subsonic speeds at lower altitude. Why *are* we going to Gander?"

"I don't understand it myself, sir."

"But you're the senior stewardess. You must have some idea," he persisted.

"No, sir." He saw the glint of annoyance in her eye.

"Very well. What time will we get to Gander? I want a connection to Kennedy immediately when we arrive."

Lydia took a deep breath and looked at her watch. "I'd say we should be in Gander in just over an hour, sir." She paused and added, "We were halfway across when the captain announced it."

"And the connection to New York?"

"I have no idea. Gander's always been an alternate. In case of bad weather, or . . ."

"Supersonic aircraft that go haywire." As soon as it was out he regretted saying it. It wasn't her fault that they had been diverted. He stuck his hands in his pockets. "Let me know immediately when I can send a personal message to Washington, Miss Olsen. It's extremely important. Surely you appreciate that."

"I understand perfectly, sir. I'll tell Captain Bartlett as soon as it's humanly possible."

He turned on his heel and strode toward his seat.

Alex Browne awoke with a start. A tall figure was standing beside her. It was the medical man, the ends of his bushy moustache raised in a smile.

"You hit your head," he said. "There's a bruise on your forehead."

She put a hand to her forehead and winced when she touched the skin. "I guess I hit the back of the seat," she said. "I never even felt it."

"It's a deep bruise," Sir Leonard said. "Quite blue, too."

"Oh," she felt a sudden spasm of alarm, but he bent close, and put his hand on her forehead. She felt only the slightest touch, like a feather against her skin. It seemed impossible that someone could touch a body so lightly.

"Does this hurt, my dear?" She felt the pressure on his fingertip increase.

"Ouch."

"So sorry." Sir Leonard took his hand away and rested it on the back of the seat. He looked down at her and she saw the cool, reassuring eyes and, strangely, something that reminded her of her father's eyes, a twinkle and, behind it, concern.

"It's going to be black and blue for a few days," he said.

She saw his eyes pass over her abdomen. "It's not going to pop soon, is it?" she asked, sudden fear welling up.

"There's no telling, my dear." He bent closer. "Is this your first?" he whispered.

"What's that got to do with it?" she asked defensively, looking around. The guy in the window seat was asleep.

"Sometimes the first one is a bit late," Sir Leonard said.

"That's a relief," she said evasively. "I want her to be born in the United States."

"You want a girl?"

She nodded. Sir Leonard smiled. "I hope your wish comes true," he said, "but nature makes the decision . . . listen, there's an announcement." He put up his finger as a voice came over the PA system.

"Ladies and gentlemen. This is Captain Bartlett speaking . . . divert to Gander International Airport . . ."

"Gander? That's someplace up in Canada isn't it?" Alex cried.

"Yes, yes. Shh. Let's listen to what he's saying."

SUPERSONIC

". . . cabin attendants. Thank you."

"I don't want to go to some God-forsaken Canadian place. I want to go to New York." She tried to stand, but a sudden pain in her back forced her into the seat. She held her back with both hands.

"The pain's coming." Her eyes widened and she grabbed Sir Leonard's arm. "Don't leave me!"

Sir Leonard bent over. "Show me exactly where the pain is."

"Here, low down. It . . . it's just like the pain I had before . . . I mean."

"I understand, my dear. I'll be right back." He went to his seat and returned with a stethoscope, and listened to the sounds in her abdomen. He folded the stethoscope and felt her pulse.

"I think you have a little more time to go. Now, why don't you try to get some rest? Can I get you a drink of water?"

"No . . . ahh . . . the pains are going."

She looked up at the lean face with the long moustache and the serene eyes and a feeling of resignation overcame her. Recollection flooded back. She saw her father trudging along the well-worn path from the barn to the white-painted farmhouse on a side road three miles out of Applefield, Wisconsin. She'd run to meet him and linked her arm around his. She felt his hand tousling her long hair and asking her what she'd learned in school that day, laughing when she'd told him "the same old thing." That *was* Applefield: the same old thing; Main Street, Maple Avenue, Orchard Road, and the service station near the school, and the Methodist Church kitty-corner with its bell that dragged out a melancholy toll every Sunday. Sameness, dullness. Nothing ever *happened* in Applefield. Just school, and church, and Sunday school, and her mother's constant scolding, "No television until your homework and housework are done." If she'd had more than one sister it would have been different; her mother's nagging would have been spread around more and she'd have sneaked off where her mother couldn't find her. She remembered her fifteenth birthday—how Dad had openly sided with her when mother made her do the chores before she would let her friends come to the party.

At sixteen she'd promised to go for a picnic with Rod Howell, the boy over on the third side road who had just bought his first jalopy. But when she had the sandwiches wrapped, her mother intercepted her as she ran out to Rod's car. "There's floors to wax, and after that you'll see if your father wants help with the chores." It was at that moment that she decided her future course of action.

The man at the Milwaukee bus terminal offered to carry her suitcase to a rooming house not far away, but she had had enough sense to spurn his offer and find a place on her own. The first few weeks were exciting: The neon and the crowds swirling in the downtown section on Saturday nights was life, and when she returned to her own room there was no scolding. She got a job as a waitress in a small diner in Oak Creek and soon discovered that, with a smile and a willingness to oblige, she could make a quarter of her salary in tips. That was how she met Sandy.

He had come into the restaurant late one Saturday night with three other boys. They cracked jokes and laughed loudly, except Sandy. He was the tallest, with dark, thoughtful eyes that regarded her trim figure with open admiration. He never made a pass, but conveyed his interest in other ways, like the way his eyes lingered on her face when she put the hamburger and french fries in front of him and the friendly smile he gave her when she brought the ketchup. By the following week, Sandy had become a regular patron, and the next week he asked for a date. She never remembered more than one or two scenes of the movie at the drive-in, but she would never forget the way Sandy's hands passed so skillfully over her body. She'd never known that she had such feelings, uncontrollable feelings. Every night he waited outside the diner, key chain whirling from his fingers. As soon as he got a raise he'd marry her, he'd promised. Next Saturday he'd met her outside the restaurant as usual and pointed with pride to a red roadster parked at the curb. It had only cost nine hundred bucks, he'd said, and the salesman had thrown in two spare tires. Now he was going to save in earnest, but the way apartment rents were going up . . . Anyway, there was a bunch of the gang having a party on the other side of town, and it would be cheaper than a drive-in. Except he couldn't go empty-handed and the bootlegger's place was only three blocks away. In six months she was pregnant. He knew a friend who knew a doctor who'd take care of everything, but it would cost five hundred bucks. In desperation she wrote a letter to her father, tore it up, thought of borrowing the money from a bank, but gave up that idea when she realized the bank would want to know what she needed the money for. She wore her waitress's apron loosely in case people noticed. And suddenly Sandy got a job in Chicago. "It's a chance to make some real money, hon. This guy, he's in pool halls . . . real big operator and . . ."

She was fired from the diner, and five months later the baby, a boy, was stillborn.

"Everything's going to be all right," Sir Leonard reaffirmed in a gentle voice. He put a finger to his lips. "I've got to see a patient in the economy cabin. Poor fellow's got concussion. Just lie back and relax."

"Concussion . . . ?"

She looked up, but he had gone. As she turned to face

forward she saw the burly form of Vincent Maxwell jump from his seat and stride through the vestibule toward the flight deck door.

Imagine, Gladys Glinker from Brooklyn being cared for by a knight. Or was a sir called a lord? A real somebody, either way. *"We'll have it in a cast as soon as we get to New York."* And the head stewardess. *"There's an Arrowhead service departs La Guardia at seven-fifty this evening, Mrs. Glinker. It arrives at San Francisco . . . we'll arrange ground transportation . . ."*

Surprising how her old line *"Did you get to Greece?"* provoked such interest in her, in *her*, Gladys Glinker, the old maid who'd never been around. Huh, the typist in the back section of the typing pool of Heimer Engineering, Incorporated, who'd sat there since God-knows-when; the skinny lady living on the top floor of the walk-up on Beeton Street; the bent figure on the bench throwing stale bread to the birds in Prospect Park on Sunday afternoons. The pregnant kid and that Mr. Ives had swallowed everything, including the lie about catching the freighter for Yokohama, and the one about the banana boat. Remarkable how much information you can get from a school atlas and make it sound believable. She'd thought she'd deceived the Church Women's group for years, explaining her occasional absences from the monthly meetings by saying she'd been "on an extended trip abroad."

She looked across the aisle. The girl was lying back, eyes closed, and Mr. Ives in the window seat had just awakened and lit a cigarette. There was something queer about *him*. Fidgety type, and looked sort of dazed. A sudden hot spasm of pain shot through her arm—she couldn't cry out or call the doctor back, she'd look a fool. Keep up the brave front,

Gladys Glinker, or everybody'll recognize you for the old fraud you are. She turned to the window and sucked in a deep breath, letting it out in a long sigh, feeling the façade of worldly sophistication she had painfully erected over the years fade into the background, like peeling away the skins of an onion until only the tiny center heart remained, exposing the raw nerve that was the bleakness of her life.

"Sorry it had to end like this. Love, Sam." Nine words on a note had changed her life. In her mind's eye she saw again the creased paper and heard it rustle as she opened the envelope. Four years, then the note. Wasted years? It was better to have loved and lost . . . ? A shadow fell across her.

"How are you feeling, Mrs. Glinker?" It was the stewardess.

"Uh, fine, thanks."

The girl fingered the arm sling. "Let me tuck in this loose end."

"Don't make a fuss. The time I broke my leg was far worse." She forced a smile. Who did she think she was fooling? An old spinster couldn't deceive a girl like this stewardess, gay and sparkling with life, playing the field, experimenting, making sure she married the right one, the best one, when she found him. All she'd had, years after Sam had left, was a second best. She remembered the first time Harrison Sloane had walked into the typing pool at Heimer Engineering, a sheaf of papers in his hand and a friendly look on his suntanned face.

"Miss Glinker, my secretary's off with the flu. I wonder if I may impose on your time to do a little job for me. This top letter *has* to go out today, but the others can be done at your convenience."

The stewardess moved away and she stared out of the window. The words glowed on the rosy lip of the distant clouds. *"I wonder if I may impose . . . do a little job for me . . . at your convenience."*

Feelings that she'd thought she'd sublimated forever had surfaced with frightening suddenness. She remembered her quick rush of breath as she looked into Harrison's brown eyes, eyes that in the next fourteen years she was to kiss as he lay in her arms in her apartment. When he wasn't there she pretended that he didn't have a wife, five children, and a mortgage; and sometimes when she was alone in the kitchen she would call out, "Breakfast coming up, darling. The usual?" She remodeled the apartment, fresh, gay wallpaper replaced the painted walls, a planter of bright flowers stood in the space near the window.

The only time she'd seen his wife was the day of the funeral. She'd worn dark glasses, which she knew was silly, because everybody present knew who Gladys Glinker was. Ellen Sloane was a tall woman, with a pinched face and thin lips. And the instant she looked at her across the open grave, she believed that she—Gladys Glinker from the typing pool —had given Harrison the only affection and understanding he'd ever had. For a time her confidence and her memories of happier times were buoyed by this knowledge. But, little by little, she slipped into the nothing-mattered attitude of middle-aged people who live alone in walk-ups in shabby parts of cities all over the world, living out what remained of their lives in resignation—quiet desperation—in typing pools, behind the counters of neighborhood ladies' wear stores, or screened by bookshelves in obscure parts of public libraries.

"Broke your leg? You'll have to tell me all about it some time." The stewardess had returned, and then hurried down the aisle. *She'd* been around. Probably around the world several times, *really* around the world, not by tracing lines with a pencil on a cheap atlas. All Gladys had seen of it was three days in London, attending the international convention of the League of Women's Councils. And all she'd had to do was present the Brooklyn Chapter's felicitations, handwritten on imitation parchment, to the head table. Nothing really important, just read the words, roll up the parchment, and hand it to the chairlady. Hardly an earth-shattering event that warranted the chapter unanimously voting to send her to England, although she could not sleep for weeks with excitement after they'd made the announcement.

"We rarely have an opportunity to honor one with such a long term of volunteer work," the president had said. "Forty years of unselfish, devoted service. Of course, London is nothing new to our much-traveled Gladys. It'll be like renewing an old friendship."

She pressed her face against the window, feeling its chill, fighting back the tears. Her body began to shake with such violence that the other voices in the cabin became a distant meaningless mumble.

SIX

"Warning to North Atlantic traffic. Boulder advises it expects communications interference from solar flares."

The Shanwick controller's voice paused, and Bartlett turned up the volume. A plop sounded in his earphones and his gut tensed. The voice continued: "Some traffic relaying through Santa Maria ATC. Request traffic west of longitude thirty report immediately if reception deteriorates."

He twisted the selector to the company wave band. "Flight Zero-One to flight operations, Kennedy. Confirm diversion to Gander due to fuel transfer problem. Request advice from technical director." He gave Kowsky a sideways glance as the airline dispatcher's voice shot back. "Roger, Zero-One. Were trying to call you. Standby."

A new sound filled his earphones—the hiss of static. Then a gravelly voice came over the ether. "Robert Ziegel to Zero-One. What's the problem, Captain?"

"Rear tank booster pumps have failed."

Ziegel's voice faded in a sputter of atmospherics. "Can't . . . hear . . . Zero-One," came through in moments of clear transmission.

"I said the rear tank booster pumps have failed. Can't get the fuel forward."

"What's your fuel reserve to Gander, Captain?" Thankfully, the transmission remained clear.

"Two percent."

Ziegel whistled. When he spoke his voice was taut and under control. "You'll get a taildown moment as the rest of the fuel burns off. Are you on autopilot?"

"Yes," Bartlett replied. "So far the taildown moment is within its range to correct." He paused and added, "We've got another problem. The visor won't lower."

"What!"

"The visor's stuck. Motor circuit's out."

"Tested the circuit breakers?"

"Yes. Breakers A-okay and holding."

Ziegel fell silent. "What about the other operational circuits? Like the solenoid switch for the nose screw jack motor?" he said at last.

"It's A-okay as far as we know."

Bartlett waited for Ziegel to go on, hoping he'd call a hasty conference of his experts. He reflected that Ziegel had a reputation for getting airplanes out of trouble. He'd once given radio instructions to the crew of a Boeing 747 to get a stuck retracted nosewheel unit unlocked as the aircraft circled Long Island Sound. Got them to disconnect the jammed up locks, which even the emergency mechanical system had failed to release, by isolating a section of the aircraft's hydraulic system and having the crew reconnect various pipes to increase the pressure on the up locks. If he was going to call a meeting he'd better hurry.

Bartlett heard him call to someone in the background. "Stand by while I get the manuals. And check the tapes of the London ground tests. Use the Gander direct telephone line to Prestwick and relay to Heathrow." Ziegel's voice returned. "Captain, I'm signing off until I get the data on your electrical circuits from the manuals and bring in Des Larson and his boys. And I've ordered a reading on London's pre-takeoff ground tests."

"Roger." Bartlett switched off. Kowsky said, "He'll be a magician if he can fix dead circuits over the air."

Bartlett said hopefully, but without feeling, "NASA boys do it. Remember the Apollo Thirteen flight that was aborted, and then the Skylab problems. The crew fixed those from ground instructions."

"Maybe . . ." Kowsky said doubtfully.

Nardini said, "Captain's right. The Apollo Thirteen crew would be corpses in orbit around the moon to this day if it hadn't been for ground control."

"Don't be morbid, Nick," Kowsky said.

Bartlett checked the moving map display. The pinprick of light had moved toward longitude forty west, more slowly now they had gone subsonic. It would soon be time to give Gander a position report.

The Selective Calling bell chimed. He moved the switch. "American Arrow Flight Zero-One. Go ahead."

"Ziegel speaking, Captain. We're organized now and Des is here. London is running through the tape. The problem may be at the main bus bar. The fuel tank transfer pumps and the visor retraction motor are on the same circuit. Connected at the main bus."

"Nick, grab a headset," Bartlett waited until Nardini plugged a headset into a ceiling outlet and adjusted the earphones. "Go ahead, Kennedy. My flight systems engineer's hooked up."

Ziegel said in the background, "Des, give us a rundown on the circuits . . ."

Bartlett interrupted. "Isn't there some way we can test the circuits in flight? Over and above what my flight engineer can do."

"Only the ground test director can do that. On-board test equipment to run through everything in flight would take up a quarter of your payload."

"Any ideas?" Bartlett fought to subdue his rising fear.

"London'll be back in a few minutes, Captain. We must check out their tapes *first*," Ziegel's voice was confident. It was all right for him, sitting in a comfortable flight dispatch office, both feet safely on the ground, checking his technical manuals, his head wreathed in a haze from his chain smoking. Ziegel had once been a passenger on the first Arrowhead pre-service tests and had left a trail of cigarette ash over the flight systems management engineer's console, examining dials, actuating switches, calculating engine performance, nozzle-gas velocities, and heat-exchange efficiencies. Bartlett himself had had to detail the maintenance staff to clean up the engineer's station when they'd landed.

"Zero-One," Ziegel's voice broke the hum in his ears, "London says the monitor tapes show an overvoltage. In both circuits." He paused. "That's damned peculiar. The fuse should . . . should . . . take care of that."

Kowsky glanced across at Bartlett, eyebrows knitted in two fringes of puzzlement.

"The fuel pumps . . . operate . . . solenoid valves . . ." Bartlett turned up the volume. "They're . . . fuel pipe gallery . . . aft baggage . . ." Ziegel's voice cut out abruptly. Bartlett adjusted the tone control. An agonizing wail screeched through his skull.

"Christ!" Kowsky ripped off his headset and rubbed his ears.

Bartlett cautiously turned up the volume. With the control at its full loudness Ziegel's voice sounded far away.

"He sounds like he's going around the other side of the moon," Kowsky said, putting the earpiece to his head.

Crackling atmospherics drowned Ziegel's voice. Bartlett selected the Gander wave band and adjusted the microphone. "American Arrow Zero-One to Gander ATC. Solar flare interfering with JFK transmission. Please relay from Kennedy." He remembered the Shanwick controller's request. "Tell Shanwick Oceanic we're having communication problems."

The earphones exploded in a cacophony of noise. He switched the selector to the Gander low-level frequency in an effort to subdue the racket, but the howling increased in volume. He switched off and turned to Kowsky. "Solar flares come in eleven-year cycles. Why the hell do they pick a time like this?"

"We're just plain lucky, Tom."

Bartlett turned to Nardini. "Those solenoid valves Ziegel mentioned are in the rear tank compartment aft of the baggage hold. It's my hunch he was going to say they had an overvoltage from the ground test. If the valve for the rear tank is stuck it might be possible to move it manually. Go take a look."

Nardini put on his jacket and made for the door. Bartlett called after him, "Remember the happy face."

"Sure, sure, Captain," Nardini said, searching for a flashlight and stuffing it in his trouser pocket.

Nardini was aware of eyes following his progress along the aisle of the economy-class cabin. He winked at the two stewardesses tidying the aft galley where plastic cups still littered the floor. Ahead, between the toilets, was a narrow door. He pulled the spring-loaded handle from its socket, twisted, and pushed. The door opened a couple of inches and jammed against something solid. He put his shoulder against it and applied pressure, feeling the panel give. The door moved enough for him to slide his slim body inside the baggage hold; as he groped for the light switch, he felt the broken baggage-restraining net against his face. Flight bags, suitcases, and golf clubs lay in a jumble in the baggage hold: women's underwear and men's starched shirts lay in a corner where they had spilled from smashed cases. And over everything were scattered folded sheets of paper.

He tore away the net, picked up a sheet and unfolded it, the stiff paper crackling between his fingers. "United States Treasury Bond" was printed in ornamental lettering across the top with a green dollar sign below, followed by the numerals 10,000. At center was a paragraph of printed matter and, lower down, the red embossed seal of the United States of America. A signature, written in the measured strokes of a bureaucrat, followed by the bold undecipherable hand of a Treasury official, were at the extreme bottom. He picked up another of the bonds. Fifty thousand bucks! He grabbed another: Jesus! One hundred thousand. He looked around in astonishment. The bonds had spilled from a blue suitcase that was sliced open, a new case with the American Arrow Airlines baggage tag dangling from the broken handle. He jumped across the heap of damaged suitcases and flight bags to inspect the name tag: Mr. Clarence Ives, c/o Box A. 1089, Grand Central Station, New York, N.Y. written with an indelible pencil in printed characters. The illegible signatures on the bonds and the painstakingly correct lettering on the tag struck him as odd. Mr. Clarence Ives was obviously, and understandably, a careful man when it came to taking precautions to insure that his baggage did not go astray. He'd even printed his name and address in the same precise manner on two labels of stout paper glued to the ends of the case. Peculiar that a man would put such valuable negotiables in his suitcase when he might just as easily have put them in a briefcase and carried them as hand luggage into the cabin, where they would be under his constant supervision. If *he* had that much dough he'd sure as hell never trust it to an airline's baggage handling crew. The old joke breakfast in New York, lunch in Los Angeles, baggage in Buenos Aires, was not a joke. It happened, and more often than airlines cared to admit. Besides, the possibility of theft, although remote, could not be denied. Odds and ends of personal clothing had been thrown from the broken case; some shirts, two or three ties, and socks. He looked again at the carpet of bonds, making a rough calculation of their worth. Mr. Clarence Ives had enough money here to buy his own executive twin jet.

Nardini tossed the paper to the floor—it felt crazy, throwing away a $10,000 negotiable bond like a bit of garbage— and surveyed the mess between himself and the bulkhead at the opposite end of the hold, trying to make up his mind as to the best way to get to the hatch that gave access to the aft section of the fuselage.

He had to move aside a score of flight bags and a dozen suitcases before he got to the bulkhead, by which time he was covered with perspiration. He swung open the hatch and stepped through, into the sudden roar of the engines in the unbaffled rear section. Swinging the flashlight to find the switch, he looked for the telephone that would connect him to the flight deck, but remembered there wasn't one. He stood in the center of the tapered compartment, with its bare fuselage frames, machined from solid aluminum, gleaming silver, and listened to the roar of the jet exhausts and the faint drumming of the slipstream on the aircraft's skin overhead.

SUPERSONIC

He looked at the rear pressure dome where two pipes passed through seals to the rear tank under the fin and glanced at an electrical conduit passing through the pressure dome, carrying cables to the flight data recorder and the cockpit voice recorder high in the fin.

Jesus only knows what secrets were being inputed into the steadily rotating tapes by the electronic sensers connected to the flight control systems, engine controls, and scores of subsystems—besides every word spoken on the flight deck and those transmitted to and received from the air controllers. What would accident investigators deduce from the recorders if they had a wipe-out at Gander? He shuddered and pushed the thought from his mind, checking the direction of the arrows stenciled on the fuel pipes.

Tracing the pipes from the dome, he bent to examine the solenoid-operated transfer valves on a platform raised above the floor. Flameproof electrical terminal boxes were mounted nearby, and he moved his finger along a conduit where it connected to the solenoid valve housing. Everything *looked* A-okay: the pipes and electrical cables shone with factory newness. He got down on his hands and knees, put his nose to the solenoid and sniffed: burned varnish. He put his nose to the other solenoids. They were odorless. The damned thing *had* been put through an overvoltage on the ground—exactly what had happened to Apollo 13! Human error, they'd said. Always human error or, in the pedantic language of the air accident investigators, "pilot error." He examined the stubby shaft that extended from the flameproof solenoid to the fuel valve and tried to twist it with his hand, but the shiny steel surface slipped through his fingers. There was no flat spot on the shaft on which to place a tool to grip it and rotate the valve. In any case, the only wrench he carried was a small adjustable type, far too small to exert enough leverage in the confined space between the other solenoids to open the valve. It was stuck solidly in the closed position, shutting off any hope of pumping fuel from the rear tank to the amidship collector tanks and into the forward tanks.

He took a quick look around, switched off the light, and stepped back into the baggage compartment. As he emerged into the economy section he saw that the stewardesses had cleaned up the galley and were now spread through the cabin, smiling and chatting with the passengers; one attendant was standing by the unconscious man near the front. He strode forward, wondering which of the backs of the heads he passed belonged to Mr. Clarence Ives.

"The solenoid's burned out, Captain. And the valve won't budge by hand. No tools aboard to shift it."

"How do you know it's burned out?"

"Smells of burned varnish. I've seen them go like that before, on DC-8 cross-feeds. They stick solid as cement."

"Any way to bypass it?"

Nardini hesitated. "I don't think so." He paused, his head turned to one side in thought. "No. It's in the pipe that comes directly from the rear tank."

"And the visor circuit?"

"It's connected at the same bus bar as the fuel transfer pumps. When they applied the overvoltage they burned out the two circuits—the one for the rear tank solenoid valve and the visor solenoid switch circuit." Nardini slowly lowered himself into his seat, a defeated look on his face. "Goddamned ground testers," he added vindictively.

"I don't understand how the pump and visor worked after climb-out," Kowsky said, running his fingers through his hair.

"It's beginning to come clearer now," Nardini said. He had taken a handbook from the shelf and opened it to a section dealing with the electrical system. "There're two ground-test circuits for both the rear pump and the visor. One solenoid switch controls the pump after takeoff and another for letdown."

"You mean there's a solenoid switch that controls the rearward transfer of fuel when we went supersonic and another *separate* one for when we transit from supersonic to subsonic and need to pump the fuel forward?" Kowsky asked.

"Check."

"And it's the switch that controls the valve for the forward pumping action that's burned out?" Kowsky went on.

"Check. When London plugged in the ground tester they must have shoved an overvoltage through the test circuit for the rear solenoid switch, the one that controls the forward movement of the fuel. When they tested the first switch they must have had it on the right voltage . . ."

"Hell! Surely they must have a safeguard for such an elementary thing as that!" Bartlett said incredulously, his hands straining to keep the yoke level.

"Why didn't they blow a fuse?" Kowsky asked.

"Search me, Pete. I didn't design the goddamned thing."

"And ditto procedure for the visor, I suppose," Bartlett said. "One solenoid switch for upward movement to cover the windshield and another to retract it. And they blew the *retract* switch with the overvoltage."

"That's the way I figure it," Nardini said, but a note of doubt had crept into his voice. "I don't understand why it didn't blow a fuse or why a circuit breaker didn't pop somewhere along the line."

"Perhaps the clever engineers forgot to put one in," Kowsky suggested.

Nardini shrugged. "Hardly." He checked an electrical diagram in the book.

"Select Kennedy, Pete," Bartlett said, taking a hand from

the yoke to adjust the volume control. "Perhaps the atmospherics have given up." He waited until Kowsky selected the company wave band before pressing the transmit button. A loud hum sounded in his headset.

"American Arrow Zero-One to Kennedy dispatcher. Are you receiving? Over." He clicked the listening-out switch and a tumultuous shriek broke through the ether. He turned down the volume and adjusted the squelch control. Kowsky gave him a pained look.

"Never heard anything like it."

"Try Gander."

Kowsky moved the selector on the radio panel. A faint voice spoke in the background, but when Bartlett increased the volume a hiss drowned out the voice. He switched off.

"Maybe they can receive," he said, checking the moving map. The display showed they were coming up to longitude forty west and latitude forty-six north, several degrees north of the Delta weather ship. If the flight had progressed normally they would have passed almost directly over the vessel as they'd slipped into New York Oceanic Control. He wondered if Arrowhead showed up on Delta's radar screens. The ship's radar, like Shanwick's and Gander's, had a maximum radius of two hundred miles.

"What's Delta's frequency, Nick?"

Nardini consulted the radio log. "One-niner-two decimal eight."

"Try it, Pete."

Kowsky turned the selector. Bartlett said, "American Arrow Flight Zero-One to Delta. Are you receiving?" A splatter of blips answered.

"Complete blackout. Another wave band?"

Nardini shrugged. "Only the marine band."

"Too bad we don't have it," Kowsky said.

SUPERSONIC

Bartlett wondered again if Arrowhead showed on the weather ship's radarscope. Possibly Delta's radio operator was as frustrated as he was, watching Arrowhead's blip creep across his scope and not able to make contact. He switched off the transmit button and checked the flight instruments and the power dials. When his eye came to the overhead fuel tank temperature gauges, he gasped and pointed. The fuel temperature needles were edging into the red danger sectors.

Nardini jerked his head up, then down. "It's the burn-off. From the forward tanks!" he exclaimed, checking his own instruments. "There's not enough left to act as a heat sink."

Bartlett's stomach tightened. He knew that even at 665 knots there was a substantial rise in temperature at the aircraft's skin surface. In his old DC-8s the skin temperature rose by thirty-five degrees centigrade at Mach 0.82. There was only one thing to do—reduce speed. But the tail would drop even lower and they'd have to apply more force on the yoke to keep the aircraft level.

"We'll try six hundred knots," he said deliberately, moving the throttles back. "Hold her, Pete."

He felt the extra weight on the control yoke as the airspeed indicator dropped. "It'll improve the fuel reserve," he told Nardini in an effort to sound optimistic.

Nardini turned to his calculator and tapped the keys. "By one percent, I'll bet," he muttered.

Bartlett rechecked the fuel temperature gauge, but the needles continued to point to the red sectors. Naturally, it would take a few minutes for the skin surface to cool, but it wasn't only the aircraft's skin heat he was worried about: the cabin pressurization system continued to pour excess heat into the fuel and still more came from the hydraulics system. The flight controls, the elevons on the wing trailing edge, were operated hydraulically by movements of the yoke and rudder pedals and every time he made a correction on the yoke or moved the rudder pedals the hydraulic system came into operation, generating heat.

"It improves our marginal reserves by one-decimal-one percent," Nardini said, handing Bartlett a slip of paper. Bartlett studied Nardini's calculations. They showed that at their present speed and flight level they'd land at Gander with just over two percent of the total available fuel load—he couldn't include the fuel locked in the rear tank—remaining in the tanks. But Bartlett realized that Nardini, trained in engine and flight management systems, had overlooked the fact that, with the aircraft poorly trimmed, Arrowhead's drag had increased. At this speed and flight attitude they'd be lucky to put down at Gander with the bottom of the wing and fuselage tanks covered with fuel. He remembered the war games off the Newfoundland and Nova Scotia coasts. How was he going to let down through squadrons of planes on antisubmarine hunts without fuel-wasting avoiding maneuvers?

"Check the weather radar's at maximum range," he said.

Kowsky touched a knob. "Three hundred miles max." He paused, divining Bartlett's thoughts. "I guess one day the eggheads will invent anticollision radar with high definition," he said. "They've been talking about it for years."

"With automatic evasive action tied in with the autopilot," Nardini added.

Bartlett gripped the yoke tighter. "Autopilot off," he said. It was time to get used to that tail-heavy action.

Kowsky moved a switch. So far the pressure on the yoke wasn't extreme although the artificial horizon told him the nose was pointing up five degrees. His mind returned to the military exercises off the coast. The Notam didn't give the number of aircraft involved and what types. If they were operating in conjunction with the Navy there'd be long-range antisubmarine reconnaissance airplanes, probably Orion P-3s, flying at the lower flight levels, below five thousand to get their subdetection radar working at optimum. But there would be other aircraft up to the ten-thousand-foot level, plus helicopters and patrol planes from the search and rescue squadrons to help any antisub planes that ditched.

"Where's the original Notam?" Bartlett demanded.

Nardini reached in his drawer and extracted a wad of paper. "Here it is," he said.

Bartlett glanced at the heading: "Air Navigation Orders, Security Control of Air Traffic, Amendment Number Thirty-Seven," then examined the thick pad. "All *this?*" he said. "Nine pages?"

Nardini shrugged. "When those Civil Aviation Authority boys get busy they get very busy, Captain."

"I don't remember the details of this one," Bartlett said to Kowsky. "Here's the Coastal CADIZ map," he continued, flipping to the back page. "Coastal Canadian Air Defense Identification Zone."

Kowsky leaned across the control pedestal and studied the map, holding the yoke against his chest. "It takes in a lot of territory off Newfie and Nova Scotia."

Bartlett glanced at the moving map display. The vertical line of longitude forty west had moved to the bright spot of light at center screen. They were at the exact point where they must transmit an ARP to Gander. He pressed the transmit button.

"American Arrow Zero-One to Gander. Are you receiving?"

Crackles sounded through the headpiece. He exchanged glances with Kowsky and switched to another frequency. Atmospherics, accompanied by a loud hum, drowned out any reply he may have initiated at Gander ATC.

"It might clear as we come up the coast," Kowsky said hopefully.

Bartlett peered at the CADIZ map. Arrowhead would be picked up by Gander's radar when they were two hundred miles from the airport and, once Arrowhead penetrated CADIZ, synonymous with the distant early warning identification zone of the military, the appearance of their blip would be flashed by teletype to the Norad Air Defense Headquarters buried under Cheyenne Mountain, Colorado, where computers in a fraction of a second would conduct a search of their electronic memories to see if Arrowhead's Flight Plan had been filed and the aircraft's progress across the Atlantic updated in accordance with the Air Report Positions and their confirmation.

The flight plans of every airliner, every freighter, every executive jet, in fact, everything that flew at a speed in excess of 180 knots toward or over the North American land mass was inputed into banks of computers. When an aircraft whose flight plan had not been fed into the computers approached the coast, a signal flashed on a hundred radarscopes in battle centers buried in obscure parts of the United States and Canada and an interrogation signal was flashed to its pilot. If he didn't respond, interceptor fighters scrambled to investigate.

"We might have to set up a daisy chain with the aircraft in the war games," he said.

"Don't tell me daisy chains! Jesus, it's years since I had to do that. And in a supersonic!"

Bartlett grinned, but without feeling, remembering a day twenty years ago when he was captain of a DC-6 from Keflavik to Goose in a radio blackout caused by a solar flare just like this. A dozen westbound planes had relayed messages to each other with the plane nearest Labrador making contact with Goose. "The TWA flight that went back to Shannon set one up," he reminded Kowsky.

Kowsky grunted and the flight deck grew perceptibly quieter and his eyes made their accustomed pattern over the instruments. He was glad when Nardini spoke.

"By the way, Captain, I forgot to mention it before but there's a lot of smashed baggage in the hold and, uh, there looks like a million dollars scattered all over."

"What *are* you talking about?" Bartlett demanded, turning to face him.

"The restraining net in the baggage hold gave way when we dived. Broken luggage is all over. There's a blue suitcase sliced clean open with dozens of United States Treasury bonds scattered about. Some for a hundred grand . . ."

"A hundred grand?" Kowsky echoed.

Nardini nodded. "Belong to a guy named Clarence Ives."

"His name's on the bonds?" Bartlett asked.

"No . . . on the smashed suitcase."

Bartlett had never invested in Treasury Bonds and didn't know if the owner's name appeared on them. How did Nick know they came from that particular suitcase? He hadn't given a thought to what might have happened in the hold as a result of the unplanned dive. "How do you know they came from that particular case?" he asked.

"Some bonds are still in it. But mostly they're scattered all over the hold."

"And this Mr. Clarence Ives's name is on the baggage tag?"

"Plastered all over in indelible pencil. With his address. Box number in Grand Central Station."

Bartlett pressed a button. A moment later Lydia appeared. "Yes, Captain?"

"There's a passenger named Clarence Ives on board. Can you find out where he's sitting. Discreetly, so that . . ."

"I already know, sir. He's in first class. In seat Eight-D." She paused, her head to one side in an inquisitive pose. "May I ask why you want to know, Captain."

Bartlett flashed a look at Nardini before replying. "Sure. Nick says there's a suitcase in the aft baggage hold belonging to Mr. Ives that broke open when we dived and scattered a million bucks' worth of Treasury bonds on the floor."

Lydia's eyes widened. "A million dollars!"

Nardini nodded. "I bet I'm not far off."

"Come to think of it, Captain," Lydia exclaimed. "I thought Mr. Ives was a bit nervous when he boarded. He sat down without taking off his topcoat and gave the impression he couldn't wait to get off the ground."

Bartlett chewed his lip and turned to Nardini. "You *really* think it's loot?

Nardini rubbed the side of his nose thoughtfully. "Yes, Captain."

"It's purely circumstantial evidence," Bartlett turned back to the instrument panel.

"If you had a million bucks in bonds wouldn't you put it in a briefcase and carry it on board, Captain?"

Nardini had a point. He turned to Lydia. "What hand baggage does Mr. Clarence Ives have?"

"A briefcase, sir."

Bartlett's eyebrows shot up.

"That puts the finger on him, Captain," Nardini said. I think—I suspect—either he couldn't get all the bonds into his briefcase and carry them on board or there's a secret compartment in the suitcase that broke open when we dived."

"You're letting your imagination run away," Bartlett said severely, turning away. "You can't accuse a passenger of trying to smuggle stolen bonds on board and . . ." But why would someone risk all that money in the baggage hold? Imagine checking in a suitcase at London Airport and seeing a million bucks disappear down the conveyor belt! And the anxiety at Kennedy waiting for it to appear from the baggage chute when they unloaded the aircraft. That was a compelling enough reason to believe Nick's hunch. But it *was* only a hunch. They had no concrete evidence. He wondered what type of man was Ives.

"Lydia. What's this fellow look like?"

"Nervous . . ."

"I mean, what's he like to look at."

"Fresh complexion. Balding head. Well dressed. Big man. Polished shoes . . ."

"Well dressed. Polished shoes." Bartlett repeated "H'mm."

"Yes, Captain." There was a hint of resentment in her voice. He knew she took pride in being able to judge people. "Looks like a businessman to me." She thought a moment. "He asked for the *Wall Street Journal* when I took the papers around."

Bartlett turned to Nardini: "There's absolutely no doubt in your mind that the suitcase belongs to this Clarence Ives guy?"

"His name's on the tag and on the stuck-on labels. Printed, very carefully, as though he wanted to make sure it doesn't get lost." Nardini's voice was so positive Bartlett found himself beginning to believe his story. A thought took shape. "Give me the manifest."

Kowsky took a sheaf of papers from his briefcase, extracted the manifest and handed it to Bartlett.

"Here he is. Mr. Clarence Ives." He looked up. "Traveling alone?"

"Yes, Captain," Lydia replied, and added, in an obvious attempt to cover herself in case it later turned out that Ives had an accomplice on board, "At least, he boarded alone."

"I don't suppose you've been able to see inside his brief-case," Bartlett said.

"No. But I saw him reading some files he took from it."

"Anybody sitting next to him?"

"A young woman, Alexandra Browne, Captain. In the aisle seat." Lydia hesitated and added, "She needs a gynecologist."

"What does that mean?" Bartlett demanded huskily. The strain was beginning to get to him. Take it easy, he told himself.

"She's about nine months pregnant."

Bartlett whirled around. "She isn't about . . ."

"Yes, Captain. Any moment or so it seems," Lydia replied.

Bartlett took a deep breath. "How the hell did she get aboard?" He paused. "Another weak-livered ticket clerk, I suppose." He added, philosophically, "Good we've got a doctor aboard. Was she hurt when we dived?"

"Bruised forehead. The doctor, Sir Leonard, has attended to her."

"Why did she come aboard if she's nine months gone?" Kowsky asked.

"Wants her baby born in the United States. And it's got to be a girl," Lydia replied.

Bartlett looked up and was surprised to see Lydia's lip quiver. She stared at her reflection in the windshield, avoiding his eyes; he recognized the signs of strain beneath her outward calm.

"How's the Secretary of State?" he asked, to change the subject.

Lydia hesitated, then turned her eyes to look into his. "He's fine. His traveling companion hit her head against the bulkhead, but nothing serious." She giggled nervously. "They're busy whispering state secrets to each other again now, sir." Bartlett smiled, and her face relaxed.

Bartlett had an urge to unfasten his harness and go aft to

inspect Ives for himself, but he couldn't leave the flight deck. He remembered the concussion case in the economy section. "What about the man who was knocked out?"

"He's still out, sir. Sir Leonard is standing by."

He rubbed his chin thoughtfully. "Is it possible for Sir Leonard to spare a couple of minutes on the flight deck?"

"I'll ask him," Lydia said, straightening up and picking a loose thread from her blouse. She gripped the door handle.

"Lydia . . ."

"Yes, Captain."

"No suspicious glances at our Mr. Clarence Ives. He's innocent until proven guilty."

"I understand, sir."

He waited until she was gone before turning to Kowsky. "What do you think?"

Kowsky put a thumbnail in the space between his two front teeth before replying. "I agree with you, Tom. Circumstantial evidence. But, on the other hand . . ." he paused. "To be on the safe side we should alert the airport police—if this communication problem ever clears up."

"What about the baggage handlers?" Nardini asked. "We'll have to stop them unloading the aircraft."

"The police'll take care of that," Bartlett said.

He checked the DME readout. Thirty-eight minutes to Gander. His eyes shifted to the map. Longitude forty-five was slipping to the right of center screen. He tightened his grip on the yoke as he thought of the scores of military aircraft converging and diverging on their secret war games below. It occurred to him that with a radio blackout the exercises might be canceled. Perhaps Kowsky, who'd once held a short-service commission, knew the Air Force drill when radio communication broke down on war exercises.

"Hey, Pete . . ." he began, just as a voice, with the clarity of a bell, boomed through his headset.

SEVEN

"Kennedy to American Arrow Zero-One. Are you receiving? Kennedy to Zero-One. Are you receiving? Kennedy to Amer . . ."

Bartlett jammed down the transmit switch. "Zero-One to Kennedy. Receiving you. Receiving you crystal clear." He turned, smiling, to Kowsky.

Ziegel's voice came on. "Boulder's reporting diminishing solar flares. How much of the transmission did you get before we lost you?"

"You faded when you mentioned the solenoid valves. My flight engineer's checked. Says there's a burned smell coming from the rear tank solenoid."

Ziegel groaned. "We hoped it wouldn't be the solenoid."

"Why didn't they blow a fuse on the London ground equipment when they put through the overvoltage?"

"Their faces are red as hell over there. Some jerk put an oversize fuse in the . . ."

Nardini, listening on his own headset, exploded. "Stupid bastards! Where the hell were the inspectors? At the local pub chatting up the birds?"

SUPERSONIC

Bartlett raised his hand to quiet him. "The company's got grounds for an official complaint and damages." He waited for the flash of anger to subside. No point in voicing recriminations at a time like this. "Have you *any* idea how we can get that fuel forward, New York?" he said in an even voice.

"There may be a way, but it'll be tricky—a long shot." A light winked on the radio console. "Zero-One to Kennedy, Gander's calling. Stand by while we answer." Kowsky changed the selector. "American Arrow Zero-One to Gander," Bartlett announced.

"Gander to Zero-One. Give position and flight level." An apprehensive note had crept into George Mercer's voice.

"Latitude forty-six north, longitude forty-seven west. Flight level four-five-zero."

"Here's a SIGMET. The warm front is pushing north of latitude forty more rapidly than forecast." Bartlett silently cursed. Did the weather boys have to put out a Significant Meteorological Report at a time like this? "It's pushing a band of cold air ahead and weather at Gander has deteriorated since we lost contact. Ten-ten cloud, temperature dropping rapidly. Ground temperature fifty-one degrees. Fog rolling in from coast . . ." A vision of Simmonds' sad face flashed through Bartlett's mind. *It won't affect you, of course, but we're rerouting the subsonics farther north.* He relaxed his grip on the yoke, but quickly tightened it as the column moved back. ". . . give ARP at longitude fifty. Remain at flight level four-five-zero."

Kowsky passed the back of a hand over his upper lip. "Fuel low, dragging ass end, blind-as-a-bat forward visibility—and now fog," he muttered.

"You forgot to mention the Air Force," Nardini growled.

Bartlett deliberately straightened his shoulders. It had the desired effect: The flight deck became silent, until Kowsky remarked, "What about MDH. We can't see forward from the side windows." As copilot, it would be his job to scan the side windows until Arrowhead descended to Minimum Decision Height. If he couldn't see the runway threshold lights at MDH he'd have to call to Bartlett to ram open throttles and go around.

"Get Kennedy," Bartlett snapped.

Kowsky twisted the frequency selector. "American Arrow Zero-One to Kennedy."

"Kennedy receiving. Gander's SIGMET just came in," Ziegel said, and by his tone Bartlett got the feeling he was purposely minimizing its importance. "Here's what we've been thinking. The fuel transfer trouble is your number one problem. Gander'll talk you down GCA and . . ."

"What about the solenoid business?" Bartlett interrupted.

"We've an idea on how you can change it."

"In flight?" Bartlett exclaimed. Nardini leaned forward, clamping his earphones closer, an expression of disbelief on his face.

"Yes, Captain. In flight."

"Go ahead."

"While we were cut off the maintenance boys tried it out on an Arrowhead that's in for a thousand-hour inspection," Ziegel went on. "Here's what you do."

There was a knock on the door. Lydia ushered in Sir Leonard Wheeler-Carthert and went back to the cabin. Bartlett swung around. "Nick, take down Ziegel's instructions and try it." Nardini grabbed a paper pad and scribbled as Ziegel spoke.

Bartlett nodded to Sir Leonard. "Pleased to meet you, sir. Thanks for your help back there," he said.

Sir Leonard raised his hands. "Glad to help, Captain," he said, alert eyes taking in the flight deck.

SUPERSONIC

"My copilot and senior stewardess have given me the general picture. What're the details?"

"The lady with the broken arm must have it set in a cast as soon as possible."

"Is the concussion case serious, sir?"

The surgeon stood near Nardini, his tall form bent under the low ceiling. "Yes, the patient's in primary shock. He needs a hospital bed right away."

"He'll get that just as soon as we land, sir."

"Now, Captain, perhaps you'll do something for *me*."

Bartlett looked up from the map where the indented coast of Newfoundland had started to creep into view. "Of course, sir," he replied, wondering what was coming.

"Would you kindly radio New York and tell someone to contact Dr. Gillespie at Roosevelt Hospital and tell him that I've been diverted to Gander. They're expecting me for an emergency consultation, possibly an operation."

"Of course, sir. You should have asked earlier. Like . . ." he looked past Sir Leonard and saw Nardini tear off his headset, pick up his scratch pad, and disappear aft.

"I've been rather busy," Sir Leonard said.

"Zero-One to Kennedy. We have on board Sir Leonard Wheeler-Carthert, a surgeon due to attend an emergency consultation at Roosevelt Hospital, New York. Please contact Dr. . . ." he looked up at Sir Leonard.

"Dr. *Arthur M.* Gillespie, head of opthalmology."

"Dr. Arthur M. Gillespie, head of opthalmology," Bartlett heard the dispatcher repeat.

"Correct. And that's *Roosevelt* Hospital. Explain that Sir Leonard is on Flight Zero-One, diverted to Gander, and we'll put him on the first flight out. Is Mr. Ziegel standing by."

"Yes, Captain. Shall I put him on?"

"No. I'll contact him when my flight engineer returns from fixing the solenoid valve."

"Roger, Zero-One."

The Gander light blinked. Bartlett rotated the switch.

"Here's another SIGMET," Mercer's voice had regained its flat tone. "Fog's rolling in from the coast faster than expected." Mercer, a Newfoundlander, allowed himself the luxury of boasting about his knowledge of local conditions. "Worst spring fog since I was a kid. It's the ice. Extends hundreds of miles out to sea. Chilling the air . . ."

"Many thanks, Gander," Bartlett drawled, switching him off.

Clarence Ives's eyes fluttered open. He searched in his pocket for a cigarette, but found only an empty package, crumpled it into a tight ball, and hurled it onto the carpet. He noticed that several papers from his file had slipped onto the floor. Unbuckling his belt, he bent down to pick them up and stuffed them into his briefcase. The young woman in the end seat turned to him.

"I hope you had pleasant dreams?" she said.

He pressed his lips tightly together before answering. She had a nerve. "Uh, yes." In the jacket pocket of his new, gray pinstripe suit he discovered a half-full cigarette package and lit one up, taking care to blow the smoke away from the girl. It billowed into a mushroom shape that was swept aside by the air-conditioner outlet.

"I guess you didn't hear the announcement," Alex Browne said.

"What announcement?" he asked, his body tensing.

"We're not going to New York. We've been . . ."

He gagged as he tried to swallow the smoke. "Not . . . going . . . New York?"

"We've been diverted."

"Diverted? Where to?"

"Gander."

"Gander! In Newfoundland?"

The girl nodded. "Yeah, that's it. I knew it was someplace in Canada."

"But . . . but we're supposed to go to New York," he said helplessly, looking around. The cabin was quiet enough; everyone seemed the same as they had been before he'd dropped off to sleep, either dozing or reading. "Why Gander?"

"Something technical." She made a helpless gesture. "I dunno. The fuel or something."

"Fuel?"

"Yeah."

Ives crossed his ankles and pressed his toes into the carpet. An acid feeling burned his stomach, and he crushed out the cigarette. Would he have to go through Customs twice, once at Gander and again at New York? He gripped the ends of the armrests and moistened his lips. The stewardess appeared.

"Say, Miss."

"Yes, Mr. Ives."

He saw Alex Browne look up expectantly. "I'm sorry, uh . . ."

"Yes, Mr. Ives," Lydia repeated.

"I was just wondering." He felt trapped. "I, uh, understand we've been diverted to Gander. Will we have to go through, uh, Customs there as well as New York?"

Why did she stare at him like that? How could she possibly know anything? The suitcase was safely stacked in the baggage hold.

"No, sir. All baggage will be placed in bond and transferred to an ongoing flight to New York."

"Oh, thank . . ." he caught himself in time and added, "you." He made a movement to get up. "I'm sorry to disturb you. I need, uh . . ."

"Yeah. Sure," Alex said, swiveling her body to allow him to pass. He took off his topcoat and Lydia folded it and took it away to hang in the vestibule rack.

He opened the toilet door, stepped inside, and locked it. He'd been stupid to ask about Customs. After he flushed the toilet he filled the wash basin with cold water and splashed his face. He tongue felt furry, so he took a paper cup from the container, filled it with water, and swished it around his mouth, but the bad taste remained. Taking a deep breath, he opened the door and stepped out. The stewardess was just outside, bending over the tubby guy who had such an important air.

"Is everything all right, sir," she asked him.

"No, things couldn't be worse, Miss Olsen," he replied in an irritable tone.

Ives moved to step past Lydia. "I'm sure Captain Bartlett explained why the diversion was necessary, Mr. Maxwell," Lydia said. She paused. "Can I get you a drink?"

"Double Scotch. And another Dubonnet on the rocks for Miss Lindenberg."

"Yes, sir." She straightened up, and followed Ives along the aisle. When Ives came alongside Alex Browne he remembered his intention to move.

"I'll sit here," he said, indicating a seat behind her as she prepared to slip sideways. "Would you pass my briefcase back?"

"Sure," she replied, handing him the case.

The stewardess stopped near his new window seat and leaned over. "Would you like a drink, Mr. Ives?"

"Uh, yes. That's a good idea. Rye and ginger." He looked

into her face, and saw the gleaming teeth displayed by her smile. He was safe. She didn't suspect anything—it had been his imagination.

"With or without ice?"

"With."

He sighed, and leaned over to examine the stewardess's legs as she hurried away.

The ragged coastline of Newfoundland showed up as well-defined headlands and bays on the map display. Bartlett checked the DME readout: 220 miles.

"Time to start descent," he said. "We need a long approach on final."

"Roger." Kowsky glanced at the DME. "We'll be on Gander's radar in a minute."

Bartlett slid down the transmit button. "Zero-One to Gander. Request descent clearance to flight level two-five-zero."

"Gander to Zero-One. Cleared to flight level two-five-zero," Mercer's voice shot back.

Kowsky swung the stem of his microphone away from his mouth so that Mercer wouldn't hear the transmission. "Makes you feel sorta wanted," he remarked.

"Sixty-five percent power," Bartlett said.

"Sixty-five percent power."

The miniature airplane on the artificial horizon dipped below the bar. Bartlett held the yoke steady, watching the altimeter figures tumble: forty thousand feet . . . 38,000 . . . 36,000 . . . The aircraft shuddered as it entered a layer of turbulent air. Thirty-three thousand feet . . . 30,000 . . . 28,000 . . . They were well into the subsonic flight levels now. Bartlett glanced out. Layers of broken stratocumulus clouds stretched below and he mentally prepared to meet more severe turbulence below twenty-five thousand feet. The convection currents inside those clouds produced frightening streams of unstable air that could throw an airplane about like a child's kite. The readout dipped to twenty-six thousand feet. He strained on the yoke. She was getting extremely tail heavy now in the denser air. The altimeter steadied on 25,000.

"Zero-One to Gander. Flight level two-five-zero. Airspeed six-zero-zero."

"Roger, Zero-One. We have you on radar now," said Mercer. "Switching you to terminal controller."

"Roger." Bartlett turned to Kowsky and nodded.

Nardini sniffed the solenoid and examined it closely. The electrical connections were in an adjacent terminal block. He checked his notes: Ziegel was right. If he disconnected the wires, he could slide the solenoid forward on its mounting after removing the four small bolts that secured it. He congratulated himself on his foresight in carrying the small adjustable wrench in his pocket, a habit he'd maintained since he'd flown the daily run from San Francisco to Anchorage on the old DC-6s.

Now check the other solenoids to find one Ziegel said could be substituted. He stood up and traced the fuel lines where they emerged from the bulkhead, cocking his head to read the stenciled labels. The red labels indicated the forward tanks, the blue the amidship tanks, and the two yellows were for the rear tank. He followed the yellows down to the burned-out solenoid and checked the blue labels that connected to a battery of solenoids controlling the valves for the amidship tanks. Ziegel said either the starboard or port amidship tank could be by-passed when the fuel was transferred forward, therefore, he must remove only the solenoid he'd specified. Checking that the valve was in the closed position, he unscrewed the top of the terminal block, exposing the wires. Be careful to prevent the wires from touching and arcing. They should have put a master switch on the circuit, but then there'd be the danger that some maintenance man would accidentally leave it off, preventing the transfer of fuel after takeoff. God, there was no end to the complications. Bet the designers of the electrical system hadn't anticipated anything like this. He removed the top of the terminal block, exposing the brass ferrule at the end of the wire. You'd think the designers of the ground-test equipment would have anticipated the possibility of accidentally applying an over-voltage. Weren't they supposed to run tests that tested the ground equipment that tested on-board equipment? Always the human element, the weakest link in the chain. Ah, that's it. Now the dead solenoid. He straightened up and wiped his forehead with his sleeve; the thrum of the slipstream whipping past the fuselage skin and the roar from the jet nozzles bore into his consciousness. He removed his jacket and laid it on the floor. Suddenly the floor tipped: they were already descending for the final approach into Gander. He checked his watch—five minutes had slipped by. Ziegel had said it took only seven minutes to change the solenoids. Resisting the temptation to hurry, he exposed the wire ends on the other terminal block, lifted out the wires, and turned to the solenoid for the amidship tank. Unscrewing the mounting bolts, for safety he put them with the others in a deep groove formed by the flange of the aluminum floor panels near an inspection hole, and slid the solenoid away from the valve, leaving the valve shaft sticking out. This was easy. Good old Ziegel. He'd heard he was something of a genius, that American Arrow had bought him from NASA at a huge price.

He transferred the good solenoid to the rear tank valve, carefully sliding it to engage the shaft. Insert the four bolts and he was home free. He turned to pick up the first bolt, but as he did so the floor dropped and the bolts flipped from the groove like Mexican jumping beans and disappeared through the inspection opening. The floor jerked and he heard the bolts rattling on the bottom skin as the aircraft bounced in turbulent air. He grasped the fuselage frame for support, kneeled down, and felt through the inspection hole for the bolts in the belly of the airframe. His fingertips swept fore and aft between the frames, feeling nothing. The bolts suddenly stopped rattling as the aircraft settled into a stable layer of air. God, now what? He wiped his hands on the back of his pants and stared at the solenoid. There was no way it would operate unless it was securely bolted down. He twisted the shaft in a desperate effort to rotate it, but again the shiny chromed surface slipped through his fingers. He rolled up his sleeve, and lay flat on his stomach, stretching his arm through the hole, but all he could feel was empty space. Take bolts from another solenoid? A sick feeling gripped his belly as he remembered that Ziegel had specifically said that only *that particular* solenoid could be switched: disconnecting any of the others would limit forward transfer of fuel. God, I've loused it up for four goddamned bolts! How can I break it to the captain? He got up, rolled down his sleeve, and fumbled to thread his cufflinks, fingers trembling as he put on his jacket and fastened the gold buttons. Closing the hatch, he stepped into the baggage hold, oblivious of the crackling of stiff paper under his feet as he went forward.

EIGHT

James Delaney sighed and looked up from the desk in his office on the third floor of Gander's Air Terminal Building, sucking the end of his ball-point pen. He bent his head again and, for the sixth time, considered how to reply to question number four on the form: As Chief, Air Traffic Control, in your opinion, did the pilot deliberately contravene Federal Air Regulations? (if so, quote section, and subsection, contravened). He pursed his lips. Roger Walker, the tower controller who'd laid the complaint, had said, "yes"—the light-plane owner had deliberately buzzed the tower. But the pilot, a man of twenty from St. John's, said that he had descended below the control tower height according to the controller's instructions. The pilot had three hundred hours flying time: more than the two-hundred-hour danger period at which point a pilot acquired a sense of overconfidence, but hardly enough to have mature judgment. He looked up again, ball-point stroking the bottom of his chin, staring blankly through the window that looked out over the roof of the old wartime hangar below. His eyes narrowed as he became aware of the patches of cloud scudding below the stratocumulus. The cloud ceiling was lowering. He made a mental note to check Met and scrutinized the small print on the form. Give the pilot the benefit of the doubt? It was the pilot's word against Walker's. The taped dialogue hadn't recorded anything more than the usual terse instructions from the man in the tower and acknowledgment by the man in the plane. And Walker, also young and only a year out of controllers' training school, was inclined to be overzealous.

His thoughts were diverted by the sound of hammering coming from the inside of a tiny single-engine airplane that had been parked on the strip of tarmac below his window for the past two days. They must be nearly ready with the installation of those long-range fuel tanks in the crop duster, he reflected, looking up at the sky. The pilot must be anxious to get off before the cloud ceiling dropped below the minimum, and by the way things looked, it wouldn't be long before it did. But that wouldn't deter the pilot. Wish I had a buck for every takeoff below the two-hundred foot minimum from Gander. Wouldn't be pushing this pen; probably be flying charters with a plane of my own down in Florida or the West Indies. Certainly away from this hunk of damp, chilly rock. Don't envy him his trip, but I do his destination, warm and sunny Santa Maria, and getting paid for it too. Global Ferry Services rewarded a man well for ferrying the little dusters and light executive planes across the Atlantic for customers on the other side. Wonder where he's heading after picking up fuel at Santa Maria? Southern France? Italy? Greece? A man gets to learn a hell of a lot about flying on the way to Santa Maria, with three steam-cleaned oil drums brimming with fuel lashed behind the cramped seat and sandwiches and a Thermos stuck below your knees. He fixed a thoughtful look on the tiny white plane with the square wing tips. It took a lot of nerve, even with radio and navigation fixes from the weather ships. Ten to twelve hours to the tiny distant dot far out over the Atlantic, depending on the wind. That's a lot of time alone, an immensity of ocean to cross, keeping awake by checking and rechecking your nav figuring and talking to yourself to stop going looney.

The telephone rang.

"Delaney."

"American Arrow Zero-One's in radar range, sir," said a precise voice.

"I'll be right down."

He dropped the ball-point on the desk, got up, and went to the door. In the corridor he glanced through the window to check the clouds, turned, and descended a flight of stairs to the second floor and pushed open a door. The familiar smell of the Air Traffic Control room engulfed him, a smell compounded of human sweat and heated varnish from the cabinets of electronic gear that were hot twenty-four hours a day. The noise of the room gave him a sense of comfort. The voices of the controllers meant all was well: It was the rare silences that gripped his stomach, when an airplane reported losing an engine a thousand miles out or the pilot of a chartered, light plane called for an emergency letdown due to icing. The hubbub washed over him—voices giving instructions every minute to scores of flight crews passing through his vast control area, directions to aircraft in his domestic sector, instructions on flight levels, Met reports, cloud ceiling at Gander, and alternative radio frequencies to use. A controller brushed past, hurrying to another radar-scope position, examining scribbled symbols on a pad; another grabbed flight progress strips from a controller-in-training emerging from the computer room. The occasional VIP landing at Gander who asked to be shown behind the scenes never failed to express surprise, and sometimes thinly disguised fear, at the apparent confusion in the ATC room.

"How can they possibly hear what the pilots are saying,"

remarked the president of a Communist bloc country whose plane had landed for a technical stop before proceeding to Cuba.

"Their earphones fit very tightly, sir," Delaney had replied, laughing.

The president had not been convinced. He'd stared down the double line where sixty controllers sat before the radar-scopes. "Incredible. They can actually hear what the commandants of the airliners are saying?"

Delaney had nodded. "Would you like to listen in?" He'd plugged in a spare headset at a controller's position and offered it to the VIP. Delaney adjusted the volume and tone controls until the president held up a finger. A smile spread across his Slavic features. After he'd taken off the headset he looked over the shoulder of the controller. A score of blips covered the radarscope. At the center of the scope was a replica of Gander's three runways, three brightly lit green strips that converged like an arrowhead, pointing roughly southeast.

"Are all those planes?" he'd asked, pointing to the blips.

"Yes, sir."

"They're going to collide!" the president exclaimed, pointing to a spot on the scope where several blips clustered. Delaney had checked the scope. To the layman the blips appeared to be on collision courses, but the accompanying flags, electronic responses to the ground radar's interception of the aircraft's on-board transponder, and the evaluation of the computer in the next room, indicated to the trained observer that the aircraft were at different flight levels, with one thousand feet vertical separation.

"They're at different heights, sir. These figures on the scope tell the controller their altitudes."

"Ah, *now* I understand," the president had said with relief, touching his heart. Delaney had tactfully led the way into the computer room where it was less busy. The noise in the ATC room brought him back to the present. He stopped behind the terminal controller, a man named Cooper, at Position Eighteen, listening to him talk to Flight Zero-One. Two parallel lines that were Arrowhead's blip had appeared inside the fourth concentric ring, the two-hundred-mile ring, at the perimeter of the scope. He turned to the console at Cooper's side. Flight Zero-One's flight progress strip was in the flight level 250 sector slot and he wondered when her captain would begin his descent. Most incoming traffic requested clearance from the twenty-five thousand foot level at the fifty-mile mark, but the supersonics, he knew, had no lift spoilers and their rate of descent was slower than the subsonics, unless they dived, when they really picked up speed. He didn't expect her captain to do that, not with injuries aboard.

"Okay, en-route controller. I have flight Zero-One now," Cooper said, letting Mercer in the radio building know he'd made radar contact with Arrowhead. Delaney rubbed the tip of his nose. How many times had he told instructors to remind controllers-in-training *not* to say okay? Cooper was a good terminal man, but still needed watching; he'd been out of training school only six weeks. He looked around for Budnick, his assistant chief. When Cooper stopped speaking he said, "Where's Mr. Budnick?"

"He slipped into the computer room, sir."

Delaney turned, as Budnick stepped through the door with a green teletype form in his hand. "Here's another SIGMET, Jim."

"Fog?"

Budnick, a big man with a red face, nodded. Delaney tactfully drew him aside. "Ed. Put Duffy on eighteen. Cooper's all right, but . . ."

Budnick raised his chin and picked up a telephone. Delaney read the teletype. As Budnick waited for the receiver to be picked up at the other end, he said, "Not a chance for the stuff to burn off with all that ice out there," lifting his head toward the east. "Is that Duffy? You free? Good, come down to scope eighteen."

He put down the telephone and joined Delaney at Position Eighteen. Delaney glanced at the ceilometer dial above the console. "Doesn't look too good," he said gloomily, drawing Budnick's attention to the instrument. The dial showed the cloud ceiling at eight hundred feet.

Delaney's mind raced ahead. Supposing the ceiling dropped to ground level in the next thirty minutes and Zero-One's captain elected to use GCA, which he'd probably already requested.

"Where's Tommy?"

"On at twenty hours."

"Get him on standby. Know where he is?" He looked at Budnick's face and saw doubt flicker behind the other's eyes.

"At home, mor'n likely. Too dull to go fishing," Budnick replied, but Delaney knew his assistant was covering up. Harry Thompson, known to everyone at Gander as Tommy, had a reputation for boasting how many weeks ahead of the legal start of the fishing season he could dip his line into the fast-flowing Exploits River, several miles west of the airport. His mind lingered on the need to get Thompson to the ATC Center as quickly as possible. He was the acknowledged expert on the Ground Control Approach talkdown position, with a well-modulated voice that carried confidence even under the worst blind-landing conditions. This quality, combined with his talent for giving a pilot instructions without superfluous words and his ability to keep up the flow without hesitation, made him Gander's most efficient operator of the Precision Approach Radar. PAR operators must not stop speaking to a pilot they were talking down to the runway threshold for longer than five seconds. If they allowed a five second gap in communications to occur, the standing instruction to pilots was to ram open throttles, overshoot the runway, and climb away. Delaney turned as a man walked with long steps along the aisle toward them.

"Ah, here's Duffy," Budnick said, and Delaney recognized the look of pride on the face of a man who knew he'd been called for a special purpose. Cooper stood up respectfully as the gray-headed man took his seat and put on the headset. Cooper moved to a scope further along the aisle in response to a controller who beckoned him. Budnick hurried away, and Delaney put the teletype message on the shelf below Duffy's console. He looked at the radarscope as Duffy adjusted his earphones and spoke into the microphone.

"Gander ATC to American Arrow Flight Zero-One. You are now one-hundred and eighty miles from touchdown."

Bartlett glanced at the time-to-go clock. Twenty-nine minutes to Gander touchdown. A new voice came through his earphones. "You are now one-hundred and eighty miles from touchdown."

"Zero-One to Gander. Roger." It was a comforting feeling to know they were visible to Gander, even though they were only a blip of intangible electrons on a screen. Kowsky must have had the same thought, for his second-in-command turned to him and smiled.

"Here's another SIGMET," the voice said. "Ceiling eight hundred feet. Outlook . . . fog."

"Zero-One to Gander. Eight hundred ceiling," Bartlett replied. Hell, Newfie was always Newfie. Fog, ice, and snow. Surely it must be fine there *sometimes*. The door burst open and Nardini entered, his face flushed.

"Forgot the flashlight, Captain."

"What's up?" Bartlett demanded. "There's a light back there."

Nardini's dark eyes were troubled.

"I changed the solenoid but dropped the mounting bolts under the floorboards. I . . ,"

"You what!"

"The bolts fell through an inspection opening when we hit turbulence."

Kowsky opened his mouth to say something, but changed his mind and closed it.

"You'd better find them fast! Twenty-nine minutes to touchdown. You've got five before we begin our descent." He thought about the war exercises and glanced at the fuel gauges. "We may have to take evasive action on approach. We're going to need that extra fuel."

Nardini looked around for the flashlight, muttering to himself. "Five minutes, Captain," he said as he left.

The flight deck fell silent. "Hope to Christ he finds them," Kowsky said at last.

"Out of fuel for the sake of some lousy bolts. Get Ziegel."

Kowsky moved the switch. "Zero-One to American Arrow."

"Ziegel here, Zero-One."

"My flight engineer's changed the solenoid, but there's a delay while he finds the mounting bolts."

"What's that?"

"The bolts fell below the floorboards when we hit turbulence."

"He'd better find them."

"He's looking." He stroked his chin. "If he can't, can he use bolts from another solenoid?"

"No. Dismounting another solenoid will cut off your remaining fuel by blocking the transfer channels. Every solenoid valve's got to be open, with the sole exception of the one I told him."

"Understood. All solenoid valves to be open." Bartlett replied grimly, thinking of Nardini in the rear compartment, searching for the bolts. It was ludicrous. More than a hundred human beings in a two-hundred-ton aircraft waiting for a man on his hands and knees scratching around for some small bolts. What if Nardini couldn't find them? He suppressed the thought and looked at the array of overhead controls, checking the switch that controlled the rear tank solenoid and booster pump; once Nick got that solenoid fixed, pressing down the switch would override the flight director computer control and send fuel in the rear tank coursing through the galleries and into the amidship and forward tanks, relieving the weight on his arms and giving them plenty of fuel to make Gander. "Will report when the solenoid's fixed."

"Roger."

He leaned forward to examine the fuel contents gauge, tapping the glass with his fingertips.

"Not exactly overflowing," Kowsky said.

"We'll be triple A when Nick's through."

Kowsky looked at the clock. "He's got three minutes."

"Take over, Pete." Bartlett waited for Kowsky to take the full pressure of the yoke before flexing his arms.

"She's getting heavier by the minute," Kowsky said, as the SELCAL chimed. Bartlett switched to the airline's Selective Calling frequency. "Kennedy to Zero-One."

"Zero-One receiving."

"Ziegel speaking. Have you found the bolts?"

"No word from my man aft yet."

"Gander says you're in radar range."

"Ceiling's down to eight hundred. Expecting more fog," Bartlett replied, wishing Ziegel would get off the air.

"Just got their SIGMET," Ziegel said.

"I'll report when my flight engineer returns to the flight deck," Bartlett said.

"Roger."

He selected the Gander wave band. "American Arrow Zero-One to Gander ATC. What's latest Met?"

"Ceiling seven hundred. Wind rising," Duffy's voice sounded strangely reassuring even when conveying bad news. "And here's another SIGMET. Torbay's just been closed. Below two hundred."

Bartlett had kept St. John's, two hundred and eleven air miles southeast of Gander, as a possible unannounced alternate to the alternate. He checked the moving map. The New-foundland coast had come up sharp and distinct, filling the left-hand side of the screen, with the rugged indentations of the Avalon Peninsula falling away to the south. Torbay, the airport for St. John's, showed as a red dot. Arrowhead would be well into their radarscopes now, their controllers listening to his dialogue with Gander. But now, with Arrowhead's tail dragging, he couldn't risk a landing at Torbay; its longest runway was only eight thousand, five hundred feet long, much too short for the type of landing to which he was now committed—nose-up, fast over the threshold and zero for-ward visibility. Too damned nose-up if Nick didn't fix that valve.

"What about the war exercises?" he asked.

"Still going on in CADIZ area below ten thousand feet."

Bartlett projected the situation forward. If the fog worsened would the military brass cancel the war games? And if they didn't, what about his clearance through the ten thousand foot level?

"Zero-One to Gander. Call immediately if any change in the war exercises."

"Roger."

He checked the clock readout. In one minute he must call back Gander for descent clearance—he couldn't afford to delay. He must lose height gradually over the final approach leg, beginning one hundred and fifty miles out. The map now showed they were less than forty miles off the coast. There was a knock on the door and Lydia entered.

"How's Mr. Maxwell?" Bartlett asked. The presidential envoy had been in an ugly mood when he'd burst into the flight deck demanding to speak to Washington. It had taken several minutes to get the White House staff to accept the radio-telephone link from American Arrow Airline's New York office, and Maxwell had boiled with rage while they'd scurried to get the president out of a national defense council meeting. Hell, you'd think they'd be better prepared than that. What if it had been a national emergency, with the president's right-hand man airborne on a commercial flight bearing intelligence that might be the turning point in a razor-edge confrontation between nuclear powers?

"I calmed him down with a double Scotch," Lydia said, smiling. "Two doubles, in fact."

"Give him a third before we land at Gander," Bartlett growled. "He may need it."

"Something wrong, Captain?" Lydia asked.

Bartlett exchanged glances with Kowsky. She'll have to know sooner or later, as would the rest of the cabin crew. "I suppose Nick told you about the rear tank problem," he said, guessing that she'd been shrewd enough to intercept Nardini on one of his journeys aft.

"Well, yes, Captain."

"We've also got a stuck visor," Bartlett said. She was silent, weighing what his statement implied.

"You mean the visor won't retract from in front of the windshield?"

Bartlett nodded. He hoped she didn't look at the fuel temperature and contents gauges. But if she did, hopefully she wouldn't realize their import and to what extent their readings, one set of gauges high, the other low, would govern their action on the flight deck in the next twenty-six minutes.

"Tricky landing, Captain?" she asked.

"Kind of." He looked up as she stood between the seats. "There's fog too. Ceiling's already low." He added, "Keep it from the passengers. I'll make an announcement later."

"Yes, sir." After a pause, she added, "I understand."

He blinked at the moving map. Longitude fifty west was a half-inch to the right of Arrowhead's light spot at center screen. Directly ahead was landfall at the tip of the Bonavista peninsula.

"What's our suspected robber up to?" he said, deliberately changing the subject.

"Clenching and unclenching his fists like a prize fighter," Lydia replied.

"He'll have time to cool off at Gander," Bartlett said.

"I'd better get back to the cabin," she said.

"Gander to Zero-One. Ceiling six hundred. When will you start descent?"

"Zero-One to Gander," Bartlett said. "Will start descent on landfall. Estimate landfall one minute."

"You are approaching tip of Bonavista peninsula."

"Roger. Can't begin descent until my flight systems engineer returns from fixing fuel transfer solenoid valve. The airline office in New York has told him what to do. He'll report back any second."

"Roger, Zero-One. Oh, Zero-One, correction on ceiling. It's now five hundred." After a pause Duffy said, "What's your fuel remaining to touchdown, Captain?"

"Twenty-eight minutes if we don't get that valve fixed."

Bartlett replied, pressing a button that subtracted the contents of the rear tank from his fuel gauge reading.

"Gander to Zero-One. Here's the rest of the SIGMET. Dew point near ambient temperature, increasing fog, and advection is causing low-level clouds. Temperature dropping."

Hell, fog on top of fog. And as the temperature dropped there'd be more fuel drain as energy demand for the wing deicers increased.

"Roger, Gander."

"He *did* go fishing," Budnick said. "Early this morning. Left around seven. Didn't tell his wife where."

"Damn him!" Delaney exclaimed. He swung back to Duffy's scope, watching the blip edging across the one hundred and fifty mile circle. Why the hell did he have to choose today to poach trout? Places where he might be flashed through his mind: the fast-flowing stream near Gambo Pond where he'd cast a fly or two himself with Thompson? He searched his mind. The streams flowing into Great Rattling Brook were too far away. On the other hand Thompson had set out early enough to get there, spend three or four hours casting his line, and be back well in time for his shift. Thompson would have checked Met before setting off, so he'd know about the possibility of fog. All the more reason he'd head west rather than south, where the fog now rolled in across the ice in Bonavista Bay.

"Where do we start looking?" he asked helplesly.

Budnick drew the back of his hand across his nostrils. Despite the air-conditioning, the heat given off by the radar-scopes and the sweating men made the air fetid. He threw up his hands.

"You know him. He could be anywhere." He paused, and Delaney knew he was reviewing, and rejecting, the places he'd thought of himself. "He'll be any place where the ice is beginning to break up. And that takes in a lot of territory this time of year."

"We've *got* to find him," Delaney said. His instinct told him that Harry Thompson had an important part to play in the safe landing of American Arrow Zero-One. In the meantime he'd keep Clifford Reynolds, the other PAR operator, on duty. He rubbed the corner of his eye with a fingertip, trying to recall the name of a nearby stream Thompson had once mentioned. "Joe Batt's Brook, Ed?"

Budnick put his head on one side, considering the possibility. "Bit close in. He'd be taking a chance. The Mounties patrol up there regularly."

"Might be the thing *he'd* do. Jonathan's Brook?"

Budnick shook his head. "Mounties thick as black flies up Highway 40."

"I don't mean near the bridge. Farther downstream, toward Gander River." A feeling that he was on the right track began to grow, Thompson was an individualist. While others poached far afield in the spring breakup, with the police knowing the likely spots to catch them, Thompson would drop his line in a stream right under their noses, where they'd least expect to find out-of-season fishermen. He turned to the radarscope. The blip was nudging the vague outline of Cape Bonavista—vague because the radar signal was distorted by the fog. He made a decision.

"Ed. Get every off-duty man after Thompson. I want him here right away."

"Right, Jim," Budnick said, and hurried off.

Delaney leaned over to listen to Duffy. "Met reports clouds building to ten thousand feet. Four hundred ceiling."

Zero-One must make its descent decision soon. With a negligible fuel reserve they can't delay, unless they can fix that solenoid valve as New York had instructed. A voice from the terminal controller at the next radarscope broke into his consciousness. "ATC to tower. Four-niner-one cleared to Santa Maria. Maintain flight level one-niner-zero." He recognized the voice of Walker, the on-duty tower controller.

Delaney grabbed a spare headset and plugged the cable into the next controller's panel. ". . . use Runway Zero-Four. Wind one-five miles per hour from south east. Ceiling four hundred. Time zero-two-three-one. Altimeter two-niner-one-four. Prepare taxi position two via alpha . . ."

That would be Global Ferry's crop duster scrambling to take off before the fog settled below the minimum. At the rate the fog was clamping down he'd just make it. The controller picked up the crop duster's flight progress strip, inserted it in the ready tray, and checked the symbols and figures on the strip against the flight plan sheet headed "Global Ferry Fl 491."

"ATC clearance four-niner-one to Santa Maria." Walker's voice sounded in Delaney's headset. "Takeoff clearance four-niner-one. Victor three-one-five to St. John's."

"Roger," said a woman's voice, and Delaney's eyebrows shot up. "Victor three-one-five to St. John's," she acknowledged.

"Use Runway Zero-Four. Wind one-five miles an hour."

She repeated the tower's instructions and Delaney reflected on his earlier thoughts about the thousands of miles of open sea and the speck that would soon be over it. What type of woman would go for a job like that? She had an attractive voice, melodious and mellow, as she called off her waypoints over the subdued roar of the crop duster's engine that came through the open microphone in the tower. "Forty-seven north, fifty west; forty-five north, forty-five west; forty-four north, forty-one west . . . Flores, Graciosa, Sao Miguel,

Santa Maria." She intended making landfall on the northern islands of the Azores group, then to head south under Santa Maria ATC until she made a second landfall on Santa Maria island. Wise move; less chance of missing those dots of land that were the only real estate between here and Europe.

The long recitation of the readback came from Walker. The pilot again repeated it. At the end of the second repetition Walker said, "Your readback is correct. Proceed on course. Contact tower on one-one-niner decimal seven when airborne. Good day."

"Roger. One-one-niner decimal seven. Good day."

He glanced at the readout from the ceilometer, the instrument on the side of Runway 04–22 that reflected a vertical light beam off the cloud ceiling and measured the distance to the cloud base. It showed three hundred feet. She'd better hurry. Met reported a cloud buildup on top of the fog to ten thousand feet, and with her fuel overload it would be a long climb to nineteen-thousand feet. She'd still be flying blind when she overflew St. John's and set course on her first oceanic leg, plotting and rechecking her waypoints. It took guts to do the sort of job she was doing. But at the end of the flight she'd probably be landing in bright sunshine, instead of groping for the land in thick Newfie fog, like a blind man feeling for the sidewalk. In the space of a second, another foggy day at Gander, thirty years ago, flashed through his mind. The way he'd liked to tell the yarn to the bush pilots in the flight dispatch shed was how he flew the biplane from *outside* the cockpit, not how he'd made his first blind landing in fog. All because he'd offered to help a man in the town who'd got news that his father was dying at Black Duck Cove, a hundred and ninety air miles nor'west. The man was prepared to track through the woods and trails on foot from the railway at Deer Lake. It was early March, the countryside snow-covered, and ice gripped the north coast.

"But man, you'll never make it. You'll freeze to death," Delaney had told him.

"I gotta go, Jim. It's my last chance to see him. I haven't seen him these nine years."

Delaney thought a moment. "I'll fly you up. Bring you back in two weeks' time. Can't do it before because I've got to pick up a guy in Maine and fly him to Ontario."

"That's awful good of you, Jim."

"Ever flown before?"

"Nope. But I ain't afeared."

Delaney looked at the sky. It was clear, except for a sliver of cloud to the north. The wind was from the northwest at ten knots and, with a top speed of 120 miles per hour, his Tiger Moth would take a little more than two hours to get the man up to his father's place. "Be up at the hangar in half an hour," he had told him.

By the time the man showed up, Delaney had struggled to get the two-seat biplane onto the snow-covered grass at the side of the runway. The aircraft had skis and he'd had to push it out of the hangar himself. The skis rested on old iron pipes and his method of "wheeling" the airplane out of the hangar had been to roll the skis over the pipes, hold back the aircraft, pick up the pipes that rolled from the rear of the skis, and reinsert them at the front end.

As he had told the tale: "I took off, picked up my heading, and started to climb. My passenger was in the front cockpit, securely strapped in, and appeared to be enjoying it. I leveled off, looked over the side to get a visual bearing, and saw some men making their way toward Drover's Pond. I fancied I recognized the way they walked, so banked a bit to take a closer look. Sure enough, I could see Gus Cook and Andy Parsons and it looked like they were going ice fishing with some other fellas. They had all the gear with them: Gus recognized the airplane, waved a whisky bottle by the neck and I waved back, checked my heading, and climbed away."

"I put my man down on the beach at Black Duck Cove, told him to be on the beach in two weeks, and took off for home. It was a grand day, clear as a bell and with a tailwind, I made easy time toward home at two thousand feet. I saw Drover's Pond glistening in the distance. There's a steep rocky island off the east shore—Little Island—and sure enough, as I came up to it I could see the boys around the holes they'd made in the ice a little way off from the island."

"I turned right, throttled back so's they wouldn't hear the sound of my engine, dived her toward the back of the island and held her in a right turn. As I came around the other side I dipped her lower until my wing tip was ten feet off the ice. Then I banged open the throttle. Boy, you should have seen the fear of God on those fellas' faces as I boomed over. Gus's mouth gaped open like a frozen cod and old Andy Parsons was flat on the ice with arms outstretched as though he was being crucified. I tightened some more, came around again and the damned engine died on me. I managed to level her off and made a dead-stick landing. She came down gently but there was no snow cover on the ice and I slithered to a stop about a quarter mile from the island. I can still hear the shouts damning me all up and down God's earth coming across the ice. A couple of the fellas started to run after me so I pulled back the throttle, cracked it open a notch, hopped out of the cockpit and stood on the ski, and stretched forward to pull the prop through. Damn me if she didn't start with a flick of the wrist and roar away on full throttle. She started to move down the ice and I felt the juddering of the skis through my flying boots as the skis bounced over ripples on the ice. Then suddenly the juddering stopped. She was airborne."

"I looked down and judged we were already about a hundred feet off the ice and turning left because of my weight outside the cockpit. She was in a full throttle climb, with the slipstream cutting through my flying suit like a steel blade. It whipped my goggles off and my face froze. For a moment I thought of dropping off and letting her go. It'd be as quick a way of going from a hundred feet as from a thousand and she was in a full-power climb by now. But I managed to get one hand on a flying wire and hung on with the other to the cockpit coaming. I couldn't get back into the cockpit because of the angle of climb: all I could see was blue sky straight up."

He leaned back in the chair and took in the appraising eyes around the counter in the old shed.

"I felt her grow mushy, vibrate, and stall. The nose dropped and she went down in a full-power dive. I could see the bush coming at me as I hung onto that wire. Then I got to thinking: If I moved my weight aft a bit, with her full power she might level off and climb. Jesus, that's just what she did do and we must've been at two thousand feet again before I knew it, pointed to the blue, and Christ, she stalled again. And all the time we were going around in this wide circle. She had plenty of gas and I reckoned this could go on forever, or just as long as I could hold on. My fingers were frozen and my face raw. Then I thought again: *When she teeters at the top of her stall and starts to drop I wonder if I could lever myself over the coaming and throw myself into the cockpit as she points earthward.*"

"So the next time she got near the stall I waited, let go of the wire, grabbed the coaming, and as she dropped—the old Tiger used to nose over at an angle—I threw myself head first into the cockpit. I landed with my face on the rudder bar and my feet sticking out of the cockpit. You know how tiny the Tiger's cockpit is." He looked around and, seeing impatient nods, continued.

"I was jammed in there like a sardine in a can, tail out of the can, with the engine roaring away and the wind whistling through the struts like a Newfie gale. The sound was magnified down there in the bottom of the cockpit. The stick was jammed between my thighs and I couldn't budge. She was diving again. Boy, was she going! So I stretched back and felt for the safety pin that locks the control column in its socket—you know how you could interchange it in front or back cockpits? By Jesus I just managed to get my fingers on it, yanked out the pin, grabbed the stick so's I wouldn't lose it, and squirmed right way up, jammed the stick back in the socket, drove the safety pin back in and grabbed that stick. Nothing ever felt better in my hands than that old stick. The airspeed indicator was winding up past a hundred and sixty and the altimeter going faster in the opposite direction. She made terrible noises and I expected to tear her wings off. But she came out. When I got her straight and level and looked out, I was buzzing the treetops, God knows where. My goggles were gone and that slipstream was like fingernails peeling my eyelids back."

"The sun had gone and, up north, cloud covered the sky. I looked for familiar signs, lakes, ponds, but it was all strange to me. The gas gauge was nudging zero: Those full-power climbs had seen to that, and the damned throttle was still stuck open. I yanked her a quarter closed and still that rev counter soared. So I closed it right back and, God help me, she still piled on full power. So I thought the best thing to do was to get some altitude. At four thousand I got the last of the sun before it dropped. And then the clouds dropped with it, too, just like that." He jerked his hand down in a sudden gesture.

"In minutes the ceiling was down to eight hundred, then five hundred, and I came down with it, heading southeast because I knew that on that heading sooner or later I'd hit the coast. And sure enough, there straight ahead of me I saw a bit of ice blink and knew if I waited until I got to the ice and then headed southwest I should spot Gander Lake. But I couldn't understand that engine. She just kept roaring away with the engine temperature up on the red in spite of the cold. Up to the ice I come and banked her over to the southwest. I'm down to two hundred now with a pea-souper coming in off the ice. Then I spotted Gander Lake, like a snake coiling through the black pines, but as I came up the fog patches got closer and closer until they were as thick and soupy as they were at the coast. Lower and lower it came until I lost sight of the lake and was skimming the treetops, hoping to pick up some bush trail I'd recognize. Jesus, how I wished I'd had a radio to call up the hangar and ask them to light a fire on the strip."

Delaney spat on the stove. There was a sizzling sound before he spoke again.

"And suddenly the trees ended and I was flying over a white blanket, either Gander Lake or Deadman's Pond. I didn't wait to identify which it was. I hoped it was the lake because of the small island in the middle of Deadman's Pond but I wasn't wasting time finding out. I pointed her down and cut the mags off and on to slow her. A long burst first to cut her speed and then shorter ones as the airspeed fell off. I still couldn't see the ice—fog all around—but I *knew* it was fog off ice."

A murmur of understanding went around the little group.

"I had my hand on the mag switch to cut her off when

up looms this clump of trees so I left it on and yanked back the stick. I recognized those goddamned trees: They were on the island in Deadman's Pond, so I knew if I flew a reciprocal and went farther back I could turn in, cut the engine and have a good run in toward the island. I turned left, flew two minutes, came around on the compass, and started feeling for the ice. The same clump of trees come at me, a bit to the left this time, but now I knew the ice would be clear to the shore. So I cut her off, eased the stick forward, couldn't see a thing through the windshield except fog, and she bumped. Did I glue her on! I could feel her tail coming up as the engine died."

Delaney shook his head and clamped his teeth on the pencil he'd been holding.

"Where did you end up, Jim?" somebody asked.

"The skis nosed up on the bank of Deadman's Pond. Just where the seaplane base is alongside Runway Zero-Four."

There was silence until the inevitable question was asked.

"How come the throttle stuck on full power?"

"A damned cotter pin sheared clean through where it hooks onto the carburetor butterfly lever. By Jesus, I swear some damn fool mechanic used the same cotter pin twice to save having to get a fresh one."

"So when you moved the throttle lever the control linkage didn't work the lever?"

"That's the size of it." Delaney paused, spat at the stove again and added, "You've got to do everything yourself these days to make sure it's done properly."

Duffy said, "Gander to Zero-One. Ceiling three hundred and lowering," and he was back in reality, on the ground, waiting for a two-hundred-ton, high speed aircraft to make a similar approach over Gander Lake. Despite the engineering advances made to aircraft since his early days, before he went into air traffic control, everything still depended on the human senses. The captain out there, twenty minutes from touchdown, despite being talked down by the GCA controller, would at the last second have to feel for the threshold just as he'd had to do in the Tiger Moth thirty years ago.

Delaney observed the blip of the crop duster making its painfully slow progress southeast, headed for St. John's, a course that would take it well clear of Flight Zero-One. His attention was diverted by the teletype clattering at his elbow, and he bent down to read it. It was from the Armed Forces Base across the road: "Military exercises canceled. ASW aircraft and support aircraft returning to bases." Good news! "Search and rescue forces standing down. Returning to base." Better still. There'd be no slow-moving helicopters with their frequent course changes cluttering his airspace. Search and rescue had a lousy reputation for getting lost around fogbound Newfie, mostly because they were piloted by Mainlanders who didn't know the difference between a headland and a cove. He looked over Duffy's console. Zero-One's flight progress strip was still in the two-five-zero slot. He glanced again at her blip, now crossing the one hundred and fifty mile circle. About twenty miles out her captain would have to alter course west to cut south of Gander Lake for the final approach and touchdown on Runway 04-22.

Several blips edged into the east side of the scope and moved in a southwesterly direction as the recalled antisubmarine Orions and escorts started to return from patrols and headed back to their Maine bases. He watched them cross behind Zero-One and in a few minutes slip from the bottom of the scope. Other aircraft, Delaney knew, would be heading back to bases in Nova Scotia, but they wouldn't show up, as they'd be outside Gander's radar range. Zero-One's blip, two parallel lines with a tiny identification flag and the numerals

250 tagging along, pressed unerringly toward the dead center of the scope; the crop duster's blip headed southeast, the gap between the two blips widening. All was clear.

For the first time since Delaney left his office fifteen minutes ago he felt a great weight slide from him. He stretched and looked around the control room, rubbing the back of his neck to relieve the stiffness. Now, if only Tommy would turn up.

"Hey, sir!" Duffy yelled.

Delaney reeled around, staring at the scope, part of his mind absorbing what he saw, another part rejecting it. A blip, minus an identification flag, but with altitude numerals, had appeared at the northern rim of the green-lit circle, creeping inexorably southward, on a course directly headed toward Flight Zero-One.

He grabbed the telephone receiver and spun the dial.

NINE

Bartlett squinted at the fuel contents gauge and pressed the button. Enough for sixteen minutes of flying time. He glanced at the fuel temperature pointers: They were stuck in the red sectors. The map display showed the tip of Bonavista peninsula at center screen. "Landfall," Kowsky announced.

"I'll give him ten seconds," Bartlett said. Kowsky turned, as if by so doing he would produce Nardini. Ten seconds passed, but Nardini didn't appear.

Bartlett sucked in his breath. "Flight Zero-One to Gander. Request clearance to eight thousand feet." At that altitude he could switch off the cabin pressurization system and stop the extracted heat discharging into the fuel tanks.

"Gander to Zero-One," Duffy's voice sounded huskier. Pilots who became familiar with controllers over regular airline routes could detect when a controller was working a hectic sector simply by the way his vocal cords tightened. Bartlett recognized the change in the quality of Duffy's voice. "Remain at flight level two-five-zero. Repeat. Remain at flight level two-five-zero. Do *not* begin descent. Unidentified aircraft on your heading from north . . ."

"Remain at flight level two-five-zero. Roger." He jerked his head toward Kowsky, his features creased in puzzlement.

Duffy's voice sounded harsh in his headset. "There's an unidentified aircraft north of your heading. Remain at flight level two-five-zero."

"Roger. Remain at flight level two-five-zero."

"The war games have been canceled . All aircraft recalled to base. But . . ." Kowsky pointed to the moving map. The thirty-mile-long sinuous curve of Gander Lake was clearly visible, an arched bow pointing north. Gander's runways slid slowly into view on the map at the northeast edge of the lake, like three intersections of a child's geometry exercise. Runway 04-22, the longest, was to the left of Airway Victor 315 that Arrowhead was following. There'd be an additional fuel drain as they turned west to vector onto the runway. ". . . we've tried to make contact but it doesn't answer. His radio must be out," Duffy continued.

"Jesus!" Kowsky exclaimed.

The door burst open and Nardini entered. A glance at his face told Bartlett he'd failed.

"I can't find the bolts. They've worked their way into the tail section," he said helplessly. "I tried shoving the goddamned thing in without the bolts, but it won't hold."

Bartlett turned to Kowsky. "Get New York."

Kowsky moved the radio selector. "Zero-One to Kennedy. Is Ziegel there?"

"Ziegel to Zero-One."

"Can't fix the solenoid valve. Mounting bolts lost. What do we do now?"

"Captain, it was a long shot," Ziegel said abruptly. Bartlett exchanged glances with Kowsky. "How's your fuel?"

"Almost on Empty. Should we switch the remaining fuel into the forward tanks?"

"No." Ziegel's voice was definite. "Leave all valves open exactly as they are. What're your fuel temps?"

"Red sectors."

"Cut cabin pressurization as soon as possible. Eight thousand feet will be safe."

"Will do. Anything else we can do? Make it fast. Expecting descent clearance from Gander momentarily."

He heard a quick intake of breath before Ziegel spoke. "Nothing, Captain. We'll listen in on Gander's wave band."

Kowsky turned the selector back to Gander's ATC frequency. Bartlett glared at his image in the windshield and, as a reflex action, pushed the visor button. Nothing happened.

"Trying one of Ziegel's long shots," he said sarcastically. "Listen while I tell the passengers a fairy story." He reached for the cabin PA switch.

"This is Captain Bartlett. We shall be landing at Gander International Airport in approximately fifteen minutes. Weather at Gander is foggy, but cloud ceiling is above the minimum." For a moment, at any rate, he thought. "Uh, due to a malfunction in the fuel-transfer system we will be making our approach in a tail-down attitude. The cabin floor will slope at a more than usual angle, like our supersonic climb-out at London, possibly steeper. Please make sure your seat belts are fastened and all loose possessions secured." He paused. Hell, weren't they entitled to know the real reason if they didn't set foot on Gander's tarmac; that there were theoretically only cupfuls of fuel to get them to the runway threshold, and that the flight crew would have to land this ass-heavy crate without being able to see through the windshield? "Thank you," he added abruptly.

He caught Kowsky's dark look. "No point scaring them to death," he remarked. Nardini handed him the *Canada Air*

Pilot opened at the plate showing the details of Gander's marker beacons, glide path, and radio frequencies.

Vincent Maxwell ran a finger around the inside of his collar and exchanged looks with Robina Lindenberg, recognizing in her eyes the fear he was trying to subdue. He glanced at the cabin floor, expecting it to tip at an angle any moment.

Miss Lindenberg stuffed the papers she was scanning into the courier's attaché case and snapped the locks. "Is it serious, sir?"

Maxwell swallowed. Nothing like this had happened before; all the hundreds of thousands of miles he'd done in Air Force One and other government jets had been uneventful. They had been confidential journeys, with himself the center of attention surrounded by two or three personal advisors or an embassy official like Miss Lindenberg. But here, in this public plane, it was different. He turned and looked at the others in the cabin.

"Aw . . ." Alex Browne coughed and waved the cigarette smoke away with her hand.

"I'm sorry . . ." Ives called from his seat behind her.

"I'm sorry," Alex mimicked Ives's self-deprecatory voice an octave higher. "That's what you always say."

"I said I was . . ."

Alex glanced across at Gladys Glinker and gave her a knowing smile. Mrs. Glinker opened her mouth but a quiver of pain shot through her arm and lodged between her shoulder blades.

"Look, land! We're nearly there," Ives blurted.

It *was* land, the tip of some headland sticking out to sea. And ice, lots of ice around the shore and spreading farther out, until the scene was blotted out by cloud. Mrs. Glinker pressed her face close to the window, feeling its coolness, but all she could see were low clouds covering the icefield. She called across to Clarence Ives. "I can't see it."

"I *did* see land." It wasn't his fault if the old biddy had bad eyesight. He took another puff on the cigarette and blew the smoke toward the ceiling. Thank God for that. It won't be long now—and he wouldn't have to go through Customs twice. He'd telephone Callahan as soon as they landed. Use guarded language in case the line was tapped. He glanced at his watch, still on London time. This airline's got a nerve, advertising a Breakfast-to-Lunch flight to New York, and here he was about to land in some God-forsaken place up in Canada. I wonder what the local time will be. Eastern Standard or Canadian Eastern or something like that. Better check the time to make sure Callahan's in. A shadow fell across his face and he looked up, startled. It was the doctor, Sir Leonard somebody.

"Won't be long now," Sir Leonard said. "We're over land —Newfoundland."

Ives forced a smile. "Yes, I saw it."

Sir Leonard passed by and stopped at Gladys Glinker's seat. "We'll soon have your arm set," he said cheerfully, caressing her shoulder. "Feeling any better?"

Gladys Glinker forced back the tears. "Mmm." She pressed her lips together. Sir Leonard turned to Alex Browne. "And how's my other patient?"

"The pains haven't come back. At least, nothing like the pains I got before. Just a sorta throbbing."

Sir Leonard patted her cheek. "I think you're going to make it. We shall be landing in a short while. They've got a good hospital at Gander."

Alex made a wry face. He looked her over, wondering if she'd pretend to show a stiff upper lip like the old lady when the time came. She puts on a brave front but you can't tell.

SUPERSONIC

Nobody knows how they'll react in a crisis until it happens. Wonder what the captain left *out* of that announcement? He looked around and saw Maxwell jump up and pace the aisle at the forward end of the cabin. Now there's an odd character. Tough as nails on the outside. Yet—can't tell. He looked along the aisle and the cabin ceiling pressed down, the walls narrowed, and suddenly he was fighting an old fear, gasping for breath, shaking off a smothering sensation that threatened to suffocate him. He was twenty-four years old, with six months of internship under his belt, a brilliant examinations record, and still vomited and felt suffocation at the sight of blood. What was the point of going on? Insistent father? Upholding the ancient family tradition? The night more than thirty-five years ago flashed through his brain. The London air raid had been heavy, the casualties a steady stream through the hospital doors. He had been in a corridor two stories up when the bomb had fallen.

"The nurses' residence!" somebody yelled.

Carmel! She was off duty. They'd kissed goodnight in the meager shelter of the doorway, oblivious to the shattering antiaircraft guns and the crunch of exploding bombs in the distance, finding warmth and security in each other's arms as he caressed her dark hair. Shouting, a scream, the sound of racing feet on tiles. Fire bells echoing through the corridor. He raced down the stairs and entered the darkened hospital foyer. An air-raid warden staggered through the door.

"Whole bloody thing's gone!" he shouted to a group of white-clad figures peering out of the double doors.

Leonard Wheeler-Carthert dashed into the street, billows of brick dust choking him, dimly aware of diffused searchlight beams. He peered at the remains of the building across the street. The three-story residence was a pile of smashed masonry and crumbled bricks. He turned, stunned and dazed, and stumbled back into the doorway where a knot of nurses huddled. One cried out.

"My sister's in there! My sister's . . ." An orderly put his arm about the nurse's shoulder and hurried her away.

A bell clanged. There were sounds of a truck pulling up. A shout, "The rescue squad's here! God, that's quick!" He wiped his face and staggered into the roadway. A man jumped from the truck, moving with unhurried purpose, giving orders, a nerve center of control that spread its influence to other rescue workers, extended a thread of confidence to the group in the doorway. Two men with a stretcher scrambled over the debris and lifted a shape that looked like a sack of flour. Wheeler-Carthert shut his eyes as they bore the grisly load past.

"Dig here," the rescue leader said, indicating a spot. Men began to shovel. A tunnel mouth appeared, and soon a man with a rope tied to his waist disappeared down the hole. The pile of debris at the tunnel's mouth got higher.

"Here's another!" Gun flashes lit up the face on the stretcher that passed him. Strands of dust-caked auburn hair hung down.

A loud cracking noise. "Everybody out! She's going!"

Men with black faces and grimy arms appeared at the tunnel entrance, standing firm, bodies braced for action.

"There's somebody alive down there! Leg's caught under a beam. She's unconscious!"

"Shoring party!"

Men crawled into the entrance, carrying timber props. Wheeler-Carthert, his thin, boyish form trembling, turned to a man beside him.

"It may be her! My fiancée!" he blurted to the figure that

towered over him. It was **Dr.** Ronald Powell, head surgeon. The big man watched the action across the street and put a hand on Wheeler-Carthert's shoulder.

"Crowbars!" Then, "Is she okay?"

The tunnel swallowed the question. The debris spewed back the answer. "Can't reach her. Need a thin chap. Really thin. A girder's got her by the knee."

A loud crack sounded from the mound of rubble, followed by the snapping of timbers. Wheeler-Carthert dashed forward. "I'll fit." The leader's eyes moved over him, hesitating. Wheeler-Carthert looked at the tunnel entrance, his heart pounding.

"The girder's settled deeper. She'll be a goner if we don't work fast."

"Bert. Tie a rope around him," the leader said, nodding toward Wheeler-Carthert.

Someone shoved a flashlight into his hand. "How long have you been interning?" Dr. Powell demanded.

"A year, sir," he lied.

"You know what's to be done? Morphine and possibly . . ."

Wheeler-Carthert tried to swallow, but his tongue was stuck. "Yes, sir."

Dr. Powell spoke to a white figure nearby, who vanished and reappeared a minute later with something wrapped in a sheet. Wheeler-Carthert felt the cold steel through the cotton. A syringe was pressed into his hand. "There's half a tube. Double dose, in the arm. Count up to sixty. Then get to work. Above the knee if necessary."

Strong fingers gripped his shoulder. "Sorry, lad. Now go to it."

"Take this stretcher," a rescue worker directed. "We'll pull when you give the signal. Three yanks on the rope."

Pale light from a hurricane lamp bounced from the tunnel

sides. The swirling clouds of dust burned his eyes and choked his lungs. He had an urge to run—run a mile, suck in lungfuls of cool night air. A voice yelled down the shaft.

"Keep going, lad."

He pointed the flashlight downward and, in the yellow beam that cut through the dust, saw a mop of black hair. "It's me, darling. I've come to get you." The figure in the dim light below did not answer.

Sweat ran down his forehead, running into his eyes as the heat in the tiny space pressed in. Muffled cracking noises came from all around and the softer shuffle of cascading plaster sounded loud in this strange new world.

"I'm going to give you morphine." He paused, letting the words come grudgingly. "Then tie you on a stretcher and they'll pull you out . . ."

Again, there was no reply from the form below. Her face was turned away from him, pressed toward a crevice in the rubble. Without hesitating he jabbed the needle into her arm. Swinging the flashlight he saw the bright glint of the girder where it had torn her nightdress, cutting into her leg, cruelly dimpling the flesh at the knee, crushing it against a massive block of masonry. A pool of congealing blood oozed where the steel sliced. He turned away, retched until his stomach hurt, and felt giddy as something danced before his eyes and dissolved into a white sheet. He pulled the shape toward him, blowing brick dust from it, and unwrapped the surgical saw. Then he burrowed deeper until he was on a level with the beam, feeling the cool steel on his arm. He poised the saw— above the knee. Silky skin, suntanned from a recent holiday. His brain reeled . . . recovered . . . the saw sagged . . . he repositioned it . . . closed his eyes . . . opened them . . . thrust his hand forward and down . . . glimpsed the skin tear, the blood spurt . . . turned away . . . retched

. . . sawed . . . the saw will tell him when it got to the bone . . . keep going . . . nearly there . . . mustn't stop now . . . press harder . . . he felt resistance in his arms . . . grinding . . . mustn't stop . . . keep going . . .

Wheeler-Carthert grasped the inert body and twisted it around in the narrow shaft. He stared at the girl's face. She was a complete stranger.

"Grab her! Steady lads."

"I'll take her." Dr. Powell's voice came from a great distance, and everything went black.

Sir Leonard staggered against the seat back, and opened his eyes. He clutched his chest, feeling the palpitations. Steady on. They mustn't see you like this. If they see *you're* afraid panic may spread like an epidemic through the cabin. He sucked in a deep breath as Maxwell strode up and said in a confidential tone, "Say Doctor, what do you make of it?"

"South over the lake. Outer marker three decimal nine miles from threshold of Runway Zero-Four," Bartlett said.

"Glide path's normal. Two and a half degrees," Kowsky confirmed. He paused, and stared at the moving map on the center console. "Jesus, when are they going to nail that bandit?"

Bartlett peered at the map. They were ten miles past Bonavista, over the bay, which he guessed was icebound this time of year. He looked out of the side window. The sky was darkening, reflecting the billowing layer below where cumulus clouds gathered like mountains, black and threatening.

Duffy's voice sounded urgent. "Gander to Zero-One. Turn right twenty degrees. Repeat. Right twenty degrees. Aircraft on your present heading still unidentified. Unable to contact."

A tremendous weight bore back on the column as he pressed the yoke down to the right.

SUPERSONIC

"Ten degrees," Kowsky said as the flight deck banked. "Fifteen . . . twenty."

Bartlett straightened the yoke, watching the turn-and-bank indicator level.

"Zero-One to Gander. Have altered course twenty degrees right. Can't you clear that bandit? Fuel reserve's almost nil."

"NORAD's onto him."

"Alert Condition Blue's on," the voice in the telephone told Delaney. "I'll call you when we get positive identification." The line went dead.

Delaney put the receiver on the cradle, wondering how the officer in the headquarters building of the Voodoo fighter base across the road could be so laconic. He looked down at Zero-One's blip as it crept on its new course and was momentarily relieved now that NORAD's communication network was in action probing the strange electronic signal. In the reinforced-concrete cavern several hundred feet below the Colorado mountains skilled operators sat before radar-scopes suddenly switched to blown-up maps of Newfoundland. At the far end of the room was the Big Board, glowing with a green translucence, on which a map of North America was etched in electronic lines. Several Air Force officers stood on a platform below the board, looking up expectantly at a red blob north of Gander.

In the pit of the air-conditioned room, below the Big Board, other operators scanned radarscopes. At the center scope an operator brought a light pen attached to a cable to bear on the unidentified red blip north of Gander. At that precise second the blip stopped, but continued to glow brightly.

"Helicopter, sir," he announced to the officer standing at his elbow. He brought the pen closer to the blip. Instantly a signal passed from the blip to the light pen, digitalizing the position coordinates of the unknown helicopter in terms of distance and altitude in accordance with the precalibrated scanning of a mammoth rotating radar antenna housed in a plastic hemisphere somewhere in Greenland. Symbols flashed on the operator's scope, and also alongside the red blob on the Big Board.

"Helicopter stationary at latitude forty-eight degrees, fifty-eight decimal one minute north, longitude fifty-four degrees, forty decimal two west. Altitude eight thousand feet," he said in a flat voice.

The officer picked up a telephone, pressed a button, and spoke to the Search and Rescue helicopter station at Halifax, Nova Scotia. "Confirm if a Search and Rescue helicopter not returned to base," he said. In three seconds a voice in Halifax spoke. "Confirm one of our helicopters not returned to base. Identity: Bravo Echo Seven-Two-Four."

The NORAD officer reached for another telephone. As he did so the group of officers on the platform broke up, vanishing into the gloom at the perimeter of the room. The officer across from the Gander Terminal Building answered his ringing instrument . . . picked up another . . . Delaney grabbed his telephone. Ten seconds had passed since he'd put it down.

"Search and Rescue helicopter from Halifax off course at eight thousand," Delaney said to Duffy, throwing the phone on its cradle.

"Why doesn't he call in?"

"Base says radio trouble and his transponder doesn't respond to interception. Of course, we know that." He pointed to the radarscope. "He's off again. Coming this way."

"Probably got a bearing of some sort. I'll clear Flight Zero-One for descent."

Delaney nodded and grabbed the telephone. In the Radio

Control Building the man collecting the teletype slips from the conveyor belt answered. "Who's monitoring the military traffic?" Delaney demanded.

"Stevens, sir."

"Switch me." The line clicked and another voice said, "Sir?"

"There's a Search and Rescue helicopter at eight thousand, forty miles north. We've got him on radar. Heard from him?"

"No, sir."

"Try all military frequencies. Looks like he's got radio trouble and is off course. The base'll tell us if he radios. But if you get him first, phone me. Understand? I'm at Position Eighteen."

"Yes, sir."

Delaney replaced the telephone. The helicopter was edging toward center scope, and Flight Zero-One nudging the fifty mile circle on the scope. He took a deep breath: forty miles from the airport was the usual place to start descending from twenty-five thousand feet. But, he reminded himself, that was for subsonic jets equipped with lift spoilers and flaps.

"Gander to Zero-One," said Duffy. "You are cleared for descent. Bandit identified. It's an off-course Search and Rescue helicopter at eight thousand feet. Resume previous heading on Victor Three One Five."

The creases around Bartlett's mouth relaxed as Duffy continued, "Helicopter has radio trouble and there's no transponder response. Position forty miles north of Gander."

"Roger, Gander. What's the ceiling?"

"Two hundred."

Bartlett tilted the yoke, watching the compass as Arrowhead banked.

"What's your fuel, Zero-One?"

Kowsky leaned over and pushed the gauge button. "Twelve minutes to the bottom of the tanks," Bartlett replied. The compass swung around to the Gander heading. He pulled the throttle levers back. The yoke pressure against his arms increased.

"Help take the weight, Pete."

"I've got her."

The tiny airplane on the artificial horizon sank below the bar, and the rate-of-descent meter showed five hundred feet per minute. Arrowhead Flight Zero-One had begun her descent. He switched on the checklist monitor and adjusted it to Approach.

"Radio altimeter."

"Checked On," Kowsky said.

"Anticollision lights On."

Kowsky's hand left the yoke and danced over the switches. "Anticollision lights, On."

Bartlett took a quick look outside. The cloud layer loomed close, with wisps of altonimbus clouds swirling above. See and be seen. "Nav lights On."

"Nav lights On."

The moving map showed a curve of jagged islands off Newfoundland. The radio became alive. "Gander to Zero-One. Helicopter looks like he intends Gander approach."

"Christ, he can't do that! Have you tried to contact him on all frequencies?"

"Yes. His transmitter's definitely out."

The cloud layer rushed to meet them and he turned up the instrument lights. Nineteen thousand feet and 550 knots. He looked at Kowsky, saw his wrists tense, the muscles of straining hands on the yoke hard like his own.

"A duck with a brick tied to its ass," Kowsky said grimly.

TEN

Delaney stared at Zero-One's blip, gauging its northerly advance across the face of the scope against the southerly creep of the helicopter, then he looked down the aisle. From where he stood at Duffy's shoulder he could see controllers tidying their consoles, removing canceled flight progress strips from plastic holders, stacking them into neat bundles, and slipping elastic bands over them. The thickness of the stacks told him that domestic flights of Air Canada and Eastern Provincial Airways had been canceled, and he visualized aircraft being towed into hangars or maneuvered into parking areas at Stephenville Airport, Deer Lake, and southwest as far as Halifax. Over in Radio Control a few high-level en-route controllers would be working the last of the westbound daily five hundred as they swung through the southwesterly end of Gander's Air Traffic Control sector and entered New York Oceanic. Budnick appeared at the end of the aisle and hurried toward him.

"Can't find him anywhere," he said breathlessly. "Dick Edwards phoned to say his boys have searched down Jonathan's Brook and the ponds in between."

"Got somebody looking around Great Rattling?"

Budnick nodded, his thin silvery hair glinting under the subdued ceiling lights. "Bert's gone in the Land Rover."

"Hope he looks down Exploits when he goes through Grand Falls."

"Told him to. And check Bishop's Falls."

"He'll have to go like a bat out of hell to get there and back before Zero-One's on final approach. Sit on that phone, Ed."

"Okay, Jim." Budnick hurried away and Delaney turned back to the scope. The helicopter had put on a burst of speed. Perhaps run into a patch of clear sky? He waited for the radial finger to sweep the scope: For a helicopter it was moving fast. He studied the vague forms caused by throwback from the fog and clutter from the high points of the terrain around the airport and he imagined the scene on Zero-One's flight deck, the eyes straining from the side windows to get a visual fix if a clearing appeared in the clouds, the quick glance over the fuel and other gauges. Complex things, those supersonics, with complicated systems so different from the subsonics. Like the fuel-trim transfer system and the drooped nose and protective visor over the windshield.

There'd been odd landings done in subsonics when forward visibility had been zero, he reflected, thinking of the Pan Am 747 en route from Frankfurt to London with two hundred and seventy passengers on board. It had been in the holding pattern at four thousand feet when the crew heard a bang and a windshield panel suddenly became translucent. They thought it had iced over. Thirty seconds later another boom and the other panel went blank. The captain had done the right thing: He got clearance to climb to sixteen thousand. Like flying the Moth in the old days—get as much air between you and the ground when something went wrong. It wasn't icing that had crazed both panels on the 747, like a car windshield hit by a stone. An electrical discharge had done it and the inquiry had never decided whether it had been a lightning strike or a static discharge from the aircraft. The captain had elected to make an automatic landing, but on the final approach the autopilot failed to lock onto the glide slope and he'd brought her down on the manual Instrument Landing System, with the first officer and flight engineer scanning for the threshold from the side windows.

Delaney rubbed his chin thoughtfully, still believing the Ministry of Transport had decided wrongly in not installing automatic landing equipment at Gander. Too infrequent periods of fog, they'd said, pointing to the Gander weather surveys that staidly reported, *Fog—relatively fog free except in spring, radiation fog in August (infrequent). Storms, none; winter, every three days.*

Delaney clicked his tongue. Those deskbound Ottawa MOT types should spend time in Gander, to feel the effect on the nerves bringing crippled aircraft down in *fog—relatively free except in spring!*

"Gander to Zero-One. Cloud layer tops off seventeen thousand," Duffy said.

Delaney leaned forward and pressed a button. The voice of Zero-One's captain broke from a speaker above the console. "Roger. Seventeen-thousand, in cloud now. What's the ceiling?"

Duffy glanced at the ceilometer readout. "One hundred and fifty."

"Zero-One to Gander. Request GCA on Runway Zero-Four."

"Roger. GCA Runway Zero-Four." Duffy pressed a button and spoke to the tower controller. "Confirm GCA for Flight Zero-One. Runway Zero-Four."

"Confirm GCA Zero-One. Runway Zero-Four," Walker replied. "Wind from northwest at fifteen."

Duffy spoke. "Cleared for landing on Runway Zero-Four. Wind northwest at fifteen miles per hour."

Delaney stepped forward and examined the helicopter blip. It had slowed, crawling over the inscribed twenty mile circle. He thumped the edge of the console in frustration. Duffy's hand swept in front of him and moved Zero-One's flight progress strip to flight level one-seven-zero. The paper strip, covered with updated ARPs scribbled over the printed longitude numbers 10, 15, 20, 30, 40, and 50, looked like a much-corrected child's exercise book with its erasures and amendments. Except for a clean, uncorrected strip in the flight level two-eight-zero sector—an eastbound Sabena DC-8 freighter passing into Gander's area from New York ATC sector—the console was clear.

"Hey, Alf," Delaney called to a controller three consoles away. "Take the Sabena Flight One-Four-Three eastbound."

"Yes, sir."

He picked up the phone and dialed. "Commanding Officer Anderson. Urgent. Delaney."

"Anderson."

"It's Delaney, sir. Any contact with the off-course helicopter?"

"No, but Halifax reconfirms it's a CH-53 Search and Rescue. Crew of two. All other CH-53s have returned to base."

"The other aircraft in the exercise, sir? The ASWs and support planes?"

"All down and accounted for, except a squadron of Orion P-3s in the air returning to Baltimore."

"You've got Flight Zero-One on your scopes, sir?" There was no harm in checking. Communication snafus had occurred between civilian and military traffic control centers before.

"Yes." There was a pause. "Tricky GCA with zero forward vision in this fog."

"And a heavy tail-down moment." Delaney fell silent, sharing a mutual feeling of concern with the officer across the road.

"I'll phone if we make contact with the CH-53," said Anderson. There was a soft click as the phone was put down at the other end.

Duffy grabbed his sleeve and pointed to the scope. Delaney watched the radial light finger sweep from north to south. The helicopter had made an abrupt change of course.

"He's heading due west!"

"He's lost for sure, sir."

Delaney looked at the flag accompanying the blip: 6,000 feet. He thought of the pilot and copilot peering through the transparent nose of the CH-53, craning for a glimpse of the rugged ground below, praying for an opening that would reveal a snow-covered hill—any solid land where they could put down.

"He's over Burnt Lake, headed toward Ten Mile Lake," Duffy said. "If he keeps on that course and loses height he'll hit the sea off Lewisport."

Delaney fell silent, and the lines around the corners of his mouth arched down as he mentally agreed with the implication of Duffy's remark: Better two dead than the one-hundred-and-sixty-odd people on board the airliner.

The voice of Zero-One's captain came from the speaker. "Passing through fifteen thousand. Thick cloud. Moderate turbulence. Airspeed four hundred and seventy knots. What's happening to the off-course helicopter?"

Duffy glanced at Delaney. "Still no contact. He's changed course. Heading due west. Losing height. Now at six thousand."

"Roger. Request course change fifteen degrees southwest of Gander Lake ready to intercept outer marker beacon."

"Cleared to course change fifteen degrees southwest to intercept outer marker."

"Roger." A hum came from the speaker. After a few seconds Bartlett's voice broke out. "Zero-One headed due west. Thirteen thousand. Moderate to strong turbulence. Visibility zero to three hundred yards. What's your ceiling?"

"One hundred," Duffy replied.

"Describe the terrain. It might lift when we break through."

Duffy adjusted his microphone and watched Zero-One's blip, now moving parallel to the helicopter's, twenty miles north.

"Low hills up to four hundred and sixty feet high two miles directly south of Runway Zero-Four. Tree-covered. Gander Lake directly south of Runway Zero-Four threshold. Outer marker on hill south of lake. Lake is still partly ice-covered this year—unusual—clear white, snow on ice."

"Obstacles on final approach?" Bartlett demanded.

"High tension cables on Trans-Canada Highway running parallel to the lake shoreline. Runway Zero-Four threshold three hundred yards from highway. They're low-strung."

"Hell—trying to catapult us on to Zero-Four?"

Duffy exchanged glances with Delaney. It was clear Duffy didn't know what to say. Against his will—he believed in letting the person in charge handle a situation like this—Delaney leaned forward and spoke into Duffy's stick microphone. "Sorry, captain. The public utility had their cables up before we lengthened Zero-Four."

There was a long silence, broken only by a loud buzz from the speaker and the subdued voices of the other controllers. At last Bartlett's voice came over the air.

"Alert airport police to meet aircraft on arrival. Suspected bank robber aboard. Passenger manifest shows name as Clarence Ives."

SUPERSONIC

As a reflex action Delaney picked up the phone and dialed an emergency number. "American Arrow Airlines Flight Zero-One diverted from London to Kennedy request police meet aircraft on arrival. Suspected bank robber by name of Clarence Ives aboard." He slammed down the phone. Christ Almighty, what a cool customer! Twenty miles out, descending through dense cloud, airport socked in, fuel low, zero forward visibility, tail dragging—and he reports a suspected bank robber aboard. He turned back to Duffy's position, for the first time aware of the small knot of off-duty controllers forming a semicircle at a respectable distance around Position Eighteen, drawn by the knowledge that Duffy's scope was now a stage on which a drama was to be played out to its inevitable conclusion. Duffy jabbed his finger at the scope.

"He's starting south, sir!"

If the helicopter stayed on that course it would miss the airport entirely. Zero-One's blip was vectored west, moving more slowly as the aircraft's speed dropped.

"Gander to Zero-One. Off-course helicopter on southerly heading, west of airport."

"He's lost all right."

Delaney peered at the two blips, trying to judge at what point the helicopter would intersect the east-west axis of the airport. Did the pilot intend to search for that line—heaven only knew how he'd find it—and then to turn ninety degrees on an easterly course toward the airport? He must be flying solely on instinct now, at four thousand. He checked Zero-One's blip: Arrowhead was passing through nine thousand. His eye moved to the ceilometer dial. It showed zero.

Lydia Olsen peered out of the little porthole in the vestibule where she'd hung the passengers' coats. A curtain separated her from the first-class cabin and she was thankful for

191

the moments alone. A hush had fallen on the cabin; even the demanding Maxwell was quiet. The captain had been right. The third Scotch had done its job. Putting her face to the window she could see the flash of the red anticollision light above the fuselage reflected on the wraiths of mist and cloud that swallowed the aircraft as it slanted downward. She hung onto the handle of the medicine chest, listening to the sound of the engines and feeling the floor throb under her feet as if the captain were fighting to keep the aircraft under control. The vanishing and reappearing red glow gave her a strange feeling of comfort but she felt chilled and, turning from the window, caught a glimpse of herself in the medicine chest mirror. With an effort, she concentrated on the image that stared back. Her face was drawn, hair a mess. Reaching for her shoulder bag on the floor, she took out a comb and straightened her hair, then touched up her lips with lipstick, and dabbed her nose with powder. God, she wished she felt the solid ground of the terminal building under her feet.

She'd never felt like this before, despite harrowing experiences with lost engines and being thrown about by clear air turbulence. This was different: The jerking floor and the dark outside, plus the barely perceptible uneven throb of the engines gave the impression that the airplane was ready to fall out of the air. The floor tilted, throwing her against the coatrack. A hanger stung her cheek. Then the floor lifted and she felt the upward pressure as the captain regained control. With difficulty she regained her footing and glanced at the mirror: A red crescent showed where the hanger had touched. Inside the medicine cabinet was a package of absorbent cotton. She wiped away the blood. Damn. She'd have to put on a Band-Aid. She swung around, clinging to the handle on the cabinet. The vestibule lights flickered and went out. Oh God, not now! The lights flashed and steadied. Through the window she saw a clear patch in the depth of the clouds and a glimpse of distant, dark hills, bare rocks, and black, ice-fringed lakes like the mouths of great caverns leading into the center of the earth. Threatening clouds quickly filled the gap, rimmed with smoky wisps that flew past the window. It was like flying inside a huge chimney filled with soot. She took another look at herself in the mirror just as a cry sounded from the cabin. She spun into action, sweeping aside the curtain.

Clarence Ives was sprawled on his stomach at the far end of the aisle, legs writhing.

"He tried to get off the plane," Alex Browne yelled. "He went crazy!"

Lydia bent over the fallen man, her own fear gone. She pulled his shoulder and saw the bulging eyes. "Get up, sir," she said in a firm voice.

Ives rose to his knees. She grasped his arm, helped him into a seat, and loosened his tie. The cabin shuddered. Empty meal trays on a shelf vibrated with a tinny sound and crashed to the floor. "Put this on," she said, fastening his seat belt.

"Let me see him." Sir Leonard Wheeler-Carthert leaned over the prostrate man. He felt the pulse and with a swift movement loosened Ives's collar and wiped the sweat from the man's cheeks with a handkerchief.

"He's under considerable nervous tension," he said. "Bring the bag under my seat."

Lydia found the surgeon's bag. Sir Leonard extracted a cellophane package, tore open the end, and took out a syringe. With a skillful thrust, he inserted the needle in Ives's forearm. Lydia glanced around. Alex was peering back over her shoulder and Mrs. Glinker had her lips pressed together, a pained expression on her face. When Lydia looked down at Ives his eyes were shut. Sir Leonard lifted an eyelid, grunted, and put the syringe back into his bag.

"Get a blanket."

SUPERSONIC

Lydia reached to the overhead rack. "Is he going to be all right?" she asked, spreading the blanket over the limp form. "If he gets a complete rest. Pulse low. Probably high blood pressure too. Can't take it under these conditions. I've put him under sedation." Sir Leonard stroked his moustache. "Keep an eye on him," he added in a confidential voice. He glanced at his watch. "We should be landing shortly?"

"In about fifteen minutes."

The stewardess's chime sounded. "Excuse me, sir."

The flight deck lights were dimmed, and the colored squares of warning lights glowed ominously. Nardini bent over the keys of his calculator; Kowsky and Bartlett gripped the yokes, their faces strained in the reflection from the visor-covered windshield.

"Move the economy passengers as far forward as possible," Bartlett said over his shoulder. "Get as many of them into the first-class cabin as there are seats available. Understand?"

"Yes, Captain."

The flight deck lurched and she grabbed the back of Bartlett's seat for support as a solid wall of cloud streamed past the side windows. He tossed his head, indicating that she should get on with it.

Lydia picked up the telephone on the wall in the vestibule. "Ladies and gentlemen. Captain Bartlett has requested that passengers in the economy section move forward into the unoccupied seats in the first-class cabin. Please remain seated until the stewardesses in the economy section make the necessary arrangements. All other passengers are requested to remain seated with their seat belts fastened. Thank you." As an afterthought she added, "It's to help make our landing more, uh, as light as possible."

Returning the instrument to its bracket, she walked down the aisle, trying not to hurry. Maxwell was fidgeting with his seat belt. Clarence Ives had slipped out of sight beneath the blanket, and Alex Browne's head lolled back. She pulled back the curtain that separated the first-class cabin from economy. Several passengers were peering out of the windows, straining to see below. She recognized the signs of fear: clenched fists, crossed feet, and white knuckles clutching armrests. The stewardess in charge of the economy cabin came to meet her. "It's to help the balance for landing," Lydia whispered. "Tell those at the rear to move into first class."

The stewardess nodded. "Okay. I'll tell them." Lydia stood near the curtain and the stewardess spoke to another attendant who stepped from the aft galley. They bent over the passengers at the rear of the cabin, pointing toward Lydia.

Lydia counted heads. The unconscious passenger was near the front. That was good. "Everybody from here back," she indicated with her arm, "please bring your personal possessions and follow me," she said, trying to keep the sense of urgency from her voice.

"Are we in trouble?" demanded a big, raw-faced man with ears that stuck out. "I was in a Seven-oh-Seven once when we had to move up front." He turned to his neighbor, a woman with a baby in a plastic cot slung on the overhead luggage stowage. "Boy, was that a heavy landing! Bumped the deck twice before we hit the runway and stayed down."

The woman put a hand over her mouth and jerked her head toward the baby. Lydia stepped forward and grasped the cot. "Please follow me."

"We hit the deck wham like that," the man continued, slamming a fist against the flat of his other hand with a resounding smack.

"This way," Lydia carried the cot into the first-class cabin. "Sit down and fasten your seat belt. I'll hand him to you."

"Are we going to crash?" the woman asked, grasping the baby.

"Of course not. This is to help balance the plane for a

normal landing." Lydia went back into the economy section.

"If you ask my opinion, it's going to be another of those hit-the-deck jobs," the beefy man said in a loud voice.

Lydia glared at him. *Keep your opinions to yourself, Mr. Big Mouth.* "Nobody's asking you, sir. Please follow the captain's instructions." The watery eyes hardened and for a moment she thought he was going to stand his ground, but he obediently picked up his flight bag in silence and followed her into the first-class cabin.

Sir Leonard got up to allow a passenger to move between him and the window. A boy squeezed past Alex.

Lydia surveyed the cabin. All the empty seats were now filled. A white-haired man had seated himself next to Gladys Glinker. "Broken?" he inquired, nodding at the trussed arm. Mrs. Glinker forced a smile and blinked behind her glasses. "Oh, it's nothing," she said. "Once I broke a leg falling from a balloon, uh, I mean a blimp. That was a long time ago, when my husband was alive. It happened in Switzerland —we used to travel a lot then . . ."

Lydia smiled and turned away, noting that the altimeter on the bulkhead was at eight thousand feet. They would soon be maneuvering into the final approach pattern. She went into the vestibule and inspected her face in the mirror. The Band-Aid didn't look too conspicuous after all.

"Cabin pressurization and heating off," Bartlett said.

"Cabin pressurization and heating to Off," Kowsky moved a lever and adjusted the heat-control knob.

The yoke jerked under Bartlett's grip. He glanced at the airspeed indicator, 390. Too fast. He eased the column back. "What's the fuel, Pete?"

"Nine minutes," Kowsky replied, pushing the button.

Bartlett spoke into the microphone. "Where's the helicopter?" he demanded.

"Still headed south. North of the airport. Uh, just a . . ." Duffy's voice hesitated. "He's stopped. Looks like he may be trying to land. At fifteen hundred feet."

"Must have found a clear patch," Kowsky said, raising his eyebrows hopefully.

"Gander to Zero-One. Helicopter is not, repeat not, landing. Changed course due east."

"That'll put him directly north of the airport," Bartlett said. The damned pilot had the instinct of a homing pigeon. Christ! Why does he have to be so cussed? Surely he could let down slowly in zero visibility and take a chance he'd settle in the trees. Far safer than putting the damned thing down on the edge of an airport building. He'd bend the goddamned machine but he'd be down. Bruised—but down.

"Keep it coming, Gander."

"Will do," replied Duffy.

"I don't want to die," Ives shouted, frightened by the glaze that covered his eyes. A voice echoed in his skull. He turned around and slowly his eyes came into focus. A big-boned man had plunked himself down in the next seat and was staring at him.

"I'm sorry. I'll give them back! I don't want to die."

"You're not going to die, buddy," the voice beside him said. "It'll just be a heavy landing. I was in a Seven-oh-Seven once. It smacked down real hard. Just like that." He banged his fist on the armrest. "She bounced back up like a rocket and hit again. Then he stuck her on like a leech. Real cool." Ives stiffened and shrank into the seat. "These jobs are built to take it. Don't worry, fella."

Lydia Olsen hurried up. "Is this gentleman troubling you, Mr. Ives?"

He struggled to see through the veil of purple that clamped down again, obscuring his vision. The face receded into a vague outline. He tried to swallow, but his tongue curled into a ball. The face came closer. "Are you all right, Mr. Ives?" A choking sensation rose in his chest. He must escape. He glanced at the big man on his left and at the window. Suddenly he rose, threw off the blanket, and, despite the seat belt, clawed at the false ceiling.

"Mr. Ives! Take it easy," Lydia cried.

"Sure buddy. Like the lady says. It's going to be okay. Just a heavy landing."

He felt hands restraining him, forcing him back into the seat. The mist cleared and he was looking at a small rectangle of plastic, which dissolved into a Band-Aid on a woman's face.

"Are you feeling better now, Mr. Ives?" the woman said. A tall man with a bristly moustache leaned over the back of the seat, offering him a paper cup. It was the doctor who'd fixed up the old lady. He took the cup and drank, spilling some of the water on his jacket.

"I'm sorry I, uh, went off like that. I . . ."

"That's all right, buddy. It's worse when you *know* it's going to happen. Now, take that Seven-oh-Seven. Nobody expected it . . ."

"Swallow this," insisted Sir Leonard, handing Ives a white pill. "It'll help your nerves."

Ives looked at the pill, hoping it would put him to sleep. He wanted reality to vanish. "I'll get more water," said Lydia, hurrying away. She came back with another paper cup. He swallowed the pill and looked at Sir Leonard Wheeler-Carthert. "I think I'll be okay now. It was just . . ."

"Jeez, it's warm in here," said the big man, loosening his tie. "Feels like they turned off the air-conditioning. Hey, Miss," he called after Lydia. "Have they pulled the wrong lever up front? It's awful hot in here." He turned to Ives and stuck out a horny hand. "Name's Stanhope. George Stanhope, from Big River, South Dakota. Sell farm machinery. Tractors and combine harvesters. The big stuff." Ives felt his hand squashed. "What're you in?"

"Me . . . oh . . ." he paused, collecting his thoughts. "Stocks and, uh, bonds."

Stanhope passed an appreciative eye over the other's well-tailored suit, spotted with water droplets. "I thought you looked a financial type. You can tell." He ran a finger under his shirt collar. "Jeez, it's real hot in here." Lydia Olsen appeared. "Say, miss. What's up with the cool air?" He put his hand up and twisted the air outlet. "There's nothing coming out of this thing."

Lydia felt under the outlet. "That's unusual." She turned the metal spout. "It's too busy on the flight deck to check now, sir. In any case, we'll be landing in about fifteen minutes."

Stanhope drew his shirt cuff across his forehead. "Yeah, I guess it will be kinda busy," he nodded toward the opposite window. "Looks grim out there to me."

Clarence Ives stared straight ahead, feeling the inner supports falling away again. Control yourself. Remember Callahan. *For once in your life you've got to stick your neck out or stay in the back room until you rot.* He searched for a cigarette, but couldn't find one. Just as well, he thought, seeing the "No Smoking," "Fasten Seat Belt" signs lit up. Lucky nobody seemed to have gotten the significance of his outburst about giving the bonds back. He shivered. Funny how this guy's complaining about the heat and I'm so cold. He looked for the blanket, but it had fallen to the floor. Hungry too. He tried to remember when he'd last had a full meal. Thinking about it, forcing his brain into action, made him feel better. He hadn't had a real meal—only that light lunch they'd served earlier on—since last night, after the bank messenger had delivered the bonds and he'd checked out of the Dorchester Hotel and into the place near London Airport.

"You look kinda better now. More color," Stanhope said, examining Ives's face. "That tall man who gave you the pill is a doctor. He looked after the unconscious fella in economy a while back."

"Unconscious?"

"Yeah. Hit his head an awful crack when the plane dived. He's still out for the count," Stanhope said, wiping his forehead again. "You're in stocks and bonds, eh?"

Ives nodded. "Yes." After a pause he asked slowly, "Why?"

Stanhope's lips parted in a toothy grin. He slapped Ives's knee. "You're a guy worth cultivating. You must know some market tips."

Ives felt his jaw relax as the pill took effect. He ventured a smile and moved his hands in a friendly gesture. "If I had any, I'd use them myself!"

"You're a wily one." Stanhope laughed. He lowered his voice. "But seriously, Mister—eh, what did you say your name was?"

"I don't think I did," replied Ives, his mind clearer now. "It's Ives. Uh, Clarence Ives . . ."

"Well, Mr. Ives. A fella in my line of business is always in need of a good line of credit. These big harvesters are mighty expensive. I'm always on the lookout for new contacts in the financial world. You must be well connected with people in banking."

"No, not really." Ives paused "I work in a broker's office."

Stanhope looked disappointed. "A backroom man, eh?"

Ives nodded. But not for long, he thought. He turned and

looked out of the window. Gray clouds raced past and rain drops streamed across the window, driven upward as the aircraft sank toward the ground.

"It's still kinda murky out there," Stanhope exclaimed. "It's gonna be a rough one, you betcha!"

Ives bit his lip and yanked the blind down.

Bartlett studied the Gander plate. PROCEDURE: turn LEFT within nine nautical miles of the OM—in his case he'd have to turn right to pick up the outer marker because he was making a westerly approach. That would save a few gallons of fuel. Glide path two and a half degrees. That was normal. Gander's radio call sign was QX—but he'd hear a continuous dash-dash-dot-dash at the outer marker. MISSED APPROACH: climb to 2,000 on track of 038 degrees. Left turn to Quebec Nondirectional Beacon. Hope he wouldn't need to do *that*. He studied the plan of the three runways and turned over the plate to the larger map on the back. The elevation of Runway 04 was 425 feet above sea level at the threshold and 452 feet at its farthest end, ten thousand five hundred feet distant on the reciprocal heading 22. It wasn't much, but as soon as his wheels touched he'd be running up-hill. Every bit helped. The runways, he noted, were asphalt. Not good. Black and less easy to spot than concrete, and slick with damp fog.

He thrust the plate at Nardini and, one by one, wiped the palms of his hands on the sides of his trousers. He glanced at the airspeed indicator. Three hundred and ten. Too high.

"Forty percent power."

Kowsky moved his left hand to the control pedestal, and pulled the black-knobbed throttles. "Forty percent power." The engine sound reduced to a distant whine.

The altimeter showed six thousand. Arrowhead's position

on the map display was exactly over Freshwater Bay, twenty-five miles from the airport. He looked out of the side window at the clouds streaking past, hoping to catch a glimpse of the sea. At five thousand feet a tremor ran through the aircraft and the yoke quivered as the stall jigger gave him warning of his dragging tail. He pressed the yoke forward.

"Mushy like a cow's nose," Kowsky said through tight lips.

"Fuel temp's down. Lower speed and switching off the cabin pressurization did it," Bartlett said brightly, nodding at the instrument panel.

"And the damn fog helps," Kowsky said.

The air was calmer now. He checked the time-to-go read-out. If he could maintain control of Arrowhead's tail-heavy attitude and the fuel kept pumping at the rate Nardini had calculated, they should be on the ground in twelve minutes.

"Gander to Zero-One. Helicopter's changed course due east. Repeat. Due east. At one thousand feet."

ELEVEN

There were times, James Delaney thought, his eyes fixed on the helicopter's blip, when he wished he'd stuck with flying as a full-time career. Air Traffic Control was a queer dichotomy of attachment and remoteness from flight operations. The pale green radarscopes, with their rotating sweeps of light and barely distinguishable blips that crept through the cloud and surface clutter from the surrounding terrain, represented tenuous links with reality. Tens of thousands of feet up and across a span of sky four hundred miles wide, the blips represented airplanes filled with human beings. In the darkened room where he spent much of his working life, in times of crisis like this, he was forced to watch and direct, nerves taut, mind alert, and make life-or-death decisions for remote pilots. But with a control column balanced in your hands and the feel of rudder pedals beneath your feet, you were your own master. Everything was a black or white decision, with no shades of gray. To go or not to go; to commit to takeoff or to abort; to move a lever or switch according to *your* judgment. But in this room, staring at the end of a stream of phosphorescent electrons crawling across a scope;

203

listening to a stranger's voice from the upper atmosphere; checking flight levels, airspeeds, and flight numbers; you had to resist the temptation to see danger in terms of nonreality. It was easy to fall into the trap of regarding the indistinct electronic signatures moving over the surface of the radar-scope as mere blips. A controller had to translate what he saw on the scope and heard through his headset into three-dimensional reality; to visualize actual aircraft filled with people, speeding through space. He pulled his thoughts back to the simulated reality displayed on the scope. Christ, why doesn't the 'copter let down now through the fog—let down anywhere? Zero-One's blip crept through the twenty-mile circle.

"Zero-One. You are now inside twenty-mile outer limit. Please squawk ident," said Duffy. The two parallel lines of the blip became solid light as Bartlett pressed the transponder button. "Thanks, Zero-One."

Duffy played it like clockwork, Delaney reflected, knowing that the request to Zero-One, although unnecessary, would have a profound effect on the flight deck. It would indicate a tangible link between the aircraft and the ground —a request to do something that the pilot would know showed up to the watchers in the darkened ATC room. The rotating finger of light on the scope, making one revolution every four seconds, swept around and Delaney observed the white oblong of Zero-One's blip dissolve back into two parallel lines.

He straightened and looked up. Two consoles away Clifford Reynolds leaned over the twin Precision Approach Radar scopes. The scopes were aglow with orange light as Reynolds warmed up his equipment and aligned his radar beam by remote control along Runway Zero-Four. Reynolds was a good PAR man, but Thompson was top class, the best he'd ever had on staff, a man with a natural talent for the work. Some controllers, like Thompson, were born with it;

others acquired a sound proficiency after many years of experience. Still others never made the tough PAR course in the first place. Thompson had only last week been through the MOTs grueling requalification test, to which PAR operators were subjected every six months. An MOT Boeing 707 had landed at Gander with two inspectors on board. One had seated himself at Thompson's elbow beside the ATC consoles, the other in the 707's copilot's seat with headset on, listening to Thompson talk down the pilot on a pitch-black night, with all runway and taxi strip lights out. In another test, the pilot had been instructed to cut two engines on the approach. Then a fuel-short condition had been simulated. For good measure the MOT man aboard the airplane had ordered the pilot to vocally interrupt the transmissions in an effort to unnerve Thompson. After the tests, filling in the official forms in the privacy of Delaney's office, the inspector who had been aboard the 707 commented, "That guy could convince me to glide home with four dead engines from the middle of the Atlantic."

Delaney studied Zero-One's blip. It was moving fast for an aircraft on instruments lining up in the final approach pattern.

"He'll overshoot the outer marker."

"What's your airspeed, Zero-One?" Duffy asked.

"Two-eight-five. She's too tail heavy. I'm holding speed until the final approach. Where're the 'copter?" he demanded.

"Headed east. He looks determined to get to the airport."

The helicopter's blip was vectoring eight miles north of the airport, Delaney estimated, half expecting it to turn south. It did just that, suddenly veering due south. Delaney stared at the blip, mesmerized by its accurate aim toward center screen.

"Try the 'copter's transponder, Duff. You never . . ."

Duffy pressed the switch, but the two parallels remained unchanged. Delaney glanced over his shoulder at Reynolds, aware of the rise in sound level of the cooling fans behind the high-powered PAR equipment. Delaney took a step toward Reynolds, watching the scopes' light finger soundlessly swishing from side to side twice a second, Reynolds's balding head fringed in an orange halo. The PAR unit had two scopes, one placed vertically facing the controller and another on the flat top of the console desk. A ground line representing solid earth was at the bottom of the vertical scope and, from left to right, a steeply sloping azimuth line on which Arrowhead would soon appear as a light spot as Bartlett maneuvered the aircraft onto the glide path. The flat scope on the console desk showed two illuminated lines diverging from a point on the left, like a wide triangle whose apex was at left screen. At the apex glowed the miniature outlines of Runway 04-22, Runway 14-32, and the short Runway 09-27. A pinpoint of light on this scope would indicate Arrowhead's heading—when the aircraft came within range—so that Reynolds could line up the aircraft onto the runway as he talked Bartlett down.

Both the vertical and flat scopes were intersected by parallel lines. From the threshold of Runway 04 the space between each line represented half a mile: at the three-mile mark was a double line—a warning to Reynolds that the last three miles were the critical ones. Beyond this, to the ten-mile mark somewhere over and beyond Gander Lake, the distance between the lines represented one mile intervals.

Duffy pressed a button and called across to Reynolds. "Feeding him into the outer marker—*now*." Reynolds raised his hand without taking his eyes from his scope.

Duffy adjusted a knob to increase the definition on his scope. The familiar permanent echoes showed up: the outer and inner markers on the approach path, the town of Botwood's water tower on a hill forty miles away that they used as a permanent fixed reference point to align and test the radar at fixed periods, and scatter from the hills in the outlying terrain. The helicopter blip crept south. If the pilot resisted the temptation to cross the airport northern boundary, Arrowhead would be safely down and taxiing in the next few minutes.

Bartlett's voice burst from the speaker. "Altitude five thousand. Lowering nose."

"Five thousand. Roger."

Bartlett nodded to Kowsky and tensed, waiting for the whine that would indicate the electrically-operated screw jack had begun to rotate. A long, silent second passed, then with relief, he heard the high-pitched sound as the mechanism rotated, lowering the nose. He glanced at the airspeed indicator. The numerals ran down the scale: 260 . . . 240, and the miniature airplane on the artificial horizon dropped to the bar. The pressure on his arms relaxed. He jammed his thumb on the visor retract button for one last try. Nothing happened. "Gander. Where's the 'copter?"

"Heading south . . . just a second. Looks like he's trying to make up his mind. He's hovering again," Duffy replied. "What's your airspeed now?"

"Two-four-zero." Perfect, Bartlett thought. When he lowered the gear the speed would fall off twenty knots. He couldn't drop below two hundred because the controls would grow mushy. He checked the compass. Arrowhead was lined up on zero-four magnetic.

"Keep it coming, Gander."

"Roger."

They'd be over the outer marker beacon in less than three

minutes. "Tell Lydia to prepare everybody as for ditching," Bartlett said, aware of a dryness in his throat.

"Yes, Captain." He heard the door slam as Nardini left.

Lydia put down the telephone and Nardini went back to the flight deck. She went up to Gladys Glinker.

"Put your eyeglasses in your handbag, Mrs. Glinker," she said.

Gladys Glinker's lip trembled. "Are we going to crash?" She shot a glance at the elderly man next to her.

"No, we're *not* going to crash," Lydia affirmed.

The man turned to Gladys Glinker and smiled. "It won't be half as bad as jumping out of that airship."

"Oh," said Mrs. Glinker. She allowed Lydia Olsen to remove her glasses and put them in her handbag.

"And take off your shoes," Lydia said. "Excuse me, sir." She knelt to pull off Mrs. Glinker's shoes. "And you, sir."

"Yes, Miss."

"Lean forward with your arms folded over your head when I tell you over the PA. Will you remember to do that?"

They nodded solemnly, and the man linked his arm around Gladys Glinker's good arm. "I'll be your anchor man," he said, forcing another smile.

Lydia turned to Alex Browne. "Cover your face with your arms folded," Lydia said. "I'll remove your shoes."

"But they're soft."

Lydia glanced down. "Okay, leave them on," she said.

She moved down the aisle, checking that seat belts were fastened. At the rear of the cabin she took the baby cot from the rail and stowed it inside the upper locker. She removed the armrest between the mother with the baby, and her neighbor.

"Put him on the seat between you and hold him back," she instructed.

"Will it be very bad?"

"A little bumpy, maybe, but nothing to be alarmed about. It's foggy on the ground and . . ." She glanced out of the window, but the blanket of gray outside reflected the cabin lights. She moved along the aisle, checking the passengers on the other side.

"Betcha he bounces twice!" Stanhope exclaimed when she reached him.

"You're on. You won't even know you're down," she said, glancing at Clarence Ives. "Light as a feather." An old fear flared in Ives's eyes and she wondered whether he was scared of the landing or about the bonds being discovered, or by both.

"You sound, well, sorta overconfident, Miss." Ives ventured.

"You heard me place a bet with this gentleman . . ."

"We didn't lay the odds, sweetheart," Stanhope interrupted. "What'll it be? A drink at Gander or a date when we get to New York?"

"Ten to one for a happy landing. Winner gets a free drink."

"You're on," cried Stanhope, slapping his knee.

She continued down the aisle. Sir Leonard's seat was empty. "Do you know where he went, sir?" she asked Maxwell.

"Checking the concussion case back there," Maxwell replied, jerking his thumb aft. "Said he'd stay with him until we're down."

She looked at Miss Lindenberg, clutching the briefcase. "Under the circumstances, wouldn't it be possible to put the case on the floor, sir?"

Maxwell nodded to Miss Lindenberg. He took a chain from his pocket, selected a key and unlocked the metal capsule that held the attaché case to the wrist chain that was connected to another that passed up Miss Lindenberg's sleeve to a shoulder harness. Miss Lindenberg put the case on the floor. Lydia checked their shoes. They had already removed them, having observed her instructions to the other passengers. "You'll take off your glasses, sir, when I give the signal." Maxwell nodded. "You can both lean against the bulkhead."

"Where will you sit?" Maxwell asked.

"I'll be on the other side 'of the bulkhead. There're a couple of seats . . ."

"Don't forget to take *your* shoes off," Maxwell said, grinning awkwardly.

Bartlett glanced at the Final Approach checklist. "Gear down." From the corner of his eye he saw Kowsky's hand move to the landing gear lever. A distant thud resounded through the airframe and a familiar thump under his feet told him the nosewheel had locked down.

"Three greens," Kowsky intoned. Their bodies strained against the harness as the speed dropped: 215 knots. The rate-of-descent meter showed eight hundred feet per minute. Perfect.

"Testing wheel brakes," Bartlett pressed hard on the toe pedals.

"Full pressure and holding," said Kowsky, checking a pressure gauge.

"Nosewheel steering."

Kowsky gripped the handle, turning it right and left. "Functioning."

"Landing lights on."

"Landing lights to On."

"Hope we can keep the tail clear when we touch."

"We'd have to land like an elephant to break through to the tank," Kowsky replied, sensing Bartlett's worry.

"Helicopter stationary," Duffy's voice announced. "You

are now vectored on Runway Zero-Four. Lined up on the center line. You should be passing the outer marker in sixty seconds. Gear down. Switch to GCA frequency one-one-eight decimal seven."

Bartlett clicked the selector to the talk-down wave band and called over his shoulder to Nardini. "Get behind me. Scan the left window."

Nardini slipped from his harness and stood behind Bartlett, grasping the back of the seat for support.

"Pete, hand over. Scan your side. Shout when you see the threshold."

The pressure on Bartlett's hands increased as Kowsky took his hands off the right-hand yoke and leaned as far as he could against the right window. Arrowhead dropped through the air like a huge duck trying to maintain its balance for landing, bill down, tail dragging at a gawky angle, feet outstretched, and the panels of the windshield that represented eyes staring blankly through the fog. In a few seconds he should hear the Morse recognition signal, *Quebec*, of the outer marker beacon as the aircraft flew through the radio signal projected directly upward from the red-and-white checkered brick hut on the summit of the hill 3.9 miles from the end of Runway 04, separated from the threshold by Gander Lake. A new voice came through the headset.

"American Arrow Airlines Zero-One commence descent NOW. The altimeter is two-niner-zero-five. Confirm you are reading me okay."

The PAR operator at last. "Reading you." Bartlett leaned forward and twisted the knurled knob under the barometric altimeter until the figures read 29.05.

"The winds on the surface are from two-seven-zero degrees at ten miles per hour, gusting to fifteen." He'll have to watch that crosswind on the threshold.

"You should be in descent. It's a two and a half degree glide path. If there are no transmissions for five seconds during this approach or unable to complete it carry out the published missed approach. Acknowledge. Over."

"Roger." Gander's approach plate flashed through Bartlett's mind. *Missed approach climb to 2,000 on track of 038 degrees, left turn to Quebec nondirectional beacon.* He mustn't miss. With the bottom of the tanks almost dry he *mustn't.*

"Heading is zero-four-two. The centerline slightly to your right. You'll have to correct that drift." Hell, did the guy have to spell it out?

"Six miles to touchdown. Your heading is zero-four. Good. It's dead on now."

"Zero-One. You are cleared to land. Check your gear is down." His eyes flashed to the three green lights. "The winds are from two-seven-zero at, uh, twelve miles per hour."

He eased the yoke forward and looked at the rate-of-descent meter. Three hundred feet a minute.

"Five and a quarter miles from touchdown. You are making a good rate of descent."

The voice in his headset fell silent . . . one second . . . two . . . three . . . four . . . "It's a two and a half degree glide path." A trickle of sweat ran under his collar. Christ, man, keep talking.

"Now, right heading zero-four, two degrees to your left." He'd drifted off again. Increase pressure on the pedal. She was like a lumbering crate with an overload of bricks.

Another pause . . . "You're holding on course four and three quarter miles from touchdown." Pressure even on the pedals.

"Holding on course, and your rate of descent looks good. Winds are from the northwest, variable, just over twelve miles per hour. Gusting still. Four miles to . . ."

SUPERSONIC

A buzz in his earphones: dash-dash-dot-dash . . . The upper red light flashed on the marker beacon panel of the radio console. The buzz ended; he was through the outer marker's cone of transmission.

"Three and a half miles to touchdown. Your heading is zero-*four*. Your rate of descent looks good. Left heading zero-two." Damn. More pressure on the left pedal.

"Zero-four is now your heading. Dropping a bit below the glide path now. Ease it up a few feet. It's a two and a half degree glide path. Zero-four's still your heading."

His wrists ached as he strained back the yoke. "You are on the glide path. Heading is now good. Two and one half miles from touchdown. You're back on course." He took his right hand off the yoke and eased the throttles back. The engine hum fell to a whisper. Beads of perspiration formed on his upper lip. He licked them away. His tongue tasted salty.

"One mile from touchdown now. And you've been cleared for landing. Check that your gear's down, again."

He flashed a look at the three greens.

"Heading and your rate of descent are both good. Zero-four is your heading. Exactly. Three-quarters of a mile. You are passing through precision limits at—this moment."

He glanced at the altimeter. Two hundred feet, the height specified as precision limits. The snow-covered ice of Gander Lake would be zipping below Arrowhead's wheels. Dot-dash-dot-dash. The middle marker pipped through his ears, the lower red light glowed and went out. Decimal six of a mile from threshold.

"Right to zero-four, looking down the left-hand side." Goddamned fool! Doesn't he know we're blind? How the hell can we look down the left-hand side? He adjusted the throttles. The airspeed dropped; 190 knots. His knuckles were knobs around the yoke. "You're now approaching the end of the runway. And you're over the end—NOW."

He tensed, waiting for Nardini or Kowsky to shout, "Threshold, flare out!" The PAR operator's voice had gone. He shouted aloud, "One . . . two . . . three . . . four . . . five."

"Overshoot!" Kowsky yelled. Bartlett rammed the throttles forward and punched the afterburner buttons. Nothing happened—then a scream as the engine compressors picked up revs. Poised on the point of stall, standing on her tail, a violent shudder shook the aircraft. Afterburner gases blasted from the engine nozzles. Grudgingly the airplane picked up speed and climbed into the fog.

"Gear up!" The yoke stiffened as the wheels retracted.

"Nose fully up!"

"Nose fully up."

"Check heading."

"Zero-three-eight and two thousand feet," Kowsky said, grabbing the Gander plate. "Turn zero-five-zero off end of runway and climb back on course."

Bartlett felt for the transmit button and rammed it down. "Zero-One to ATC. No threshold visible. For Christ's sake, doesn't your PAR man know our visor's stuck?"

"He does, captain." It was Duffy's voice. "He says he was using normal terminology."

"Request clearance to come in short of the outer beacon. May not have enough fuel to go around."

Silence followed. Bartlett pressed the yoke left as the airspeed rose to two hundred and twenty knots. He fought the aircraft's tendency to yaw.

"It's inadvisable, captain. The outer marker's only three decimal nine miles from the threshold . . ."

"I know, I know, but . . ."

"We might not be able to cut you in sharp enough to vector you onto the heading, captain."

SUPERSONIC

"Where's the 'copter?"

"Headed southwest. At eight hundred feet."

The scream of compressors suddenly thrust into maximum revs and the thunder of the jet blast, amplified by the damp fog clinging to the ground, rolled across the snow-patched grass and tarmac, penetrated the ATC building a mile away, and reverberated around the room. Delaney glued his eyes on the helicopter's blip. The pilot must be nuts.

"That heading'll take him over Zero Four's threshold!" he shouted to Duffy from Reynolds's PAR position, where he'd stationed himself.

"Shall I cut Zero-One inside the outer marker, sir? Give him a chance to get there first."

Delaney had to think fast. The wrong decision meant the difference between getting a hundred and sixty or more passengers safely on the ground and . . . Clearing Zero One to take the shortcut around the outer marker meant the captain would have to lose height rapidly, two thousand feet in less than half a mile. With a dragging tail and heavy stick forces that would be a tough maneuver—and taut nerves on the flight deck wouldn't help. On the other hand, if he took him out for the full approach to the outer marker beacon, he'd make his approach at a shallow angle, controlling the rate of descent by a touch on the throttles, trusting to God that his fuel would hold. The landing in the Moth over Deadman's Pond flashed through his mind, finger on the magneto switch, engine blasting full power . . . switch on . . . switch off . . . thick fog streaming past the windshield . . . skis skimming the treetops . . . feeling for the ice . . . skis bumping . . . engine dying . . . slewing up on the bank . . .

"Vector him through the outer marker."

"Zero-One," Duffy said, making a deliberate effort to keep

his voice under control. "Continue on present heading until I turn you *south* of the outer marker."

"Roger."

A door slammed and running feet sounded from the end of the room. Delaney spun around. A wiry man with a crown of bobbing, sandy-colored hair, dressed in a grubby parka, raced past the darkened radarscopes. Budnick lumbered behind, panting, mouth working.

"Found him . . . neighbor's garage . . . fixing car!" Budnick gasped. "Came back early from fishing . . . before the fog clamped . . ."

"Tommy, take over this talk-down!" Delaney said, pointing to the PAR scopes. Thompson sat down as Reynolds moved away. "It's a diverted supersonic. Fuel short. Tail-down attitude, fuel's locked in rear tank due to transfer problems. Got it?"

"Yes, sir." Thompson nodded, breathing heavily. He glanced at the consoles. "Runway Zero-Four, eh?" He rubbed his hands on the front of his parka before adjusting a knob.

"And his windshield visor won't retract. No forward visibility. Limited side vision only."

Thompson spoke out of the side of his mouth. "It's ten-ten sitting on the ground anyway, sir."

"He's made one shot at it. Couldn't see the threshold. He's on his go-around now. Duffy's feeding him through the outer marker."

"I get the picture, sir. What's his flight number, sir?"

"Zero-One. It's American Arrow. An Arrowhead." Delaney waited for the rest to sink in before mentioning the helicopter. Thompson rotated two small handles on the side of the console and watched a purple light on the console's metal edge grow in intensity. A mile away, near the end of Runway

04, the PAR antenna rotated on its bearing. Thompson continued to adjust the brilliance of the light until he was satisfied he had the antenna aligned to scan Flight Zero-One the second the aircraft flew through the outer marker's cone of transmission. Then he adjusted the definition and contrast knobs on both the vertical and horizontal displays. He glanced across at Duffy's scope.

"What the hell's that?" he exclaimed.

"A Search and Rescue 'copter with dead radio. He's lost and trying to put down," Delaney explained.

Thompson's eyes bulged. "But Christ, sir! He's headed for Zero Four's threshold!"

Delaney felt the veins in his temples thrum. For the first time since he'd left his upstairs office he found nothing to say.

"What about feeding Zero-One *inside* the outer marker? I mean, sir . . ."

Delaney shook his head. "We decided against it. Too risky. She's tail-down, heavy to maneuver. Has to land fast to prevent a stall-in."

Thompson was silent for several seconds, fascinated by the sight of the helicopter blip approaching the end of the runway. "The 'copter's practically on the ground, sir," he said. "Six hundred feet."

Duffy spoke. "Zero-One, turn one hundred and eighty degrees on to magnetic heading zero-four-zero for landing on Runway Zero-Four."

"Roger."

Bartlett shoved upward with his left hand and checked the compass. The aircraft came around in a steep bank, protesting the demands on her aerodynamic characteristics, primarily designed for Mach 3 flight and shallow approaches, not for high-powered maneuvering within the confines of an airport's outer perimeter.

"Gear down."

"Gear down." Several seconds passed. "Three greens," Kowsky said in a cracked voice.

"Nose fully down."

The screw jack whined. "Nose fully down. Locked." The airspeed indicator turned to 200 knots.

"You're nine miles south of the outer marker. Heading directly on zero-four," Duffy said.

"Where's the 'copter?"

"Heading southwest. At six hundred feet."

"On my reciprocal?" Bartlett demanded.

"Yes, sir."

For a moment he was too stunned to reply. "What the hell's the idea?"

"You'll reach the threshold before him."

He exchanged looks with Kowsky, whose face visibly whitened.

"Handing you to the PAR controller, captain."

Kowsky changed the frequency selector.

The yoke quivered. Bartlett glanced at the airspeed: 190. He eased the throttles forward and glanced at the fuel gauge. It showed a hairbreadth above Empty.

"*Altimeter two-niner-zero-five. Winds from two hundred and seventy degrees at ten miles an hour. Confirm you are reading me okay.*"

Yet another voice. This one was crisp, clear-cut, with a reassuring tone.

"Roger. Reading you."

"*Commence your descent—NOW. You are above the glide path. I'll keep you advised as you approach it . . . and if there are no transmissions for five seconds during this ap-*"

proach or unable to complete it carry out the published missed approach. Acknowledge. Over."

Go around again? On fuel fumes? "Roger."

"You're seven miles from touchdown. No need to acknowledge any further transmissions. You should be in descent."

"Start scanning." Bartlett felt Nardini's breath on the back of his neck.

"It's a two and a half glide path and you're still above it. Zero-Four's the heading. You're at six and three-quarter miles from touchdown."

Delaney watched the orange light spot that represented Arrowhead on the PAR console creep down the sloping line of the electronic glide path. On the flat PAR scope the corresponding light spot edged away from the centerline.

"Zero-Four's the heading. Right two degrees. The on-course is slightly to your right." Bartlett moved the yoke. The controls responded heavily. *"You're correcting slowly but nicely back to it."*

Smoothly done, Delaney thought, watching the light spot move back on course.

Hold her there. Bartlett's mind balanced on a razor-edge of decision. Level the yoke. Ease throttles back. Gently does it.

"Six and a quarter miles from touchdown. Still slightly above the glide path."

"Ease the stick forward," Delaney muttered, watching the spot above the glide path. Ah, he was moving down.

"Maintain that rate of descent. I'll advise you when you intercept."

Control column forward. That much? The tendons on Bartlett's wrists stood out. His muscles ached. He resisted the temptation to check the fuel gauge.

"Turn further right to heading zero-four."

Bring that compass around two degrees. That's it.

SUPERSONIC

"On course, nicely now. Five and three-quarter miles from touchdown. Very slightly above the glide path. Stand by to adjust your rate of descent."

Delaney's lips formed two thin lines. Just a touch on the throttles.

"Five and a half miles from touchdown. Flight Zero-One is cleared to land. Check gear down and locked."

Bartlett flashed a look at the three green lights.

Delaney craned his head toward Duffy's scope. The helicopter blip crawled inexorably closer to Runway 04's threshold with each rotation of the light finger.

"You've intercepted the glide path now. Readjust your rate of descent for a two and a half degree glide path."

Bartlett's right hand shot out. Steady on the throttles. The rate-of-descent meter showed two hundred feet per minute.

"Five miles to touchdown."

Delaney stared at the helicopter's blip, mesmerized by its unerring movement.

"Heading Zero-Four. Turn right heading one degree now."

Damn that drift: the crosswind. Altitude eight hundred. Yoke down to the left. Not too much.

"Four and a half to touchdown. You are maintaining a good rate of descent. Say again, you have been cleared to land. Check gear down and locked."

This guy made it sound like a normal talk-down. Three greens.

"Heading Zero-Four, correcting nicely to the extended center line and you're maintaining a good rate of descent. Four miles until touchdown."

Dash-dash-dot-dash in his earphones. Red glow on the radio console.

"Three and three-quarter miles. Descent is good. You're on the glide path. Course just slightly to your right now."

SUPERSONIC

Delaney watched the radial finger crawl around, outlining the clutter. He estimated the two blips were five miles apart, on reciprocal headings set for collision.

"*Three and a half miles to touchdown. Very nice rate of descent.*"

Bartlett watched the rate-of-descent dial. The engine rev needles steadied. Maybe the 'copter would find a clear patch and put down, the pilot still had time.

"*Winds are now from two hundred and seventy degrees at twelve miles per hour.*"

Delaney's eyes riveted on to Duffy's scope. The helicopter's flag showed three hundred feet. Get the hell down! He dragged his gaze back to Thompson's scopes.

"*Three miles to touchdown.*" Thompson pressed a button and the vertical and horizontal PAR scopes suddenly expanded: The glide path and heading lines from three miles out to the threshold blew up to a bigger scale, with Runway 04 shown by well-defined boundary lines.

"*Two and three-quarter miles to touchdown.*"

The nerves in Bartlett's wrists twitched. He concentrated on the voice.

"*Rolling out nicely on course. Rate of descent good. I say again you have been cleared to land. Two miles to touchdown.*"

Two miles. Three thousand, five hundred and twenty yards. He glanced at the engine rev counters, amazed that they hadn't dropped to zero. The altimeter read 600 feet.

"*Zero-four's your heading. A mile and three-quarters.*"

Delaney's glance took in both PAR scopes. Both read dead on. A perfect GCA.

"*Holding nicely on course and on the glide path. A mile and a quarter to touchdown. Good rate of descent . . . one mile to touchdown.*"

Bartlett poised his right hand above the black throttle levers. One mile: A man can run it in less than five minutes. A good man, in top shape, properly trained.

"Three-quarters of a mile and passing through precision limits—NOW."

Delaney tore his eyes away from Thompson's flat scope and looked at Duffy's. Two blips a mile apart. Christ! The 'copter's speeded up. The finger crept around, sweeping a trail of bright light behind it. Runway 04 glowed in clear outline.

"Zero-four's your heading."

Nardini's breath was hot on the back of Bartlett's neck. Dot-dash-dot-dash sounded in his ears as the middle marker light flashed on and went out.

"Very nice rate of descent. Half a mile to touchdown."

Delaney grabbed the phone. "Erect arrester cables for approach on Zero-Four." He heard Walker in the tower answer, "Yes . . ." and slammed the phone down.

"You're on course. On the glide path."

Kowsky and Nardini, you've got to see it this time. Yell it loud.

"Approaching the end of the runway."

Delaney stared at the blip, filled with a feeling of awe and helplessness. The 'copter was down to less than a hundred feet. The goddamned idiot was determined to put it on Runway 04.

"You're over the end of the runway—NOW."

A blinding flash of blue light shot through the window on Nardini's side, flooding the inside of the flight deck. Bartlett snapped his face away from the brilliant glare.

"Threshold!" Kowsky shouted.

He eased back the yoke, eyes narrowed, focusing on the airspeed indicator. A distant bump told him the main wheels had touched. A voice in his ears, Duffy's voice. "Arrester cables erected." He glanced out of the window. White runway lights centered in blurred halos shot past. He pulled back the throttles, and waited for the thump of the nosewheel making contact. The inclination of his seat and the artificial horizon told him they were ballooning at a steep angle. He shoved the yoke forward. Another jolt reverberated through the flight deck, but the nose remained pointed skyward. Glue on, you bastard! Another bump behind him, then he was suddenly floating through the air.

"The blip's gone!" Duffy cried. His scope flickered and dimmed until all light faded from it.

Delaney's eyes widened to adjust to the sudden darkening of the room. An alarm bell jangled. Three seconds later the room lights came up and the fluorescence came back into Duffy's scope. Delaney stared as the light finger swept around. The helicopter blip had vanished. The other blip was moving down the exact center line of Runway 04. Moving fast. He wasn't down yet—not with that speed on. Cut engines, man. Halfway down the wet runway and still no solid contact. Get her down and reverse thrust—if you've got enough fuel . . .

Another thud. Tires screamed, skidded as Bartlett pressed the toe pedals with every ounce of strength in his legs. He shoved the yoke forward, thrust it hard against the limit stop the moment the wheels again crunched the asphalt, and yanked the throttle levers toward him through the reverse thrust gate. A second later a roar as the buckets opened at the rear of the engines, diverting the jet exhausts forward. Then, quite suddenly, all noise ceased. He looked at the fuel gauge: there was a row of zeros and the needle of the double-reading instrument was hard against the bottom stop. The airspeed showed one hundred and twenty . . . 110 . . . 100

SUPERSONIC

. . . He stood up on the brake pedals as far as his harness would allow, with Kowsky doing the same on his side. Ninety . . . 80 . . . 70 . . . He could hear wheels rumbling and felt the jouncing motion as the two hundred-tons of aluminum, titanium, and high-tensile steel that was Arrowhead settled lower on the landing gear shock struts. Sixty knots . . . 50 . . . 40 . . . The nose tipped, the nosewheel touched—lifted —and an explosion like the crack of a giant whip sounded in front of the windshield. Impulsively he let go of the yoke to shield his face. He felt the harness bite his flesh and his head jerk forward, then back. They'd hit the first arrester cable and snapped it against the visor—it must've ridden up over the drooped nose. Thank God for the stuck visor! He grabbed the yoke, pushed it hard against the instrument panel. Thirty on the clock. They were out of runway now. The next cable would snag them. Hope the passengers had their heads tucked down. He saw Kowsky's hand gripping the nosewheel steering control, correcting for the slew when the cable caught. A tearing strain on his hands and arms as the second cable snagged the nosewheel, ran under it, and grappled the main undercarriage structure. His neck snapped forward. The coaming of the instrument panel dipped drunkenly, tee-tered, and fell level. All forward motion stopped, and the only sound was of dying gyros and the hollow echo of a Dixie cup rolling across the floor. He looked at Kowsky leaning on the yoke, eyes closed, and heard the scream of a distant siren. He didn't speak for a full ten seconds. "That must be some sort of record," he said, in a voice barely under control. He swal-lowed and added, "Ziegel probably never knew supersonics could glide engines off."

Kowsky unbuckled his harness and sat back in his seat. "I wouldn't try it at seventy thousand feet if I were you."

Bartlett swung around. "You okay, Nick?"

"Sure, Captain," said a voice near the floor behind him. "Just a cut on my arm."

· "Hope we haven't got more casualties back there," Bartlett said, jerking his head aft. He pressed the transmit button.

"Flight Zero-One to Gander ATC. We have just landed on Runway Zero-Four. Request tow vehicle to the terminal area—we're out of fuel." He paused. "And say. That's one hell of a blinding location flasher you've got on the threshold. How come it didn't work the first time around?"

TWELVE

"I told you it'd be a heavy one!" cried George Stanhope for the third time, slapping Ives on the back. Ives clung to the airline counter, resisting the pressure of the milling crowd. He ignored Stanhope and called to the ticket clerk.

"What's happening to the baggage? I heard they've changed their minds and we've got to go through Customs here after all. Is that right?"

"Yes, sir."

Ives's heart pounded against his chest. He took a deep breath. "When will I be able to get my hands on my suitcase?"

"It'll be at least another half-hour, sir. They're towing the aircraft in now. Your buses were lucky. They found a short cut in the fog around the taxi strips."

Ives made a pretense of looking at his watch. "It's important I get my baggage as soon as possible. I have to get the first plane out to New York."

"Won't be for some time, sir." The clerk tossed his head. "That fog'll have to burn off. Doubtful if there'll be any planes flying until tomorrow."

SUPERSONIC

George Stanhope grasped Ives's shoulder. "See what I see?" He pointed across the concourse where a neon sign, "Big Dipper Bar," glowed with the promise of comfort and warmth. "We'll drink to solid ground," he said, stamping the terrazzo floor. "That reminds me, that gorgeous stew owes me a drink. Speak of the devil—I mean angel—hi, Miss."

"Hi, there," Lydia said, emerging from the crush of people. She anticipated Stanhope's question. "I've got some things to attend to. Getting the injured passengers looked after, and . . ."

"I understand, Miss." Stanhope held Ives's arm. "My friend and I'll be in the 'Big Dipper.' See you later."

"Don't get too dipped!" Lydia laughed, and hurried away.

Several passengers were stretched out on the brightly colored seats around the concourse, silent and limp. Hospital orderlies carried an inert figure on a stretcher toward an exit and passengers had begun to drift from the counter and stood in little groups, talking excitedly, drawn together by a bond of shared danger that they had survived. A crowd moved toward the restaurant, shouting for others to follow, and a voice, shriller than the others, rose in protest.

"I can *walk*. It's my arm that's broken, not my leg!" Gladys Glinker jumped up and down in the wheelchair, pushed by an orderly, who wheeled the vehicle through the groups of people with a commanding "Make way there," toward the same exit as the stretcher party. An airport official ran across the floor to intercept Maxwell and Miss Lindenberg. "This way, sir. The VIP lounge's ready. There's a private telephone . . ."

"Thanks," Maxwell interjected.

The airport official went on. "I've arranged accommodation at the Holiday Inn." He cleared his throat. "But, uh, you may sleep over in the VIP lounge if you wish, sir."

"I've got to get to Washington right away."

SUPERSONIC

The official shook his head. "The fog's sitting solid, sir. There won't be a plane out of here until tomorrow."

Maxwell stuck out his jaw. "Get me to the phone," he demanded. "We'll see about that."

Bartlett put two fists on the counter in the Operations Room and regarded them with surprise. Slowly he uncurled his fingers, turned to Kowsky and Nardini, and then to the dispatcher.

"First Officer Pete Kowsky and Flight Management Systems Engineer Nick Nardini," he said.

"Pleased to meet you sir, and sir," the dispatcher said, gripping each man's hand in turn. Two assistant dispatchers also shook their hands as the door opened and Delaney entered.

"Captain Bartlett," he said. "James Delaney—I'm in charge of Area Control."

"We owe you our deepest thanks, Mr. Delaney," he said, surprised at the feeling in his voice. "But that blue flasher on Zero Four's threshold. It's not marked on the operation plate."

"That's no flasher on Zero-Four," Delaney said in a quiet voice. He paused. "The 'copter hit the high tension cables."

Bartlett's jaw dropped and the place suddenly became very still. The dispatcher and his assistants stared at the floor. For several seconds silence hung like a pall in the room, until the rat-tat-tat of the teleprinter in the corner broke the hush.

"Hell, no!"

Delaney nodded. "Complete wipe-out. They didn't stand a chance. Smack on the Trans-Canada Highway."

"How many?"

"Two. Pilot and crewman. The Armed Forces just phoned."

"Oh, God," Kowsky groaned. He removed his cap and ran his fingers through his hair. "Poor bastards."

Bartlett looked around the little group. One of the assistant dispatchers crossed to the teletype machine, tore off the message slip, glanced at it, and put it in a file tray.

"What about your electric power? Did it cut out?" Bartlett asked.

"The scopes faded completely for a few seconds, until the emergency standby generators cut in," Delaney replied. He looked up at Bartlett. "We thought we'd lost you."

Bartlett suddenly felt chilled. The dispatcher coughed and bent to peer over Bartlett's side of the counter.

"You'll be wanting to clear that paper work, Captain?"

"What? Yes." Bartlett picked up his briefcase and dropped it on the counter. Kowsky did the same with his case.

"Thanks again for everything, Mr. Delaney," Bartlett repeated.

"It's Tommy you *should* be thanking. And Duffy."

"Tommy?"

"Harry Thompson, the talk-down man. Duffy's the terminal controller, Captain."

"Where can I find them?"

"In the ATC Center on the second floor, Captain. I'll take you up when you're through down here."

"I've been looking for you everywhere, Sir Leonard," Lydia called, running to the surgeon as he strode across the concourse. He carried his medical bag, and *Yachting World* was tucked under his arm.

"Another patient? I thought I was finished." He glanced at the hands of the big clock on the wall. "I *must* get a plane to New York as soon as possible."

"There won't be anything leaving today, sir. The airport's completely socked in. They say maybe in the morning. By midday for sure. There's a front . . ."

"Where can I make a long-distance telephone call?"

"I'll take you to the airport manager's office."

He looked down at her. "Why were you looking for me?"

Lydia felt her temples throb. She tried to look away, but the kind blue eyes held hers. Impulsively she stood on tiptoe and kissed Sir Leonard on the cheek, feeling the moustache prickle her skin. "To thank you personally for everything you did. I—I don't think I could have managed on my own."

"Nonsense, nonsense, my dear. Shall I tell you something?" Sir Leonard glanced over his shoulder and bent low. "I was scared stiff," he whispered.

"Drink up, Clarence. Here's to terra firma. The more firma the less terror! Ha, ha!" George Stanhope raised his fourth rye toward Ives. "And a special toast. To a *soft* landing in New York!"

Ives lifted his glass and sipped the golden liquid absentmindedly.

"Come on, Clarence. Down the hatch!"

Ives made an attempt to smile. "Here's, uh, to a happy landing in New York."

He looked through the open side of the bar that led onto the concourse and wondered where the Baggage Claim carousel was located. They must be unloading the baggage by now. He turned to Stanhope.

"I need my toothbrush and things. Freshen up, you know. Maybe they've unloaded the luggage." He made a movement to slip off the stool.

Stanhope put a restraining arm on Ives's shoulder. "This'll freshen you up, Clarence. Waiter, same again for me and my friend."

"No—really." Ives touched his forehead, feeling faint. "I'm sorry. Two's about my limit."

"Come on, Clarence. One more for little old New York.

For Wall Street. That's it, for Wall Street and all those beautiful stocks and bonds."

Ives stared at the glass the barman slid before him, then raised his eyes. The rows of colored bottles behind the barman merged. He shut his eyes and wobbled unsteadily on the bar stool.

"You okay, Clarence?"

"A bit dizzy. I need something to eat."

"One more and we'll go satisfy the inner man."

Clarence Ives opened his eyes. The bottles slipped back into focus and he reached uncertainly for the glass. As he did so a hand descended on his forearm.

"Excuse me, sir. Are you Mr. Clarence Ives, traveling on American Arrow Airline's Flight Zero-One, London to New York, diverted to Gander?"

Ives looked at the owner of the arm and found himself staring into the youthful face of a tall, large man dressed in a brown uniform with a polished leather belt and peaked cap. There were yellow words on the shoulder flash and through a haze he read "Royal Canadian Mounted Police." His eyes dropped toward the floor and he saw the breeches with broad yellow stripes and silver spurs on the man's boots.

"Yes," he said in a barely audible voice, without raising his head.

"Please accompany me to the office across the way, sir." The man's fingers tightened around his arm. Ives nodded and slipped off the stool. "Er, sorry George. There's something I've got to explain . . ."

"Hey! What's up, officer? Clarence was only having a friendly drink . . ."

James Delaney closed the door of the ATC Center and mounted the stairs to his office on the third floor. He stood in front of the window, peering at the swirling fog, then turned and slumped in the chair behind his desk, eyes closed, feeling drained. A mechanical scream rose and fell in the distance and he recognized the peculiar pitch of the siren of the Armed Forces' crash tender. He opened his eyes and looked at the papers on his desk, picked up the MOT form, and studied the unanswered question: In your opinion, did the pilot deliberately contravene Federal Air Regulations? With swift strokes of the pen he printed in block letters: NO . . . and in the ATC center one floor below Duffy turned back to his scope and switched it off. He picked up Flight Zero-One's flight progress strip and slid it out of its plastic holder. In the section between longitude 50 and longitude 60 he wrote, "Landed at Gander." He glanced at the clock that showed Greenwich Mean Time and wrote "*zulu*," followed by the time.

He stared at the eight-inch-by-one-inch paper slip for a full half-minute before handing it to a pale-faced controller-in-training.

"File this under Awaiting Investigation," he said in a quiet voice. "And make a photostat copy for Mr. Delaney."

Bartlett picked up the ringing phone on the table in the deserted Crew Room.

"Here's your call to New York, Captain," said the operator.

"Cathy! It's me. Tom."

"Are you all right? The airline office called to say you'd been diverted to Gander. Are you speaking from there or . . . ?"

"Yes. I'm at Gander. We, uh, had a bit of a problem with the fuel system. Cut our range. Nothing serious. What's the news?"

"It's benign. He's been moved into a private ward. Dr. Lieberman . . ."

Bartlett's shoulders relaxed. He looked up as the door opened and Kowsky and Nardini entered. They fell into the comfortable armchairs that lined the room.

". . . said it looks very promising."

Bartlett shook with relief. "Oh, Cathy, that's terrific!"

"When will you be home?"

"The Met boys say the fog'll clear by tomorrow, about . . ."

"Tomorrow! The office didn't mention fog."

"I'm not surprised. They're always optimistic," Bartlett said, suddenly feeling lighter. "We should be taking off about midday."

"I *am* disappointed. I thought we could both see him tonight."

"Explain I'll be there as soon as I get in." Bartlett looked at the slouched figures in the armchairs, as the door opened and Lydia swept through the doorway. "Take care, honey. See you tomorrow. Give him my love."

He replaced the receiver as Lydia announced, "The crew bus is waiting. They're putting us up at some place called the Albatross Hotel."

Kowsky stirred and stretched. "Jesus, sounds ominous to me. Albatrosses bring bad luck."

Lydia giggled. "You've got a morbid imagination," she said. "It only brought bad luck when the Ancient Mariner shot the darned thing." She paused before adding, "Talking of bad luck. Did you hear about our pregnant passenger?"

Nardini opened his eyes and rubbed his chin. "Don't tell me."

Lydia nodded. "I heard the news in the airport manager's office. They managed to get her into the town hospital in time. Guess what?"

"Twins," Kowsky ventured.

"A boy. Eight and a half pounds."

Kowsky made a helpless gesture with his hands, yawned,

and got up. He turned to Bartlett. "The concussion case is going to be okay. I met the surgeon in the corridor."

"Yes, I checked earlier, and the old lady's having her broken arm set in the town hospital." He turned to Nardini. "Did you get that cut on your arm attended to, Nick?"

Nardini nodded. "Sure, Captain. It's nothing."

Bartlett paused, lost in thought. "We were lucky—damned lucky," he repeated. "And only a few scratches from the landing." He bent to pick up his briefcase and looked around the trio of faces. A feeling of gratitude welled up inside him. After a long moment he said, "You've all been wonderful. Now, let's get going. The driver's waiting."

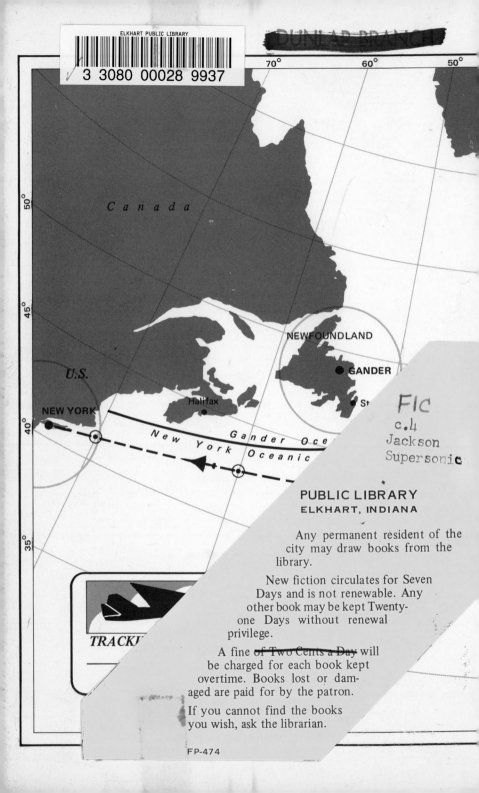

70°   60°   50°

50°

45°

40°

35°

C a n a d a

NEWFOUNDLAND

GANDER

U.S.

NEW YORK   Halifax   St

New York   *Gander Oce*

New York Oceanic

TRACKI